PRAISE FOR TIM PRATT

"Fun, funny, pacy, thought-provoking and very clever space opera – a breath of fresh air."
Sean Williams, author of *Twinmaker*

"Pratt's thoughtful worldbuilding, revealed little by little, continues to impress… This well-imagined universe, populated by original and empathetic characters, has enough energy to power what could become a long-lived series."
Publishers Weekly

"Brilliantly fun space opera that reminds me of Killjoys but with more Weird Alien Cool Shit."
Liz Bourke for *Locus*

"A really good read that was intelligently written and skilfully put together."
Two Bald Mages

"The engaging, inclusive, and entertaining Axiom series, may be his best work yet… witty, heartfelt sci-fi romp."
Tor.com

BY THE SAME AUTHOR

Tim Pratt

THE FORBIDDEN STARS

BOOK III OF THE AXIOM

ANGRY ROBOT

ANGRY ROBOT
An imprint of Watkins Media Ltd

Unit 11, Shepperton House
89 Shepperton Road
London N1 3DF
UK

angryrobotbooks.com
twitter.com/angryrobotbooks
Waking Nightmare

An Angry Robot paperback original, 2019

Cover by Paul Scott Canavan
Set in Adobe Garamond

ISBN 978 0 85766 769 4
Ebook ISBN 978 0 85766 770 0

Printed and bound in the United States of America by Penguin Random House.

9 8 7 6 5 4 3 2 1

For Zoe

CHAPTER 1

Callie and Ashok crouched back-to-back in a dark passageway deep in the heart of an ancient space station – which wasn't as abandoned as they'd hoped. The walls were smooth, made of a dark and lusterless metal not even the sensors embedded in Ashok's face could identify; the ceilings were so low they both had to hunch over to avoid scraping the tops of their heads; and even at its widest point the passageway was too narrow for them to walk side-by-side. The artificial gravity here was heavier than Callie would have preferred, too, so every movement was a conscious slog of drag and effort. Callie felt like a mouse infiltrating an anthill.

Being this deep in the Axiom station was a lot like being in a coffin. That aliens were trying to murder them didn't do much to dispel the feeling.

"I'm starting to doubt the benevolence of the Benefactor."

"You're just starting now? You're way behind schedule." Ashok's voice carried low and clear in her helmet's comm. There was an atmosphere in this station but it wasn't anything humans could breathe –

not even humans with as many filtration systems as Ashok had. "The note said this place would be, quote, 'interesting,' not pleasant."

Callie saw the perturbation in the air and lifted her arm just before a Liar appeared from nowhere, as they did, just two meters in front of her. The tentacled, squidlike alien wore a suit of shimmering chameleon tech, and it raised a pseudopod holding a complexly curved weapon, but Callie was faster, and she fired a needle full of paralytic fluid into the Liar's center mass.

The alien flopped to the ground, writhed briefly, then stiffened, all sprawled and ungainly, no bigger than a human toddler. "Back away!" Callie shouted, and Ashok obligingly shuffled along the passageway so she could retreat before the Liar – assassin? guard? – burst into sudden white fire, a ferocious heat that burned itself out in seconds and left nothing but scorch marks on the floor.

That was the seventh alien to attack them so far, and all seven had self-immolated despite Callie and Ashok's best attempts to subdue them non-lethally. The ancient aliens known as the Axiom had built this place but they still had servants among the Liars, some willing and some brainwashed, and Callie hated killing them when she wasn't sure which was which.

More intel in general would have been nice. The Benefactor's note had led them to this Axiom facility, but their mysterious source of information wasn't too forthcoming with details. Callie enjoyed blowing things up, but she preferred to know *what* she was exploding before she lit the fuse.

"Why the fireworks show?" Callie said. "If it's an anti-interrogation thing, why don't they just poison themselves?"

"Dramatic effect? Actually, I bet it's practical. The Axiom hate sharing their toys. These Liars have short-range teleportation technology in their suits, and it gets burned up along with the users, so we can't steal it." Ashok sighed. "I'd really love to steal it."

"We already *have* that technology." They only had one personal teleportation unit, stolen from a Liar cultist a long time ago, and Callie was always nervous it was going to teleport her inside a wall or something, but still.

"This tech is totally different, cap."

"How so?"

"We use wormholes to connect distant points. These guys… I guess my fancy cyborg eyes are better than your squishy jelly blobs." He tapped the nest of lenses on his face. "When these Liars pop out, there's a vertical split in the air, like someone took a seam-ripper to space-time. There's no wormhole tunnel. They just tear a hole in reality and step through. You can actually *see* the place they're coming from. It looks like a big room made of white stone. There are columns in there. It's kind of churchy. Or ancient-temple-y."

"You saw all that in the half a second they take to appear?"

"I can replay what I see in slow-motion and watch it with the bits of my brain I'm not using to watch your back."

"Huh." Ripping holes in reality. That sounded bad, but Callie found the revelation of unprecedented advanced technology more interesting than surprising at this point. The Axiom could generate wormholes, create artificial gravity, disassemble planets into raw materials, control inertia, and manipulate minds. There wasn't much she'd put past their capabilities. It was a shame they were genocidal monsters bent on immortal galactic domination. "Is the churchy place somewhere on the station, you think?"

"I doubt it. Let me show you." He brushed the translucent diamond housing on his prosthetic forearm with his gloved fingers, and the surface went shiny black, then displayed an image. "This is a zoomed-in frame-grab from my clearest look through one of their portals."

Callie squinted. There were the pillars, oddly fluted and narrow, and the gleaming white stone walls, inscribed with glyphs or words or decorations she couldn't make out in detail. At the top of the image, there was a section of what appeared to be a glass dome in lieu of a ceiling, with towering fingers of jagged black rock outside… lit by the weak light of an alien sun, clearly visible through the glass.

"Could be viewscreens," Callie said. "We've been on space stations and asteroids that had fake domes like that, with screens for panels so you could feel like you were under a real sky."

"Could be, but Occam's Plasma Grenade says the simplest and most potentially deadly answer is probably the right one. If that *is* some other planet, it kinda makes you wonder where it is, doesn't it? Is it a home base for assassin death squid devoted to slumbering alien monsters? That seems like the kind of place we might want to find, so we can blow it up."

"And steal their stuff."

"Well sure. It's not like saving the universe from a secret alien threat usually pays all that well, and I need to get new toys somehow."

"Let's focus on exploding one thing at a time." They continued and reached a branching corridor, just as low and dark as the one they were in now, and moved carefully to their right. They'd planted explosive charges at key points in the station and only had one charge left, meant to go right in the center. They'd detonate the bombs from their ship the *White Raven* and create a beautiful chain reaction that should turn this whole facility to glowing dust. If they didn't get murdered first.

A doorway stood open and dark at the end of the

passage and Callie did a careful pirouette to let Ashok take the lead while she covered the back. He peered into the darkness with his augmented sight and said, "It looks clear, which just means nobody's popped out of thin air yet. But, oof, it's a mess in there."

Callie slipped in after him, pleased to enter a chamber with a ceiling over two meters high and wide enough to stretch out her arms if she wanted. The space was filled with cylindrical incubators of a sort she'd seen before in other Axiom facilities, meant to breed Liars. These incubators were almost all broken, though, crusted with the dried remnants of fluids or partially melted by electrical or heating mishaps, and even the few that looked intact were empty. This facility, like most Axiom facilities they'd found, looked like it had been abandoned centuries or even millennia before, when its creators went into hiding or hibernation. "Do you think the Liars who've been attacking us are the survivors of those who originally staffed this station? Or their descendants?"

"Probably descendants," Ashok said. "Unless they were in cryosleep and only got activated when we broke in. Liars can live centuries, but not millennia, as far as we know. Though their ability to share memories with their offspring does let them take a long view of things…

"We could ask these guys about their family history if they didn't burn themselves to death first. I'd love to chat. I almost never get to practice speaking the Axiom language, and Lantern makes fun of my accent a lot." He gestured with the cluster of multi-jointed manipulators he had in place of a right hand. "There's another door – that's probably the hub of the station through there. Big bomb boomtown." Ashok pushed ahead without waiting for Callie's order. He was an incredible engineer, a good friend, and a terrible subordinate.

She grabbed his shoulder. "Hold up. They've been attacking us more frequently as we get closer to the center of the station. The Benefactor said there was something dangerous here that we needed to destroy – the Liars could be trying to protect a weapon. If I was them, I'd save the last of my forces for a final ambush to protect their prize."

"If there's a weapon here, why don't they just take it to their weird white temple for safekeeping?"

"I don't know. Maybe it's too big. Maybe this whole station is the weapon, and there's a red button that says 'destroy the universe' in the middle. How would I know? It's Axiom shit."

"There is no ambush." A deep voice, mechanically simulated, emerged from the space beyond the doorway. "I am the only guardian who remains."

"You speak our language?" Callie move to one side of the door, her back to the wall, and Ashok mirrored her on the other side. No reason to give an enemy a clean shot through the doorway.

"I do not. The station has scanned your vessel and its data banks and it is translating my words to you, and yours to me. You are enemies of the Axiom."

"The Axiom are enemies of every thinking creature in the galaxy. Maybe the universe."

"Is the crashing wave enemy to the sand?" the voice mused. "Is the boot enemy to the ant crushed beneath its heel? Is the lightning enemy to the tree, struck and burned in the storm?"

"That's some good translating," Ashok said. "Idiomatic and everything. I wouldn't mind getting a peek at the code he's running in this place." Ashok surreptitiously crouched and pushed a button on his artificial thigh, making a panel slide open. Something smaller than Callie's palm scuttled down his leg, then darted through the passageway. One of his little drones.

"The Axiom is not your enemy," the voice said. "They do not hate you. They do not think of you at all. That is the only reason you survive. If the Axiom noticed you, they might brush you away, brush your entire *species* away, as you would brush away an insect. If you destroy their works, though… they will notice."

Callie snorted. "They aren't as attentive as you think, or as numerous. We've been blowing up their shit for a little while now, and they're all still sleeping."

"Some of their works are abandoned, yes. But if you destroyed *this* place… they would notice."

"So let them notice. Did you ever hear of the Dream? We destroyed that station, and every Axiom hibernating there."

"Did you? Good. The Dreamers with their reality engine were enemies of my faction, with long-term goals incompatible with those of my masters."

"That's pretty cold," Ashok said.

"Why don't I come in there, and we can talk face to face?" asked Callie. "Or face to whichever part of your body has the most eyes on it, I guess." The Liars tended to have the same basic physical form – a central trunk surrounded by pseudopods – but details like the number of limbs and eyes varied. As a species, they were as devoted to self-improvement and customization as Ashok was.

"If you wish to cause the deaths of your entire species, by all means, enter," the Liar said. "If you value the preservation of your people, leave this place, and never speak of its existence."

"I can see what he's guarding." Ashok spoke into her suit comm, not projecting his voice where the alien could hear. He held up his arm, showing her the view from the drone. "Looks like an old-fashioned key."

A shimmering crystalline object hung in the room beyond, floating in a beam of blue light, and it *did* sort of look like the kind of key people used back when mechanical locks were all the rage, though oversized – as long as her longest finger, with a central cylindrical shaft and teeth at the top. Callie couldn't remember when she'd ever seen an actual stick-it-in-a-lock key in the real world, but the shape was used as the 'lock' icon on plenty of computer systems, so it was familiar enough. There probably weren't a lot of keys made out of glass, though, and the 'teeth' on the end were hard to focus on – they were sparkling, scintillating, coruscating.

The drone's camera panned and revealed four more Liars, armed with various weapons, arrayed around the key in its beam of light. *No ambush. Last of my kind. Well, they* are *called Liars.* Callie was sure they were lying about the imminent extermination of her species, too.

"If they're trying to protect that key, why don't they just grab it and tear a hole in the air and go to their temple?" Ashok said. "We couldn't follow them."

"It's a mystery." She switched to public address. "You can teleport. You should do that now. We don't want to hurt you. Your masters are long gone. This is a new galaxy. Go. Be free."

"I am the last guardian. I will never stop protecting the treasures of my masters."

"Okay, then. I tried." Callie had plenty of empathy, she really did, but it was wrapped in a generous insulation of pragmatism. "Blow the drone."

CHAPTER 2

Callie turned away, Ashok's lenses went dark, and a moment later a flash and a boom erupted in the room beyond.

They rushed in and found the key still floating in the beam of light, undisturbed by the blast. Callie couldn't tell whether it was held between opposing magnets, levitating in some kind of alien stasis field, or hanging from a string. Four of the Liars had been reduced to scorch marks, damaged enough in the explosion to trigger their self-immolation systems, but the last was intact, sprawled unmoving against a wall. "Looks like its suit got damaged in the explosion," Ashok said. "Must have messed up the self-destruct system."

"Is it alive?"

Ashok prodded the alien with his foot, then shook his head. "Doesn't look like it." He crouched and began examining the suit.

Callie went to look at the key. Her suit's sensors weren't as impressive as those in Ashok's face, but she could tell there was no nasty radiation coming off the key. Didn't mean there weren't protective countermeasures

19

in place. She walked around it, marveling.

The key was exceedingly strange. What had looked like a crystalline sparkle on the viewscreen was much more peculiar than that. The end of the key seemed to change shape, extruding pyramidal spines that then sank back into the central orb, only to reemerge elsewhere – a constant, flowing, eerily beautiful procession of shapes. The Axiom didn't usually make beautiful things. They made strange things, ugly things, spiny things, *wrong* things. This key didn't seem wrong, but it did seem otherworldly.

"Got it." Ashok peeled open the dead Liar's suit, and drew out a sort of bracelet with a greasy-looking black crescent attached to it. "It looks like the same material the wormhole generators we've seen are made of, but this one's not a black box. It's a black... moon? Scythe blade? Talon? Our death squid was wearing this around a pseudopod, like a bracelet. I bet it opens a portal to that temple place."

"Unless it's the self-destruct button. Remember, when you assume, you're an asshole."

"I don't think that's how it goes, cap. Anyway, I found the self-destruct. It's a unit grafted right into their nervous system, it looks like – if they hit some threshold of damage, or lose muscle control or whatever, whoosh, up in flames they go. The explosion just knocked this one's unit offline–"

He stumbled away as the Liar burst into sudden,

searing flame, and Callie winced and shielded her eyes.

"Temporarily offline, apparently." She stepped toward the remains, which were more intact than usual. The tentacle Ashok had prised from the suit was entirely whole, albeit severed and burned on the end. The explosives must have been threaded through the suit, and since the tentacle was outside containment, it had survived. The Axiom were truly terrible employers.

"I was just thinking… they didn't take the key out of here, even though it's small enough to carry." Callie picked up the severed tentacle in her gloved hands and carried it over to the beam of light, then pushed it gently toward the key. The tentacle arched, bent, and curved around the beam. She tossed it aside. "They couldn't touch the key at all. The field pushes them away. The Axiom didn't trust their employees, or slaves, or cultists, or whatever, no matter how thoroughly subjugated they were."

"I wonder if we could touch it? I might be able to disable the security. I've seen Axiom barrier fields before, and, unlike these cultists, I'm not brainwashed into thinking the Axiom are infallible unstoppable super-monsters who'll crush me if I look at them funny. I know they're occasionally fallible intermittently stoppable super-monsters who'll crush me if I look at them in any way at all."

Callie nodded. "We probably shouldn't touch it. We should set the last charge and blow this place up, key and all. I don't trust the Benefactor, but we seem to have a mutual interest in destroying Axiom tech, and they said whatever we found here was a danger to all life in the galaxy."

"Huh." Ashok looked at the key closely for the first time. "I don't know if blowing up the station would destroy the key. I don't think it's entirely in this dimension."

"Elaborate."

"Look at the head, how it seems to shift and change shape. Given the capabilities the Axiom have demonstrated before, it wouldn't surprise me if they could create and manipulate extradimensional objects." He sounded excited, which usually meant he'd found something he wanted to attach to his body, or a way to make things blow up in new and interesting ways.

"So the key is… like a tesseract?" Callie wasn't a mathematician but she remembered enough of what she'd learned in school to follow him that far. Tesseracts were theoretical objects that existed in four spatial dimensions, not just the three dimensions she could perceive: they were to three-dimensional cubes as cubes were to two-dimensional squares. Not that she could actually envision what that would look like.

"Right," Ashok said. "But I think this is a five-cell, not an eight-cell like a tesseract. It's a pentachoron."

"I don't know what you're talking about."

"If a tesseract is a four-dimensional cube, a

pentachoron is a four-dimensional triangular pyramid, an object bounded by five tetrahedral cells." He pointed at the emerging and subsiding points. "See?"

"Not even a little bit."

"Hmm. Tesseracts are square-y, and pentachorons are triangle-y."

"Okay, slightly better. But what about that makes the key explosion-proof?"

"Parts of the key aren't in this dimension to *be* blown up, is the thing. Imagine you've got a whale with its head inside your house–"

"Ashok, your metaphors are horrible."

"You could blow up the house, right, and destroy the whale's head, but the rest of the whale's body, sticking outside, would be fine. Apart from being dead I guess. Anyway. Now imagine you can't even *perceive* the world outside your house." He paused. "Maybe it's not such a good analogy, I concede, but do you get what I mean?"

"Yeah, I get it. Even if we destroyed the visible part of the key the rest of it would be fine."

"I really shouldn't have mentioned the whale. There's a good chance nothing we do would affect this key, if it's a key, at all. It could be indestructible, unless you have an interdimensional anvil and hammer and tongs."

"So how do we get rid of it, assuming it's a dangerous weapon we need to eliminate?"

"We could hurl it into a star."

Callie nodded. "That will destroy most things."

"Well, no, that wouldn't destroy it either, but at least then the key would be in a secure location. Nobody's going into a star to get the key back." He paused. "Unless the Axiom have technology that allows them or their servants to go inside stars. Not ruling it out."

"Hmm. Even if we blow up the station, the key will probably just remain here, unharmed?"

"It might just keep drifting in space, yeah."

"So sending us here to blow this place up might, theoretically, have been a way to clear out all the obstacles between the Benefactor and the key, so they could swing by and scoop up the floating extradimensional object of their desire after we left, with us none the wiser."

"You have a suspicious mind, Callie. That's why you're the boss."

Callie sighed. "Do you think the key actually opens anything?"

Ashok held up the black crescent on the bracelet. "I kind of do. Maybe something on an unknown planet." He grinned. "It's been *ages* since we opened a mystery box. Could be gold in there. Could be spiders. But don't you want to know?"

"It has not been ages since I made a dangerous decision driven by curiosity. It's been, like, a month. But all right. See if you can lower that field."

"Sure. But first–" Ashok reached into the pillar of

light with his left hand... or tried to. His fingers hit resistance. He gritted his teeth and pushed, then sighed. He tried with his right hand, the one with manipulators instead of fingers, and had no more luck. "Oh well. Worth a try."

"Was it? You could have lost your hand!"

She couldn't tell, because of his complex optics, but Callie was sure he rolled his eyes anyway. "Oh no. Whatever would I do. I'd have to get an amazing new hand, maybe with that integrated miniature cryo-beam I've been working on with Lantern. What a potential tragedy we have narrowly averted."

"You'll never get promoted, talking to your captain like that."

"I'm okay with ship's engineer being my terminal rank. Ambition was never my problem. Guess we go with our original plan, huh?" He knelt to place the last explosive charge, this one right on the base of the pedestal that held the key.

"Maybe it'll destroy the key anyway," Callie said.

"We'll find out," Ashok said.

They blew the station from the *White Raven*, and watched it explode into small fragments from a safe distance.

"I'm not seeing anything unusual in the debris field," Janice said. She was half the cockpit crew, running communications and the sensor array, and was famed for her ability to inject just the right note of despair and cynicism into any conversation, no matter how hopeful. "You probably ran low on oxygen and hallucinated this magical key."

Drake, the pilot, was her other half – not in the sense of romantic involvement, because they weren't, but in the sense of sharing a body with Janice, which he did. Years ago they'd been in a catastrophic spaceship accident, and should have died, but an unknown group of Liars with a propensity toward medical experimentation had put them back together again from their surviving parts and mysterious tech. Drake, being the more optimistic of the pair, thought the aliens had meant well, and just hadn't known what humans were supposed to look like. Janice held that the Liars were mad scientists amusing themselves with human experimentation. "Could be floating there, hidden in the mess," Drake said. "It's small."

"True," Janice said. "I haven't run diagnostics on my magic key detector in ages either."

"Shall," Callie said from her seat at the tactical board. "Send a drone out to look for anything that scintillates and coruscates, would you?"

Shall, the AI that ran the ship's computer – sort of *was* the ship's computer – said, "Will do. It's been ages since I went outside."

CHAPTER 3

Callie and Ashok were floating in the cargo bay as the small drone returned, bearing the key in its manipulator arms. "Just floating there, unharmed, as you predicted," Callie said. "Think it's safe to touch?"

Before she could stop him, Ashok gripped it in his manipulators, then tapped the shaft gently with one bare finger of his other hand. "Feels like glass. Cool and smooth. I would avoid touching the in-and-out-of-reality triangles though. You might lose a finger."

Callie took the key and held it up, watching its teeth dissolve and erupt. "Those Liars were willing to die to protect this. They've been guarding it for millennia, probably, passing on the directive to guard it to generations of babies."

"Let's see why." Ashok stroked the greasy-looking crescent he'd strapped to his wrist, and a slit appeared in the air. "Activates just like the short-range teleporter."

Callie sighed. "Please don't open holes in space-time on my ship again without asking first."

"You *don't* want to go?"

She sighed again. "Shall, let everyone know Ashok

and I are leaving the ship to check something out."

"Are you taking the canoe?" That was their small boarding-and-landing vessel, currently in the cargo bay.

"No, we've got an Axiom toy that opens doors in the air."

"Better go quick before Elena finds out," Shall said.

Elena Oh was the ship's executive officer, doctor-in-training, and the love of Callie's recent life. She was generally very supportive, but even she had her limits, and Callie thought this might just brush up against them.

Ashok gestured at the tear before them. "Rank has its privileges."

Callie took a breath, then moved through the slit. It was nothing at all like passing through a wormhole bridge. It was much more like pushing through a curtain made of rotting meat. Even through her spacesuit, something about the texture of the ragged air, pliably giving way against her body, made her shudder.

Ashok followed and the slit sealed up behind him. He looked at the screen on his arm and whistled. "This is… we're in the same place we were before. Like, coordinates-wise." He looked around. "Cap, I think we're *in* the fourth dimension."

Callie looked around. Fluted pillars, white walls etched in what she now recognized as the eye-twisting script of the Axiom, a smooth white floor, and that dome overhead, the alien sun a little lower now. "Up, down, side-to-side – I still just count three dimensions, unless you include time, which we're wasting. Besides, I don't remember much undergraduate math, but I know the fourth dimension isn't a place, it's a dimension of space we can't perceive."

"Yes, true – I was being dramatic, but the situation warrants it. We've moved from our local space-time into a… not adjacent, exactly, but overlapping? No, that's wrong too. This thing doesn't teleport us, at least not to another point in our space-time. It doesn't make a wormhole. It's a phase-shifter. The Liars were using them to sneak up on us, ducking in here, then emerging in another place in our usual spatial reality." He looked around. "I wonder how they control where they come out." He touched the crescent and another opening appeared, showing their cargo bay. He sealed it up. "Opens in the same place we left from. Good, but boring. Hmm. This looks like the same room I glimpsed through the portals on the station, even though we're kilometers from that position. I don't think this place bears any relationship to our spatial coordinates. It's some kind of pocket universe."

"A pocket universe with its own sun? Seems a lot more likely we're in an unknown system."

Ashok looked at the ceiling and whistled. "Look, there, and over there." He pointed. A couple of small panels in the immense dome were black. "I think you're right. I think that dome *is* a viewscreen, just projecting an image. Maybe that moonscape is where the cultists used to live, or something. I don't believe there's really a sun or moon outside."

"Then what is outside?"

"Um. Possibly… nothing. Literally nothing."

"I'm not sure that makes any sense," Callie said.

"Me either, to be totally honest – I'm an engineer, not a theorist. But we're here, and I don't think *here* is a place you can get to in a spaceship. It might not even be a real place, as we understand places. And reality. This could be an Axiom construct, a little extradimensional hideaway created to keep… That."

He pointed past her. Callie turned, and whistled. There was a vault door set in the wall behind her, an archway of golden metal five meters high and three meters across, with a hole in the center about the height of her head and the size of her fist. She looked down at the still-shifting key. "You think this key opens that door?"

"Occam's Plasma Grenade."

"But a lock, and a key, it's so… old-fashioned. The Axiom could manipulate constants of space-time. Why would they lock something in a *vault*?"

"A vault hidden in another dimension, with a key that exists in *multiple* dimensions. Why not? That vault's not hooked up to any kind of computer system, so it can't be hacked. I'm guessing the biggest bomb

TIM PRATT

we've got wouldn't put a scratch on it – it's probably extradimensional too. You can't pick that lock, unless you have lockpicks that exist in four dimensions, and I don't. One key, to open one vault, protected by self-destructing zealots. We would never have gotten here with the key if the Axiom hadn't abandoned that facility, for whatever reason, however many centuries ago, and let their operational security go to shit." He grinned. "So do we open it?"

"The Benefactor's message said this station was one of the most dangerous Axiom facilities in the galaxy," Callie said. "Given some of the things we've encountered… that sounds pretty dangerous. The Benefactor told us this station should be destroyed, for the sake of all life in the galaxy. Or it could have been a trick to get the key so the Benefactor could open the vault and get whatever's inside. Either way… I doubt there's anything nice behind that door, Ashok."

"But it's a vault, and we have a key. How can you not be tempted?"

"I never said I wasn't tempted." Ashok's curiosity was notorious. He'd fly into an exploding starship if he thought there was interesting tech hidden inside. Callie was more pragmatic… but she was also vulnerable to the allure of the unknown. Her ex-husband used to say Pandora had nothing on her – Callie would have opened that box without hesitation. "But just… imagine you're an alien, and you land on Earth, and you find a

31

mountain, and there's a steel door in the mountainside. The door is covered with pretty little symbols, triangles inside circles… all in yellow and black. You might be tempted to look inside, but it would be a bad idea."

"You think there's toxic waste behind that door?"

"I think the Axiom fought wars with each other that destroyed star systems. I think they launched long-term projects designed to alter fundamental characteristics of space-time – some of which are still ongoing thousands of years later, as we've discovered. I think they plotted to survive the heat death of the universe. I think anything *they* locked up, with a key like this, in a place like this, could be something we don't want to fuck with."

"It could be something *amazing*." He gazed up at the door, and then frowned. His mouth was still human enough for that. "Huh. There's more writing up there, over the door."

Callie tilted her head back, and saw more of the Axiom script, following the arch above the vault. "Can you read it?"

"Lantern taught me some of the language, and I've got a visual dictionary loaded in my external memory. I recognize most of the words… let me see… that's the imperative case – no, wait, it's got a warning inflection, hold on. I think it says something like… 'Open only on the last day of the war.'"

They both stood silently for a moment, looking at the vault.

"Which war?" Callie said.

"How would you know it was the last day?" Ashok said.

Callie shivered. "We can't. We just... Ashok, we can't. Whatever's locked up in here, we should leave it locked up."

"I get where you're coming from, but maybe it's a weapon we could use against the Axiom."

Callie shook her head. "The last day of the war? If we're guessing, I'd guess it's a weapon of last resort. Like, our enemies have taken the capital, the palace is about to fall, let's blow everything up ourselves so there's no country left for them to conquer."

Ashok slumped. "You know how I tweaked my risk-assessment engine to be *real* comfortable with dangerous activities? Even *it's* telling me we shouldn't open the door. This is officially the worst, though."

"Make a hole, Ashok."

He obliged, tearing another rip in the air. They slipped through and sealed the temple up behind them.

"What do we do with the key?" Ashok said.

"Once we get underway, I'll load the key and the phase-shifter onto a torpedo and launch them both into the nearest star. Your idea was a good one. The phase-shifter will burn up, and the key will be safe there, at least until heat death, and by then everyone will have bigger problems. Maybe the star will become a black hole and the key will be *really* locked away."

"Oh captain, my captain," Ashok said glumly.

The next day, she and Ashok stood in the *White Raven*'s observation deck and watched the flare of the torpedo's propellant drive it toward the sun. They stood silently for long moments after the torpedo vanished from sight. A while later, the screen on Ashok's arm flashed. "Impact," he said. "The world is a little safer now. A little more boring, but safer."

"Sometimes that's best," she said. "Being thrown into a volcano is probably exciting too. Exciting isn't always good." She clapped him on the shoulder. "Next time we find an alien vault, I'll let you open it, for sure. Okay?"

"Promises, promises," he muttered.

Back in her quarters, Callie made sure the door was sealed, then opened up the strongbox bolted under her bunk. It wasn't a four-dimensional vault that could only be opened by a pentachoron key, but it was pretty secure, with a code to enter and biometrics both.

She opened the lid, and gazed at the key inside: crystalline, shifting as her eyes played over it, beautiful and strange and not entirely of this world. Shooting a torpedo into the sun – and talking about their plan to do so on unencrypted comms – had been a necessary deception. Callie had no doubt their mysterious 'ally' the

Benefactor was still watching them, but she was confident her quarters were secure, at least for the moment.

If the Benefactor *had* sent them to clear the path in order to take the key, better to make it seem like the key was beyond reach forever. She wasn't about to get rid of it – not until she had a better idea of what it was for. The answer could be in some Axiom database. In the meantime, she'd keep the key locked away. The universe was full of dangerous things, and Callie liked having them under her control.

Ashok made sure the door to his machine shop was locked, then took the cloth-wrapped bundle containing the phase-shifter from underneath a pile of scrap in one of his work table drawers. Callie had told him to keep the device safe, and to try to figure out how it worked, if he could. They'd discussed destroying it, but what if the Benefactor had a dimensional ripper of his own? They might need to get back to that temple eventually.

Because maybe someday there would be a war. And maybe someday that war would have a last day.

Ashok settled down with his instruments and began to study the device.

CHAPTER 4

"I think we should go," Ashok said.

Callie looked at the three letters they'd received from the mysterious Benefactor, pinned by magnets to the table in the *White Raven*'s galley, the crew's unofficial conference room. They had an actual conference room at home on their asteroid Glauketas, but this was an all-hands meeting and Drake and Janice preferred to stay on the ship and away from the artificial gravity on the station. Weight made them hurt.

Callie shook her head, her great cloud of hair floating around her. She usually kept her hair ruthlessly pinned down in microgravity, but living someplace where 'up' and 'down' were meaningful terms had made her lax. Also, Elena liked it when her hair floated around that way, and Callie liked being something Elena liked. "It's probably a trap, Ashok."

He nodded. "Yes."

"You want us to fly into a trap."

"I could live without the trap part, but I can also live with it, too. If we never flew into obvious traps we'd never go anywhere. Besides, *this* note worked

36

out." He tapped his finger on the second note the Benefactor had left, the one Ashok had found in his machine shop on Glauketas – the note that provided coordinates for the space station where they'd found the pentachoron key and the vault.

"That intel was good, sure," Callie said. "And the first few times you play cards with a con artist, they let you win, so you'll be stupid and bet big later, and *that's* when they fleece you. That exemplary trustworthy note basically said 'Go check out this place on the edge of the very normal and pleasant Nommo system, home of gorgeous colony worlds and excellent music and food,' right? Whereas *this* note says, 'Go visit the haunted nightmare system that has devoured every ship that visited in the past hundred years.' You see the difference?"

"Sure I do," Ashok said. "The difference is, the Nommo system is boring, and the haunted nightmare system is interesting."

Callie wished Stephen, her old XO, were still around. His realism, pragmatism, and habit of expecting the worst had provided a wonderful rudder (and occasional anchor) for the crew. Of course, then he'd gone completely against type and fallen in love with an environmental artist on Owain in the Taliesen system and decided to get some pleasure out of life instead of sticking his head into alien space stations to see what might bite it off. There was no accounting for some people's baffling life choices.

To Callie's surprise, her new XO, Elena, chimed in with a rather Stephen-like observation: "It's obvious the Benefactor has their own agenda. Your theory about them trying to use us to get their hands on that key... thing... makes a lot of sense. If they want us to go to the Vanir system, they have their own reasons, I'm sure."

"Right," Callie said. "And why should we do anything to further the Benefactor's undeclared interests? I don't mind taking jobs, but I do like to get paid for them at least, and it's helpful to know what the jobs even *are*. I'm glad Elena's on my side."

"Er," Elena said. "I am on your side, always and forever, absolutely yes. That said... our mission is to destroy everything related to the Axiom that we possibly can, right?"

"I see where this is going," Callie said.

"What if that's the Benefactor's mission too? They clearly have intel, but maybe they lack the resources to do anything about that intel, and that's why they need us."

"Or maybe the Benefactor just thinks we're expendable. They could have come to us in a spirit of partnership and alliance, and instead they hid on our ship, spied on us, and left these creepy secret admirer letters. Why not meet us face-to-face? Why all the cloak-and-laser-pistol stuff?"

"Maybe they can't take the risk," Shall said from the ceiling speakers, entirely too reasonably. "It could be dangerous for the Benefactor to approach us directly. Or maybe they're testing us, to see if we've got what it takes to make use of their information. If Lantern is right about the Benefactor's identity, they have to proceed cautiously."

They'd speculated at length over who the Benefactor might be, and so far their best guess was a rogue Liar in the cult of truth-tellers. Who else could know the locations of multiple Axiom facilities? The cult was mostly compartmentalized, with the cells in each system never interacting with each other. Their friend Lantern — herself a secret traitor to the sect, a double agent now working against the Axiom while pretending to lead the cell of truth-tellers in the Sol system — theorized that the Benefactor must be one of the handful of elders who made up the central council of the truth-tellers. Lantern didn't know where that council operated, who was on it, or even how many it numbered – the Elders just sent orders to the individual cells, and those orders were followed without question.

"Yeah, maybe," Callie said. "I–"

"Speak of the alien," Shall said. "Incoming call from Lantern. She seems excited."

"Put her up on the screen," Callie said.

Lantern was transmitting from her own space station off in the Oort cloud. They were practically neighbors, by cosmic standards, and the communication delay was minimal. The small seven-armed alien appeared on screen and undulated her tentacles in a gesture that Elena doubtless recognized but Callie couldn't. Elena wiggled her own arm back, grinning. "Good to see you again," she said.

"I have interesting news," Lantern said.

Callie grimaced. Interesting could mean lots of things. "About the note?"

"Oh yes," Lantern said. The third note the Benefactor had left, in the room Lantern used when she visited Glauketas, had been written in Axiom script, and had proven to be a series of passwords Lantern speculated would give her access to a secret truth-teller database. "I had to be very careful, in case the codes were a trick, a – what do you call it in your language, Ashok?"

"A honeypot," Ashok said. "If you think someone might try hacking your system, you can set up an isolated and monitored section of the site that looks legitimate, and when your hacker gets in, you can trace them back to their source, or even flood them with malicious software to take over their systems."

Lantern undulated. "In the language of the Free we call systems like that *ratatoks*, after a kind of carnivorous stationary hunter on one of the planets we settled. It smells sweet, but tries to eat you when you come too close." Liars didn't call themselves 'Liars,' of course – among themselves they went by the Free, because they were no longer slaves to the Axiom.

"Comparative linguistics is fun," Callie said, "but what did you find out?"

"The codes allowed me to access an old, abandoned truth-teller database. There wasn't much data there, but I did find a map marking various locations around the galaxy, in inhabited systems and uninhabited both. The map wasn't annotated, so I was unsure what the locations were until I noticed one of the markers matched the location of *my* station, and another was the site of the truth-teller base we found in the Taliesen system… and a third marked the location of the Dream."

Callie whistled. "You're saying we know the locations of the other truth-teller cells, and of the Axiom facilities?"

"Some of them, anyway, though maybe not all, and some of the locations may be other things, but… they are certainly worth investigating. I'm especially interested in the locations marked outside systems inhabited by humans."

Callie nodded. The truth-tellers were the Liars who'd given humans the wormhole technology that allowed them to colonize the galaxy – but only in twenty-eight systems that were relatively distant from Axiom facilities. The Liars had carefully corralled and managed the humans to keep them from disturbing Axiom projects, while making them think humanity had the run of the galaxy. Callie and her crew – and a few distant friends on Owain and in the Jovian Imperative – were the only humans who knew the Axiom existed. Most of the truth-tellers were tasked with making sure humans didn't stumble onto Axiom secrets; one had destroyed a space station that was home to fifty thousand souls in a failed attempt to kill Callie and her crew after *they* discovered Axiom wormhole technology. "There are no truth-tellers in uncolonized systems, right? So those must be something else. Like maybe Axiom facilities. We've gone from having no idea where to go next to getting a to-do list of places to investigate."

"All thanks to the Benefactor," Ashok said. "Which is why I say we go check out their first tip." He tapped the first note, the one Callie had found in her cabin on Glauketas not long after they destroyed the Axiom facility called the Dream. "How about we vote? I vote yes."

"I'm shocked," Callie said.

"We also vote yes," Drake said from behind the silvery privacy screen of the mobility chair he and Janice used to get around. "Janice and I are both intrigued."

"I'm not intrigued," Janice said. "I just like doing things, because then I'm not sitting around dwelling on the essential horror of the human condition. No offense, Lantern. I'm sure your condition is horrible too."

"I... none... taken?" Lantern said.

"You know we're going to go, Callie," Elena said. "I mean… the Vanir system. It's been almost a hundred years since the rest of the galaxy heard a word from the place. Three-quarters of a million colonists went through that gate before it was sealed off, and no one knows what happened to them. It's like the lost colony of Roanoke times ten thousand."

Callie wrinkled her forehead. "Was that a historical reference? You know we're shaky on our ancient history around here." Elena had been born in the twenty-second century, gone into cryo-sleep for a long space voyage, and been thawed out five hundred years later, just in time to fall in love with Callie. Sometimes the universe was wonderful, but dating someone whose cultural references were half a millennium old could be tricky.

"Never mind. I'm just saying, the Vanir system is a mystery box. You can't resist a mystery box. We know this about you."

Callie crossed her arms. "Maybe I'm not so prone to outbursts of suicidal curiosity anymore. Maybe I'm growing and evolving as a person."

Elena twinkled. "Mmm, no. I sleep with you every night. I think I would've noticed if you'd done any evolving."

"Come on. Give me some credit. I didn't open the weird fourth-dimensional vault, did I?"

"True," Elena said. "But you did go and *look* at the vault first. We're literally the only people in the galaxy with a shot at figuring out what's wrong in the Vanir system. We can solve one of the great mysteries of our time. How can we not?"

Callie picked up the note, the one she'd found on her pillow, written in an unknown hand. It said,

> *I've been watching your progress, checking in on you occasionally since you set out for Ganymede in that ramshackle pirate ship, and watching you closely once you reached Taliesen. Did you sense me? I thought you might have, once or twice. You're very perceptive, for a human. You did excellent work dismantling the Dream. For your next project, you might visit the Vanir system. What you find there should interest you... and certain members of your crew.*

Callie *had* glimpsed shimmers and corner-of-the-eye disturbances on their voyage to Taliesen, visual glitches she'd put down to stress and fatigue. Either the Benefactor or their agents had hidden away on the ship and watched her, or they had access to enough information about what happened on board her ship to make it *seem* like they had.

The note was signed 'The Benefactor' – a nom de plume she still found the opposite of reassuring – and beneath the signature was a stylized blue drawing of an eye. That part gave her chills.

Once, when traveling very slowly through the tunnel of an ancient Axiom wormhole bridge, strapped to the back of a drone, Callie had seen something strange: a section of the tunnel that looked like a window. Behind the window sat something dark, and slumped, and rounded, with a single fist-sized eye the blue of Cherenkov radiation.

She'd only glimpsed it for a moment and had assumed it was delirium – she'd been under a lot of stress and fully expected to die – but later Stephen's friend Q had mentioned seeing something from the *White Raven*'s observation deck when they passed through the bridge: a blue eye that glowed. Then they'd gotten that letter from the Benefactor, with a drawing of a blue eye. The connection was obvious – the Benefactor was either the entity in the wormhole or wanted them to think he was.

Callie's first impulse after finding the note was to clear their ships and the asteroid and run full decontamination protocols, the kind of deep-cleanse procedures reserved for pathogen outbreaks, meant to kill anything on board ships or stations from microbes on up. But if this Benefactor had stealth and teleportation technology good enough to creep around her home and evade notice, and the skills to blank out their AI Shall's security cameras without Shall even noticing the tampering, then the Benefactor could easily slip out with the crew and make Callie's whole plan to decontaminate the interloper into oblivion moot.

Her second impulse had been to destroy the note and pretend she'd never seen it, because she didn't like being manipulated, and this wasn't even subtle manipulation.

"Shall?" Callie said. "What do you think? Do we go to the system of no return?"

"I do like expanding my data banks," Shall said. "And going to the Vanir system would definitely do that. So I say yes."

"Lantern?"

"The map I found has *two* locations marked in the Vanir system, one just outside the orbit of the twin colony planets, and one quite distant, several degrees outside the path of the ecliptic. I'm curious to find out what those are. I'd like to go and see."

"So even if I vote no, I get overruled," Callie said. "This is what I get for giving you all ownership stakes in our little concern, isn't it?"

"Demonstrably," Elena said.

"Then for the sake of unit cohesion and morale, I vote yes as well," Callie said.

As if she were ever going to do otherwise.

CHAPTER 5

"There's a probe approaching Glauketas," Janice said into Callie's comm.

"Are you sure? We haven't gotten any alerts here on the station." Callie was in the room she shared with Elena on Glauketas, out beyond the orbit of Neptune, trying to pack for the possibly one-way voyage to the Vanir system. She'd never had any trouble packing before – pants, weapons, it wasn't hard – but she'd never traveled between the stars with someone she was in love *and* lust with, and these days many more options were variously appealing.

"The *White Raven*'s long-range sensors are superior to those on Glauketas, captain," Janice said. Callie smiled. *Captain*. When Janice was polite and formal it usually meant she thought you were being stupid but was exercising great restraint. "The probe is still some distance away, but it's coming. I can't figure out where it came from, either. I backtraced the trajectory, but there's a point where the probe just appears from nowhere. It must have launched from some vessel that's not using a transponder, running dark."

"And we're sure it's a probe, and not, say, a missile?"

Janice didn't answer for a long moment. Then she said, "That silence you just heard was my withering scorn at even being asked a question like that, captain."

"Understood. What's it look like?"

"A ball of metal the size of your head with lots of electronics crammed inside it. Someone wants to take a look at us, or – hold on, the probe just sent me a burst of unencrypted text. It says 'first letters of first letter.' And... now it's sending a splintercast, but I can't tell you what it says, because we don't have a decryption key."

"Wait. Try..." Callie started to look up the Benefactor's first letter from her terminal, then realized she knew it by heart anyway. "IDIYYFW."

"Pretty weak decryption key, but I guess there's nobody else out here on the frozen outskirts to intercept it anyway... okay, that string works. The message says, 'The Benefactor sent me to assist you.' Huh."

Callie whistled. "This is a definite escalation from leaving notes on my pillow. How long until the probe gets here?"

"Couple hours."

"Understood." She flipped comm channels. "Ashok, I need you to make me something, and I need it made in about ninety minutes."

"Is it a perpetual motion machine?" Ashok said. "I always thought I could make one of those, as long as I had a really impossible deadline to motivate me."

"We have very large guns pointed at you, Benefactor." Callie spoke from the bridge of the *White Raven*, transmitting on the same encrypted channel the probe had used before. Ashok had finished building the thing she wanted in about forty minutes, so they'd had time to take the ship out on an intercept course to meet the probe. If this gift from the Benefactor *was* full of murder, harboring secret technology that even Janice's paranoid sensor array couldn't recognize as weapons, they'd be able to fight back better with the *Raven* than on the asteroid.

"I am not the Benefactor," the probe replied, in a pleasantly deep but overly ingratiating tone, like an insurance salesman who saw you as his last opportunity to avert bankruptcy. "The Benefactor is my employer. He said you might be skeptical. Permission to board, so we can talk directly?"

He *said*? *That's one more data point about the Benefactor's identity than we had before. Assuming this thing can be trusted, which is a big if.* "We can talk just fine from here," Callie said.

"That's a bit rude," the probe replied.

"There's no communication delay at all," Janice said on private comms. "That voice must be transmitting from somewhere close by, astronomically speaking."

"My name is Kaustikos," the probe said.

"I know that word," Elena muttered. "I think I saw it in one of the medical texts I've been studying. His name is… 'one who burns'? So he's flammable?"

"Not quite the right translation," Shall's voice was apologetic. "Kaustikos means 'capable of burning,' but in the sense of *causing* burns, not burning itself."

"I didn't choose the name," Kaustikos said. "The Benefactor did. It's a working pseudonym. A code name, if you prefer. The Benefactor has a flair for the dramatic, if you hadn't noticed."

"You let your boss change your name?" Callie said. "You should have negotiated a better contract."

"You call *me* Shall," Shall said over her private comm. "You got everyone else doing it too, even though my name is Michael."

"That's because you have the same name as my ex-husband, and it got annoying," Callie said. Shall was an AI based on a template of her ex-husband's mind, and was very similar in personality and temperament, with notable differences, like the fact that Shall had been in space with her often while Michael was back home on Ganymede. Also, Shall had never cheated on her a dozen times.

The probe replied, "Given what the Benefactor is paying me, he can call me anything he wants, and I'll hop when he answers. Captain Machedo, I can be a great help to you. Without my assistance in the

Vanir system, you and your crew will likely die." He paused. "Honesty forces me to admit that, even with my assistance, you'll probably die anyway. But at least it will be for a good cause."

"Go back to the part where you get paid," Callie said. "Why don't we get paid? If the Benefactor wants us to go to the Vanir system, he can fund the expedition. He'll have to pay our usual 'stupid code name' surcharge if he wants us to rename ourselves after medical terminology."

"Dibs on 'Diaphoresis'," Ashok said. "It just sounds so pretty. Like diaphanous." He was listening in from the machine shop.

The probe sighed. "The Benefactor believed you were on a sacred mission to save the galaxy, and feared you would be offended he suggested you might take money in exchange for saving countless lives. It seems he overestimated your zeal. Fortunately, I am authorized to pay for any costs associated with outfitting your ship and crew for the journey, and to transfer a sizable sum to your accounts upon your successful return from the Vanir system."

"I prefer payment in advance. My reputation is good enough that I usually get it, too."

"Money won't do you any good in the Vanir system. Even the Benefactor isn't entirely sure what's happening there – he knows more than you, of course – but it's safe to say that normal economic systems are no longer in operation."

Callie grunted. "Pay us anyway. I plan on returning to a system where I can spend it. Or do you have to call your boss first?"

"I have a certain amount of discretion. There."

"Shall?" Callie said.

"Did you want to buy one of the minor moons of Saturn?" Shall said. "Because we *could*, if we pooled our shares." He flashed her the total amount transferred to their account, and Callie grunted. She could turn Glauketas from a lightly refurbished mining station into a gloriously modern space station just with her share, and have enough left over for a pretty nice dinner afterward.

"As far as good faith gestures go, that's a pretty good one," Ashok chimed in.

"Now can I come aboard?" Kaustikos said. "Since we're co-workers?"

"If you're so vital to our mission, why didn't you come yourself, instead of sending a probe?"

"Ah. I see the confusion. I am not transmitting remotely. I *am* the probe. I am a fully autonomous artificial intelligence."

Callie frowned. AI were rare and expensive – Shall had been an extravagant anniversary gift from her very wealthy husband, meant to keep her company with a version of his personality while she was off on long space voyages. More importantly, AI took a *lot* of processing power to run properly. Shall was comfortable enough on the *White Raven* and Glauketas, but when he ported a copy of his consciousness to a drone or probe he lost a lot of speed, cleverness, and access to data, because the hardware just wasn't sufficient to let him operate at full capacity. "You're AI? Don't you feel a little cramped in that steel ball?"

"The Benefactor has access to rather impressive microtechnology, Captain Machedo. I have a full copy of my consciousness here, with plenty of room to incorporate new and interesting experiences."

"Who's your template?" Shall asked.

All the AI in the galaxy that bothered to talk to people were built on the templates of human minds, with those personalities, thought patterns, and memories acting as seed crystals and stabilizing agents for the machine mind. Attempts to create pure computer intelligences had been unsuccessful, because while such entities could sometimes attain consciousness, they had no more interest in talking to people than people had in talking to slime molds... and just as little common ground for communication. AI based on humans weren't truly copies of those people, at least not for more than the first microsecond, when their experiences started to diverge. Just the speed of their thoughts, and their instantaneous access to information, ensured they would become different from their models but they did retain enough humanity and memories to stay interested in people.

"Oh, who remembers?" Kaustikos said. "My template wasn't very interesting, and that transition was a long time ago. All you need to know is, I have qualities the Benefactor thinks will be useful on this mission – the ability to improvise, patience, and being a highly motivated self-starter."

"So you've got a code name *and* a secret identity," Callie said.

"You must admit," Kaustikos replied, "secrecy does seem to be our employer's preferred method of operation."

Callie bristled at the 'our employer' bit, as she had at being called a 'co-worker,' but, then again, she did intend to keep the money, and that meant trying to carry out the job in good faith to the best of her abilities. "You can come on board. But I don't trust you, so first we're going to send a drone out to meet you and fit you with a little insurance policy our engineer built."

"Oh, dear, any addition to my body would simply ruin my pleasingly symmetrical contours."

"I took aesthetics into account when I built it," Ashok said.

"Even so. What if I refuse?"

"Then you can fuck off back to the Benefactor and tell them we don't want your help."

"What if I tell you my accompaniment on this mission is a condition of your employment?"

Callie laughed. The whole crew laughed, even

Elena. "Shall, you have an MBA, do you want to answer that?"

"One traditionally negotiates the terms of a contract before making payment in full," Shall said. "For reasons that are likely obvious."

"And if the Benefactor demands their money back?"

Shall didn't have a tongue to cluck, but he made the sound anyway. "Our verbal contract, such as it was, specified that we would go to the Vanir system, funded by the Benefactor. We will do that. He has no grounds to demand repayment."

"Would you go to war with the Benefactor over this? Knowing the resources he must have?" Kaustikos sounded genuinely curious.

"Would I go to war to maintain our independence?" Callie said. "To show that we can be hired, but never owned? Of course I would. It's up there among the top five reasons I'd go to war."

"Fair enough," Kaustikos said. "I assume you want to strap some sort of bomb to me, so you can destroy me if I turn out to be a traitorous villain?"

"Now you've gone and spoiled the surprise," Callie said.

CHAPTER 6

Shall sent out a drone with the device Ashok had made, a palm-sized curve of shiny metal that matched Kaustikos's carapace and attached almost seamlessly. The attachment was full of inward-pointing explosives that would vaporize the probe without doing much damage to anything in its vicinity. Once affixed, the bomb couldn't be removed with anything short of *another* bomb, or Ashok's proprietary homemade nanotech solvent.

"The constant terror of death won't impact my job performance at all," Kaustikos transmitted as the drone finished installing the failsafe.

"You've got a copy of your consciousness somewhere else," Callie said. "You're way more immortal than most of us."

"And yet I'm very attached to *this* version of my consciousness, which has already diverged from my earlier state in such enjoyable ways. Why, if you blew me up, I'd lose all these deeply pleasurable memories of meeting *you*."

"That would be a tragedy," Callie agreed. She felt

better. "You have permission to come aboard."

Kaustikos followed the drone to an airlock, then floated inside, where Callie and Ashok waited to meet him in the cargo bay. The shiny ball of artificial mind maneuvered with spinning reaction wheels, turning to face them with an array of lenses that reminded Callie of Ashok's.

"Tell me everything you know about our boss," Callie said.

"Aren't you going to show me to my rooms first?"

"You're a floating metal ball. You can live in that empty crate strapped to the wall over there. Speak."

"What is there to say?" The probe rotated to direct its array of lenses at Callie. "The Benefactor is a concerned citizen of the galaxy who discovered a terrible existential threat – the Axiom. My employer judged that you could be an effective tool to combat that threat, and decided to offer information and other assistance to your mission."

"What does the Benefactor know about the Vanir system?"

"Our employer has reason to believe that it wasn't a natural disaster that closed the Vanir gate, or even human sabotage, but the intervention of alien beings – the Axiom, perhaps."

"If the Axiom know about humans, why hasn't he sent a million murder machines through the bridges to every inhabited system and wiped us out?" That was the big fear, and the reason the Liars hid the existence of the Axiom from humanity – because if the ancient aliens were ever disturbed, they would likely take steps to eradicate the disturbance, and they could destroy planets as easily as Callie could squash a bug.

"That is an *excellent* question, and one the Benefactor wonders about as well."

"Damn it, spaceball, the letter your boss sent said the Vanir system would be of particular interest to people in my crew. What does *that* mean?"

The probe bobbed. "I'm afraid our employer has not shared that information with me. He keeps secrets, as we've discussed. Believe me when I say the Benefactor wants you to succeed in destroying whatever force has closed off the Vanir system, if it proves to be related to the Axiom, or their servants. I'm sure he has a good reason for his reticence."

"I'm not reassured."

The probe bobbed, lenses shifting. "Even if the Benefactor *is* somehow nefarious, captain, surely you can accept that you share a common enemy? Let's say the Benefactor is a crime boss, or a cult leader, or an aspiring warlord, or something else that would make you scowl in disapproval. Whatever his business, he can't do it in a galaxy scoured of life, which, as I understand it, is the worst-case scenario outcome if we fail in our mission to destroy the Axiom."

"I'll work with the Benefactor as long as our interests coincide," Callie said. "But I don't like spying, or secrets, or manipulation."

"Alas, those are the Benefactor's primary tools," Kaustikos said. "That's how he knows so much, I'm sure. But in my role as liaison I will attempt to disguise those tools to make them more palatable to you – like a parent putting spinach into their child's fruit smoothie so the little treasures will eat something more nutritious without screaming about the taste."

"The human who provided the template for you must have been a real asshole," Callie said.

"Perhaps," Kaustikos replied. "Or perhaps he was a wonderful humanitarian, and my experiences as a second-class citizen since becoming an AI, discriminated against in nearly every polity despite being clearly superior to humans on every measurable axis, have made me bitter and ungenerous. I suppose you'll never know. When do we leave for the Vanir system?"

"We're nearly ready," Callie said. "Go to your crate until we call for you." She spun and propelled herself out of the cargo hold. Once she was out of earshot she opened a private channel to Shall. "Is everything operational?"

"The spyware in the bomb is working fine," Shall said. "Any communication Kaustikos tries to send should be intercepted. Though if it's encrypted, we won't be able to tell what it says. We can also jam his comms entirely at will, but he'll notice."

"Let him talk for now. I'm curious to hear how he describes our meeting."

But Kaustikos didn't attempt to send any messages before they got underway.

Callie and Elena strapped themselves in at the nose of the ship, behind Janice and Drake's control center. Ashok and Lantern were in the machine shop, and Kaustikos was in the cargo bay, according to the transponder hidden in the bomb. "I'm sure we're forgetting something," Callie said.

"We've got food and weapons and tools and medicine," Elena patted her arm reassuringly. "Anything else we need, I'm sure we can get it. We're in a warship."

"Skirmish-ship at best," Janice said. "Recon ship, for sure. We've got enough guns to slow people down so we can run away from their superior firepower, but don't go thinking we're indestructible."

"We can always teleport out of danger," Elena said. "The bridge generator transports us to safety automatically if we get grievously damaged, so we kind of *are* indestructible."

"Ha," Janice said. "Except after we jump, for all those long hours waiting for the bridge generator to recharge. That's when I'd try to kill us, if I was a horrible alien menace."

"Good thing you're on our side," Callie said.

"Ashok, are the coordinates punched in?"

"Sure are, cap. We should pop out of our wormhole on the far side of the Vanir system, about as far away from the bridgehead as we can get while remaining in the system."

"Good." The Vanir system wasn't technically inaccessible, as far as the scientists could tell. The big wormhole bridgehead out by Jupiter could open up a passage to the Vanir system just fine, and, for years, the system had been a perfectly ordinary colony, trading with its interstellar neighbors via the bridges. The problem was, for the past hundred years, no one who'd gone through the bridge to Vanir had ever come *back*, including military ships and probes. No one knew if the bridge had malfunctioned or if something on the other side was keeping the ships from returning. All the human-occupied systems had agreed that *whatever* was going on there was too dangerous to investigate further, and the Vanir system had been formally interdicted and closed to civilian traffic. The Jovian Imperative still sent occasional military vessels, packed with guns and humanitarian supplies both, but none had ever returned.

The closest colony systems had dispatched unmanned probes to see what was going on in the Vanir system but, traveling conventionally, it would be centuries before they arrived. The Vanir system was remote even in terms of galactic scale. Earth's solar system was on the Orion Spur, a minor offshoot arm of the Milky Way, not even one of the main spirals. Most of the other twenty-seven colony systems were in the Perseus, Outer, and New Outer arms, close neighbors in astronomical terms. The Vanir system, though, was way on the outer tip of the Scutum–Centaurus Arm, just about as far from Earth's neighborhood as you could get while remaining in the galaxy.

There was lots of speculation about why the system had gone dark, and whether it had something to do with its relative remoteness, but that had always seemed unlikely to Callie. Absent the wormhole technology of the twenty-eight bridges, *all* the colony systems were impossibly distant from each other, and if they were suddenly forced to rely on conventional methods of space travel it would take centuries to send a letter even to the nearest colony.

"If there's something right outside the wormhole gate turning spaceships into neutron paste, we'll be spared," Callie said. "If the whole *system* is some kind of Axiom area-denial weapon, or full of hungry nanomachines looking for raw material… well, with luck we'll be far enough away from the big nasty to avoid being caught up when we come out. All right. Ready when you are, Ashok."

After a moment, the spreading black inkblot tendrils of the wormhole gate opened before the ship, and the eddying arms of darkness stretched out to embrace them. They moved into the familiar but eerie darkness beyond the gate – it looked like a round tunnel, interrupted by bands of white light at regular intervals. Callie watched the twenty-one second countdown begin on her screen. No matter how far you went, to the colony next door or the far side of the galaxy, the journey between two ends of a wormhole bridge always lasted exactly twenty-one seconds.

That's why she was rather surprised when they emerged spinning wildly into ordinary space after only seventeen.

CHAPTER 7

Unfamiliar stars whirled on the viewscreens. "Stabilize!" Callie shouted, but Drake was already correcting the nauseating spin and getting the ship steady.

"What a good idea," he said amiably.

Callie ignored him. "Elena, report!"

Elena wasn't just XO but also the ship's medical officer, though in terms of experience she was *maybe* a third-year medical student at this point, and that was with a whole lot of neural enhancers and many cramming sessions in medical education simulations. "All crew life signs are green – just some accelerated heart rates and adrenal spikes, and *that* makes sense."

"Shall, report!" Callie barked.

"The ship is fine," Shall said. "All systems functional. Or, I mean. They appear to be."

"Janice, where are we?"

"Not where we're supposed to be," she snapped. "Give me and Shall a minute to try to figure it out, would you?"

"Ashok, Lantern, what the hell happened with the bridge generator?"

"It malfunctioned in a *really* interesting way, didn't it?" Ashok said cheerfully. "This isn't a case of punching in the wrong coordinates – we got booted out of the wormhole *early*. How does that even happen? It would help if we understood how the bridge generator worked in the first place. I sure wish the Axiom had left some diagrams, or maybe a repair manual or two."

"Is the bridge generator broken?" Callie's nightmare was being stranded far from any human-habitable world, with safety and resources beyond the reach of their Tanzer drive.

"I'm not seeing any errors," Ashok said. "As far as the bridge generator's logs are concerned, it took us exactly where we wanted, and, once it finishes cooldown, I don't see any reason it can't take us somewhere else. Maybe even a place we're trying to go next time."

The fist of Callie's heart unclenched. "Good to know. Lantern, do you have any insight?" Lantern knew more about Axiom technology than they did, since the truth-tellers used selected parts of it, though the more devout treated the devices like holy relics than technological tools.

"I am very confused," Lantern said. "I have never heard of something like this happening. We will investigate."

"Report if you come to any conclusions. Or even wild speculations. I'd take anything at this point."

"You aren't going to shout 'Kaustikos, report?'" The drone AI sounded amused.

"Cargo doesn't have any responsibilities," Callie said.

"And yet. The Benefactor worried something like this might happen."

Callie tightened her fingers on the armrests of her chair. "What? You knew the bridge generator might malfunction, and didn't think to mention it?"

"Oh, don't make it sound so sinister." Kaustikos sniffed. "The Benefactor didn't say 'oh dear, you might get kicked out of a wormhole, be careful.' He just mused that whatever aliens disabled the bridge in the Vanir system might have taken steps to prevent incursion from small wormhole generators like yours as well. He theorized that they might, at the very least, be able to detect such arrivals, and suggested we emerge on the outskirts of the system to avoid detection. Since that was already your plan, I felt no need to mention the Benefactor's suggestion. Indeed, I was afraid if I *did* mention it, you might choose to do the opposite out of spite or contrariness."

Callie started to object, then noticed Elena trying not to laugh and settled for scowling instead.

Kaustikos went on. "It seems that whatever entity or group runs the Vanir system now has more... *robust* methods to prevent intrusion than expected."

"It's gotta be a force field," Ashok said. "Some kind

of barrier around the system that interrupts wormhole bridges and makes them terminate short of their destination. Or maybe space caltrops."

"Okay, we know where we are now," Janice said. "The good news is, we're closer to the Vanir system than we were before. Much closer. Very much. The bad news is…"

"Let me guess," Callie said. "Space is big."

"Just like it says in the Bible," Janice agreed.

"I think that line comes from Shakespeare, actually," Drake said.

"Isn't it from the *Epic of Gilgamesh*?" Ashok said. "Or, wait, no, one of Aesop's Fables?"

"It's the Bible," Janice said. "Proverbs. Right? It sounds like a proverb."

"The source is a little later than any of those," Elena said. "I don't think the man who wrote that line ever thought it would become a *proverb*, but–"

"There's a ship approaching," Shall interrupted. "I've never seen anything like it. No matches in our database at all."

"Let's take a look at it." The ship was a long way off, far beyond visual range, but the *White Raven*'s sensors scanned it and put together a composite of what it would look like.

Callie grunted as the image assembled itself onscreen. The ship approaching them was roughly spherical, twice the size of the *White Raven*, covered in spines and fins and needles, and apparently made of gleaming black glass.

"It's a scourge-ship." Lantern's voice was awestruck. "I've seen drawings in the museum of subjugation. The Axiom had a fleet of those ships. They're made for scouring worlds. They were sent out for... the Axiom called it 'cleansing.' Eradicating sapient life, or life that showed signs of sapience to come, before they could pose a threat to the Axiom. Those ships burned whole ecosystems, whole *planets*, down."

"Now we know for sure the system wasn't taken over by a doomsday cult among the colonists or an isolationist human warlord," Callie said. "Score one for the Benefactor's mysterious source of information. Do these ships usually travel alone, Lantern?"

"No. It's formidable enough on its own, but it took a fleet of dozens to destroy a planet, and they generally traveled in packs."

"Just one here, though," Callie mused.

"It makes sense," Kaustikos said. "If our adversaries built a fence around the system, why not have a guard dog to chase anyone who tries to climb over the fence? What now, Captain Machedo? Run away as fast as we can?"

"Oh, no," Callie said. "That ship is a valuable source of intelligence, and we're going to suck it dry."

"Scourge-ships were typically crewed by my people,"

Lantern said into Callie's suit comms. "The truly loyal ones – fanatics, who believed they owed their existence to the Axiom, that slavery was the proper state for any creatures the Axiom permitted to live, that service was glory. Axiom officers would oversee the fleet remotely."

"So it's not likely to be fully automatic? Good. Punching a control panel is so much less satisfying." Callie crouched aboard the scourge-ship, in a narrow corridor that showed bright new welds where the interior had been repaired or retrofitted sometime in the not-so-distant past. This wasn't an Axiom relic mothballed for millennia, but a working ship in active service. The lighting was shaded a lot farther into the red end of the spectrum than humans preferred, and the bare metal all around took on a rust-colored hue. They had artificial gravity here, not too heavy, but enough to keep her feet on the ground. She'd released a handful of Ashok's scuttling spider-sized drones and they were beaming a map of the ship's interior back to her as they explored. They were also probing the ship's automated systems in the hopes that Shall might be able to hijack the ship, or at least interrupt its functions. Shall thought it was possible, assuming the scourge-ship ran on the same protocols as the other Axiom machines they'd encountered and studied.

Callie wore her prized possession, an experimental spacesuit with the best stealth technology humanity had yet developed – almost entirely undetectable to scanners or biological eyes, but so ruinously expensive that her old bosses at the now-defunct Trans-Neptunian Alliance had never created more than the single prototype she'd been selected to test. She'd boarded the ship using the personal, short-range wormhole generator Lantern had given her, a piece of rare and highly restricted technology, much prized even among the truth-tellers. Callie was a perfect stealth and infiltration machine, and she *loved* it.

She crept along a corridor the drones had assured her was clear. Shall kept whispering in her ear, keeping her apprised of the situation outside. The *White Raven* was running, and the scourge-ship was chasing. "It's gaining on us, but slowly," Shall said. "It absolutely bristling with weapons, but it's not firing on us."

"They must want some intel too," Callie said. "We're probably the first people to ever trip this little alarm of theirs, and they'll want to know if we're a one-off or the vanguard of a larger force. Being isolated in the Vanir system goes both ways – no information gets out of there, but precious little information goes in, either. You're scanning the *White Raven* for intruders, in case they sent in a boarding party of their own with personal teleporters like mine?"

"I've been ludicrously vigilant ever since you found out the Benefactor had been skulking around," Shall said. "No signs of any space-time anomalies here.

They could be scanning for the same thing, though – they might know you're there."

"That's why I didn't linger after I 'ported over. They might know I'm on the ship, but they won't know exactly where. They can play cat and mouse but I bet I'm better at it than they are."

Most of her drones had dead-ended into bulkheads, but one had found the engine room – that could be useful – and another was slowly making its way toward Lantern's best guess for where the control room would be. The ship was roughly spherical, covered in hooks and spines that Lantern said served no known purpose, apart from looking wicked. Elena said the ship looked like a sweetgum seed pod. Apparently they were black and spiky too. Callie thought it looked like the head of a medieval morningstar mace. Lantern speculated that the cockpit was in the center, the most protected and armored place, the nut in the shell. Lantern had no idea how many crew members a scourge-ship required, but Callie hadn't passed anything that looked like cabins, or a galley, or a gym, or even an infirmary – just armor plating and storage rooms and access panels.

She froze and watched her feeds as one of her drones went dark, and then another, and then a third. but on that last one, she got a flash of what killed it: a scuttling thing with spindly black metal legs, and a central body bristling with lenses and spikes. It was just a robot, but it gave her the same visceral revulsion that particularly leggy and hairy insects did. She slid into an alcove, crouched, and checked her weapons.

Callie might have missed it, because the hunter was walking on the ceiling, but she made a habit of scanning her *whole* environment, and glanced up at the right moment. The hunter-drone stopped directly above her, lenses rotating, antenna bending this way and that. Callie had faith in her suit – it mimicked her background, hid her heat and sound and breath, and was invisible to every kind of sensor she knew about. She should be completely undetectable unless the nasty spider thing actually brushed up against her –

The hunter dropped, and Callie rolled out of the way just before it struck the space she'd occupied. The drone made an annoyed chittering sound and its antennae waved wildly.

Callie decided she was tired of being the mouse. She sprinted down the corridor and tossed an electromagnetic pulse grenade behind her. The grenades had a small radius – wouldn't do her much good if the blast disabled her own suit – but enough to knock the thing's systems offline long enough for her to more permanently disable it.

She turned to watch the grenade pulse green for a moment (Ashok's concession to her desire for some indication the thing had actually gone off), and the hunter obligingly dropped, its spindly legs motionless, its glowing lenses dark.

Then half a dozen pseudopods popped out of small round portholes ringing the central orb and it rose up on obviously biological limbs and started running toward her.

She'd seen Axiom biotech, and Axiom robots, but this was some combination of both, or else it was a Liar in some kind of armored suit. Callie tossed a stun grenade this time, a burst of electricity that should scramble the nervous system of just about anything that had one. The hunter tumbled and slid to a stop in front of her, tentacles twitching.

"Is there anybody in there?" Callie resisted the urge to rap her knuckles on the thing's carapace. It would probably explode or give her cancer or inject her with a neurotoxin or something. Instead she took out a marble-sized green ball from her belt and tossed it onto the hunter. The marble burst on impact, gooey filaments spreading across the hunter in a web and sticking to the floor and the walls. Ashok used the same goo to seal hull breaches, and, while the material wasn't indestructible, it was tough enough to keep the little monster secure for a while.

Callie was running blind now, her drones eaten up, and the ship knew *something* was here, hunting its hunters. Callie decided time was becoming precious, so she took a perpendicular corridor and started working her way to the ship's creamy, murdery center.

Several hunter-drones scuttled past, converging on the one she'd disabled, some with their organic parts undulating wildly, others looking as purely robotic as her original victim had at first, and Callie crouched and pressed herself against walls and at one point crawled underneath a pipe to let them move past without making physical contact and discovering her.

She finally reached a sealed round door with Axiom script written above it in red. "Translation?" she asked, sending her view back to the *White Raven*.

"The scourge fleet had its own dialect," Lantern said. "I think it translates as something like, 'Heart of Correction'? Or 'Core of Punishment' might be more accurate."

"Sounds important." Callie stuck plastic explosives to the door, backtracked around a corner, and hit the button. The boom reverberated through the corridor, and when she peeked around the edge she saw the shaped charge had done its job — blown the door *inward*, spraying a lot of shrapnel in the process. She moved through the opening low and fast — and then stopped, staring at the pilot dying on the floor with a gaping hole in her torso.

Callie turned and tossed a few more marbles of expanding sealant at the remains of the doorframe, and the material obligingly filled in the hole and hardened, giving her some temporary security and privacy. Seconds later, she heard the scratch and scuttle of hunter claws trying to breach the barrier, but she barely spared the bio-drones a thought. She knelt instead by the dying pilot, and said, "I'm sorry." The pilot didn't reply, and Callie watched the light disappear from her eyes.

Her human eyes, in her human face.

CHAPTER 8

Callie numbly operated the controls of the scourge-ship, following instructions, intuitions, and guesses from Shall, Lantern, and Ashok. Once she successfully loaded Shall's control software into the system, everything got a lot easier.

She disabled the internal security and the scuttling of the hunters stopped. Then she transferred the ship's navigational data back to the *Raven*, so they could see where it had come from, and how it ended up here. The scourge-ship, presumably, could come and go from the Vanir system at will, and might reveal a path they could follow. Worst case, they could travel in this vessel… but Callie didn't want to do that. She couldn't remember when she'd been more unsettled, and she wanted to get off this ship, and away from its dead pilot.

Looking at her was worse than glimpsing the clawed hand of an Axiom protruding from an improperly sealed pod on the Dream. That, at least, was fully alien. This was more like seeing Elena's old crewmate Sebastien with metal Axiom implants in his skull and his eyes glowing red, but worse.

Once she'd done everything that needed doing, Callie sat down on the floor – the pilot's chair was covered in blood and less identifiable fluids – and told her friends what she'd found. "The pilot is a human female. About my age, I'd guess."

"*Human?*" Lantern said.

"Does she have implants?" Ashok said. Axiom mind-control technology typically involved a lot of hardware sticking out of the skull. The tech they'd encountered didn't work very well on humans because it was designed for Liar physiology, but the Axiom in the Vanir system could have perfected their technique in the long decades since the system sealed itself off. They'd gone in another direction, though.

"I don't see any visible technological implants, no. It's… her *arms* are gone. Her human arms, I mean. She has limbs, and they're attached to her shoulders, but they look more like the pseudopods of your people, Lantern – grafted on, or something. She died from the explosion when I breached the door, a piece of shrapnel put a hole in her torso, and I can see her guts…"

"Oh, Callie," Elena said softly.

The pity in her voice put some steel in Callie's: "No, that's not what bothers me. I mean, it *bothers* me, but I've seen people with holes in them before. What's bothering me is that her guts are all wrong. No pink coils of intestine… instead, there are all these bright yellow strands, as thick as my pinkie fingers. This isn't just a case of strange prosthetics. These changes go deeper, fully internal. But her face, her head, her legs, everything else, looks human. Someone did this to her, changed her, put her on an Axiom ship, and sent her to murder or capture other humans." Callie shuddered. "We're going to find out who did this, and we're going to make sure they never do it again. Ashok, you and Lantern get over here and start pillaging the data banks, and then disable the ship. One less operational scourge-ship in the galaxy is a net good. Shall, send a drone… one big enough to carry this body back to our ship."

Once Ashok and Lantern had looted everything of use from the scourge-ship, Callie ordered Drake to get under thrust in a random direction away from their point of arrival – just in case more scourge-ships came to check on the one they'd so thoroughly disabled. Ashok couldn't remove the scourge-ship's bridge generator because it was rigged to destroy itself in the event of tampering, but that was fine for their purposes – he tampered with it anyway, and reduced the greasy black cube to a ruin with concave sides. They pulled all the ship's data they could access and brought it home. Once they translated and analyzed that they'd have a sense of where to go from here… if they could go anywhere at all.

They had plenty to occupy them in the meantime.

Callie joined Elena in the infirmary, looking down at the dead scourge-ship pilot on the exam table, her body-cavities open to the air. Callie had made a good start on that with the explosion, and Elena had finished it more deliberately with bone saws and rib-spreaders.

Elena wore a white plastic apron, diagnostic lenses, and a baffled expression. A rack beside her held specimen jars where various disgusting things floated in equally disgusting cloudy fluids. "Have you figured anything out yet?" Callie said.

Elena shrugged. "I'm not quite a doctor – even with the neural enhancers and access to the medical database, I need another six months of intensive work in the Hypnos residency suite before I can even try to get certified – but I *am* a biologist, functionally even a xenobiologist, and this is a lot more like dissecting an unknown animal than autopsying a human. I do think this pilot started as a baseline human, and the changes were made later, probably in her adulthood. The brain is intact, and the original sense organs, but almost everything else has been altered to one degree or another."

"Altered how?"

Elena began to point, though Callie didn't recognize much of what she pointed at. "She still has lungs, but she doesn't have a heart, a liver, kidneys, or a reproductive system… She has blood, but it's not *just* blood. Most of the tests I can do here just say her new fluids are 'unknown contaminants.' She has other organs, new organs, like nothing I've seen before. I think this one does the job of the heart." She prodded a gray shape in the woman's chest cavity, like a flower made of valves. "She must have other systems for processing waste, too, assuming there *is* any waste. She doesn't have a stomach or a bowel! At first I thought her digestive system had just been damaged in the explosion, but that's not it. The system has been replaced. I don't know where she gets her energy, but it's not from food, or at least, not the same way we get it from food."

Callie gazed down, trying to keep her face impassive, but somehow seeing a person so profoundly changed was worse than seeing one merely dead. "Why would anyone do this to a human?"

"I think they're improvements," Elena said. "Why else go to all this trouble? Maybe this faux-heart is more efficient than her old one. Maybe food that's edible for humans is scarce in the Vanir system now, and they had to make alterations to use calories more efficiently. It could just be adaptation, altering their bodies to better fit their environments. Instead of terraforming a world to make it more hospitable to humans, you change the human to suit the environment."

"That doesn't fit what we know about the Vanir system – the planets there are supposed to be perfectly habitable, and one was supposedly a verdant paradise."

Elena nodded. "That's not the only inconsistency. I've checked the database, and the alterations made to this woman are way beyond any technology humans have now. By my ancient 22nd-century standards, modern surgeons are basically wizards – we were still struggling with reliable organ replacement back in my day, and someone with implants and augmentations like Ashok was the stuff of science fiction – but what I'm seeing here? Whoever did this makes your best doctors look like children poking roadkill with a stick."

"Axiom biotech, then."

Elena nodded. "It must be. We've seen their biological drones before. This is… some horrible extension of the same science."

Callie turned away from the body on the table. She'd killed humans before. She'd killed aliens before. She'd never killed someone who was *both*. "I can think of another reason to change her digestive system, besides increasing efficiency or whatever."

"What's that?"

"When I was a kid, there was this fad for home-grown pets, and you got to tinker with their genes during incubation, adding certain traits, suppressing others. You could make, say, blue mice with vestigial wings, or glow-in-the-dark ferrets, or miniature potbellied stegosauruses, or whatever. The company that made the kits, being composed of rapacious assholes like most companies, made sure you couldn't feed your winged mice regular cheap-ass mouse food. You had to use the company's special food, which included some custom-made enzyme or protein or something... or else the creatures you made would die. While making very pitiful and pathetic noises, naturally." She gestured in the direction of the body. "If you changed a person for your own purposes, in horrible ways, and you wanted to make sure they obeyed your orders, making it so they couldn't even *eat* if they tried to escape would be pretty effective, wouldn't it?"

"It would." Elena started to strip off her gloves and apron. "You think she was forced to pilot that ship and attack us?"

"I think she's my age, or thereabouts, which means she was born something like sixty years after the gates to the Vanir system closed permanently. She grew up under circumstances we can't even imagine, in a world that would have seemed absolutely normal and ordinary to her, no matter how horrible and twisted it looks to us." Callie sighed. "I think I can't even begin to guess at her motivation, but it makes me feel a lot better to think they had to force her to hunt us."

"Since when do you have faith in humanity?"

"It's individual humans I don't have faith in. If I didn't have faith in humanity as a whole, would I go to all this trouble to save the galaxy for them? I've even expanded my concept of humanity to include AI like Shall and aliens like Lantern, who just want to live their lives without the threat of the Axiom looming over them. Whether the definition of humanity stretches to include people who've been changed like our pilot here… I sure hope so. Killing Axiom is very uncomplicated for me, emotionally. But this…" A torn-open torso full of alien organs, beneath a human face. "This is a little rough."

Elena silently took Callie in her arms and held her for a moment. Elena knew when to talk, and when not to, and that was part of why Callie loved and counted on her so much.

After a moment, Elena released her. "I think I've learned all I can from the body. We've got scans and diagnostics and samples if I want to go deeper. What should I… do with her?"

"Cremate her, and we'll hold onto her ashes. Maybe she has people in the Vanir system. I'm going to see if Ashok and Lantern have found anything useful in the data they took from the scourge-ship. Maybe they even found her name."

CHAPTER 9

Ashok's machine shop was simultaneously neat and jumbled. The walls were covered in tools, coils of cable, random lengths of metal, spools of wire, jars of bolts and screws and rivets, but everything had its place, even if the system of organization was mysterious to anyone else. He sat on a stool at his workstation, cords running from the base of his skull into a terminal, and he was humming a horrible Luna-Pop song that had been aggressively popular when Callie was a teenager. "Hey, cap." He didn't turn around. "Just finishing up."

She floated closer and hooked her toes under his worktable. "How's it look? Can we get to the Vanir system?"

"In theory. That scourge-ship sure did. It's gone back and forth from this position to the Vanir system dozens of times. It looks like there's one very specific set of coordinates we can use as our destination – every other possible position is blocked off, and if we tried, we'd just pop out of the wormhole in the wrong place again… Probably right back in *this* place. I have no idea how their multidimensional electric fence works, and there's zero information about the force field or caltrops or whatever in the scourge-ship's system, so I don't have any hope of circumventing it."

"There's just a single point of entry and exit into the system? So it's functionally like the big wormhole bridges. So much for the amazing advantage of our forbidden technology that allows us to go anywhere at any time and appear without warning. How long would it take us to get to the Vanir system with our Tanzer drive? Forget wormholes – how about good old hard-burning space travel?"

"We'd die of old age four or five times before we got there, cap, sorry. Whoever's running things over there put up a *big* fence. On the plus side, that means they're not exactly in regular communication with the scourge-ship, so our dead pilot isn't missing a check-in or anything. There's no way they're talking via conventional communication at this distance."

"So it's wormhole or nothing. And if it's wormhole, we have to stroll through their front door."

"Well… one of their many front doors, I suspect. The set of coordinates I found is probably specific to *that* scourge-ship. You wouldn't give all the ships in your fleet the same position for coming and going. They'd open wormholes right on top of each other, and there would be breakage." They'd seen wormholes open in the middle of ships before. There wasn't much left of the ships afterward.

"Hmm. So there are probably lots of safe coordinates. Can we extrapolate other potential safe landing sites?"

Ashok pulled a cable out of his skull and grimaced. "When you're extrapolating from a single point of data, cap, it's not really extrapolation. We call that 'making a wild-ass guess' instead. I could assume all the scourge-ships come and go from roughly the same region – some kind of alien shipyard or mustering area or whatever. That's assuming there's more than one scourge-ship, so we're two asses deep already – keep up. After that, I could calculate the dimensions of a reasonable safe zone around each ship, since you don't want to open and close wormholes too close to your neighbors. From that point, I could come up with a list of likely coordinates that maybe probably aren't blocked... but I can't guarantee there's not already a ship sitting at that spot, and it wouldn't be good for *us* to appear on top of them. There's only one set of viable coordinates that we *know* is currently unoccupied by another ship, because we disabled the ship that belongs there and left it floating over there." He waved his hand.

"Ugh. If we *hadn't* wrecked that ship, we could use it to go back, flying under false colors, space pirate style." She cocked her head. "I don't suppose you could... unscuttle it?"

Ashok sniffed. "You wound me, cap. You tell me to break something, and it stays broken. Which is to say, sure, I could fix the ship, if you gave me a hundred repair drones and a week, but we'd have to hook *our* bridge generator up to its navigation and propulsion system, since I scuttled theirs."

Callie groaned. "The ship was an abomination, but I wish I hadn't wrecked it. Why do I have to destroy every abomination I see?"

"Hindsight is a bastard," Ashok said cheerfully. "I *did* loot the transponder from the scourge-ship, though. We can use it to make any control systems on the other side perceive the *White Raven* as the scourge-ship instead. We can even configure our stealth technology to make us look like the ship to scanners."

Callie blinked. "We can *do* that?"

"We'll be able to do it in a couple of hours, when I finish fiddling with the program," Ashok said. "Our Liar stealth tech can already hide us from sensors while projecting an image of our ship off in the distance to draw fire to the wrong place. It occurred to me recently that if the system could generate a convincing image of the *White Raven*, maybe it could generate a convincing image of something like a Jovian Imperative Depredation-Class dreadnought? That could be useful for scaring people off – puff us up to look bigger than we are, like cats or lizards – so I started tinkering in my free time. I am now tinkering much more diligently so we can look like a scourge-ship instead."

"Ashok."

"Yes?"

"Are you going to make me say it?"

"Nah, that's okay. I know you love me. Now, if someone actually looks out a window with their biological eyes, or, Kurzweil forbid, tries to board us, they'll realize we're not what their computers claim we are."

"Even so, we just went from one hundred percent doomed to maybe, what, eighteen percent doomed? I'll take it. Before I go – what's the word on Kaustikos?"

"He's just hovering around. Seems to be behaving. No attempts to hack into our systems, no attempts to send messages – not surprising at this point, since we're a billion kilometers from anywhere, but it's weird he didn't try to chat with his boss before we wormholed here. I'm thinking of the guy as cargo, pretty much."

"Suspicious cargo, Ashok. Always be suspicious."

"I learned that from the best, cap."

Callie clapped him on the shoulder and started for the door, then paused. "Where's Lantern?"

"She's in her cabin, going over all the data I didn't. We kept distracting each other with our cries of horrified horror as we dug into the information, so we decided to work separately. She took the really distressing stuff and let me focus on the navigational issues. I owe her."

Callie toggled to a private channel and said,

"Lantern? Up for a visit and a preliminary report?" Callie would barge in without hesitation on Ashok, Drake and Janice, and Elena, because they were her crew, and Kaustikos was an interloper with no expectation of privacy, but Lantern was different – she ran her own station, with her own crew of truth-tellers, and she was here helping out as a kindness, and at great personal risk. She got to stand apart from the usual chain of command.

"Of course, Callie. Please come at your convenience."

Now was convenient, so Callie scaled up to the crew quarters and rapped her knuckles on the cabin door. It was the XO's cabin, technically, the second-best on the ship, but Elena shared the captain's quarters with Callie, so they let Lantern have it. Drake and Janice's cabin had special accommodations, and Ashok slept in the machine shop half the time anyway, so nobody's feelings were hurt.

The door slid open, and Callie stepped in to find Lantern tethered to the floor, pseudopods manipulating half a dozen terminals at once, leaving one tentacle free to flutter in a gesture that Callie was *pretty* sure meant 'anxiety'. Elena had been trying to teach Callie the body language of the Free – and it really was a component of their language – for months, with minimal success. Callie had never been great with languages, though she was fluent in rude gestures.

"Ashok said you were going through the non-navigational data?"

"Yes. I was hoping to find out what's happening in the Vanir system. News, memos, even entertainment would give me some idea... but there's nothing like that. The data is extremely sparse, and very mission-focused. It seems this scourge-ship is one of several that take turns patrolling this region of space – or else they leave this space unpatrolled for long intervals, which seems unlikely. There are patrol guidelines from an entity designated 'Command,' but nothing personal or non-mission-oriented at all. As far as I can tell, the pilot just... sits there, when there's nothing to chase. Like a motion sensor that hasn't been tripped."

"Ugh. Do you know when this ship is expected back?"

"It looks like they go on patrol for roughly a month at a time, and there's another week or so to go on this one's shift."

"Hmm. Coming back early could trigger alarms, but it can't be helped. We'll just have to move fast. Anything else?"

"Nothing definitive, but I did find some things that are... suggestive. The logs are a mixture of human language, the language of the Free, and the Axiom alphabet... sometimes mingled all in the same message."

"That's weird," Callie said.

"I had assumed we were going to a system where human life had been exterminated, but something else is happening there," Lantern said. "I fear the humans may have been enslaved, as my people were, long ago. The sort of changes wrought in the human pilot… in the museum of subjugation, there are accounts of the Axiom altering my people for specialized tasks and environments, albeit not to such an extreme."

"I've been having similar thoughts. I don't suppose… did you find out the pilot's name?"

Lantern's tentacles fluttered in some complex way Callie couldn't parse. "Yes. No. Sort of." A long pause. "Her name is Subject SS-802."

CHAPTER 10

"I'll call you Sadie." Elena sealed the combustion chamber. "SS-802 is a terrible name." She took a deep breath. "Sadie, I'm sorry this happened. Callie wants to save people – even people she doesn't like very much – not kill them. I wish we could have helped you. I can't imagine what you went through. What your life has been like. If you suffered, and I think you did, I am glad your suffering is over, and sad you didn't have the chance to live free."

That was the best she could do. Elena punched in the sequence and turned her back before the panel opaqued and the chamber beyond heated up. The combustion system was meant for destroying medical waste. She'd never used it to cremate the dead before.

"May I come in?" Kaustikos's suspiciously smooth voice sounded over the room's comm. She glanced at the screen and saw he was hovering outside the door.

"I can't see why," Elena replied. "You don't need a doctor. If you're malfunctioning, talk to Ashok. He's the engineer here."

"Ha, no, I just thought we could have a conversation."

"About what?"

"About what happens next. Your captain has been rather... reluctant to share her plans with me. Which is to say, she doesn't even respond when I attempt to open communications with her."

"She's been pretty busy, infiltrating an Axiom ship and gathering intelligence. I'm sure she'll talk to you when she has time. Is that all?"

"Not entirely. I understand *you* were new to the crew, not so long ago, and yet you've integrated beautifully into the whole. I seem to be having a hard time making connections with my crewmates. Any advice?"

Elena snorted. "My situation isn't comparable to yours, Kaustikos. Your mysterious employer has been helpful, which is why you're here, but the Benefactor done a lot to build trust. That lack of trust extends to you. We think you know more than you're telling us."

"Doctor Oh, doesn't everyone know more than they share? I should hope so. Otherwise every interaction would become quite tiresome as people rambled on, sharing the pertinent and impertinent alike. I would point out that the Benefactor is our *mutual* employer. It seems I have to point that out quite often."

"I hope that's not too tiresome. No one is happy when their employer sends a spy to keep an eye on them. Callie and the others are professionals. Just let them get on with the mission, and if you know something useful, share it."

"I am not a spy. Or, at least, not just a spy. I am an underutilized resource. I gather you and the captain have an... intimate relationship. I assume you care greatly whether she lives or dies. I would appreciate it if you could use whatever influence you have to convince her to avail herself of my services. I am useful in the field, I am useful as a strategist, and, indeed, I am useful as a *friend*. Shouldn't we all be friends?"

"Sure. Let's be friends. My name's Elena. What's yours?"

"You may call me... ah. I see. If I am reluctant even to divulge my name, what basis can there be for a friendship between us? Fine. My name is... John."

Elena thought for a moment. "You're lying, aren't you?"

"Elena, my employer wants me to exercise a certain amount of discretion–"

"My friends call me Elena," she said. "You can keep right on calling me Doctor Oh." She muted the comms.

Something about that floating lying surveillance orb really gave her the creeps.

Kaustikos came floating into the machine shop and

Ashok waved. "Hi! Could you go away? You have a bomb on you and I like to be *outside* the potential blast radius. Even with an inward-pointing charge there's always a chance some piece of shrapnel will come bouncing in my direction, and while I don't tend to fear injury, I'm pretty busy just now."

"I came to see if you needed any help interpreting the data recovered from the scourge-ship."

"Are you a data analyst?"

"I have a full suite of software–"

"Pfft. So do we. Anyway, nah, we're good."

The orb bobbed. "Does that mean you've found a way to penetrate the Vanir system?"

"Penetrate! Why does that sound so pervy when you say it? Something about your voice, it's got this oily quality, like you're an evil lawyer in an immersive about the problems rich people have. You might want to consider a different suite of vocalization software–"

"This voice is an emulation of the one my human template had," Kaustikos said.

"Ouch. No reason to be stuck with the garbage nature gave you, though. Look at me – it's not like I kept most of my original equipment."

"Nevertheless, my voice has some sentimental value for me."

Ashok nodded. "I definitely get a super sentimental vibe from you, like as a rule."

"This interaction is most vexing. My dossier assured

me you like *everyone*, yet you're very hostile to me."

"I do like everyone! I don't even dislike you, Kaustikos. I just dislike corporate oversight, and you are the personification of corporate oversight. Everyone on this ship fled the kind of world where there's a boss who tells your manager what you need to do so your manager can tell you to do it. You're… middle-management, Kaustikos. Everyone hates middle-management."

"I am a fellow freelancer! Just because I act as a liaison doesn't mean I'm management. Have I given any of you orders?"

"You tried to give a couple, yeah, when you first showed up. That didn't work out, so now you're trying to buddy-buddy things. I get it. Unfortunately, you kinda spoiled things with that first impression. It's not me you need to win over, anyway – it's the captain. I don't have much hope for you, but let me give you some advice about dealing with her. If you have something important to say, you say, 'I have something important to say, and you should really listen.' At that point she will listen, and then you should say something *that is actually important*, and also something she doesn't already know. Do that successfully a few times, and she might not wince every time you speak. Okay?"

"That is… genuinely helpful, Ashok. Thank you."

He shrugged. "I'm an engineer. I fix broken systems. You're a loose ball bearing bouncing around inside a

TIM PRATT

machine that otherwise functions extremely well. We're *all* watching to see if you're going to bounce into the gears at the wrong time and mess things up. So… try not to do that."

"I will make myself scarce until I have something of value to offer, then."

"Great! Also, people are nervous about being around someone with a bomb attached to them, but I'll grant you that part is not entirely your fault." He paused. "Say, can you tell me something?"

"If I can."

"What color are the Benefactor's eyes?"

Kaustikos paused. Ashok had a rough idea of the kind of computing power packed into that probe and knew a pause of any length was either faked for purposes of anthropomorphization… or the result of millions of calculations, extrapolations, and branching probability trees being analyzed rapidly under that silvery surface. "Blue. Very bright blue. And the Benefactor only has one eye."

"So you *have* met him."

"I have seen him on a screen. I have not met him in person."

"Thank you for sharing, Kaustikos. This could be the beginning of a beautiful something."

"One hopes." The orb bobbed once, which Ashok decided to interpret as a friendly nod, and then floated away.

97

"Blue," Ashok muttered.

"Is everyone where they're supposed to be?" Callie asked from her chair at the tactical board. The crew chimed in to confirm their positions. "The bridge generator is recharged and ready to make another jump. We're going to aim for the Vanir system again. We don't know what we're jumping into – it could be a nice bit of empty space. It could be a fleet staging area filled with thousands of scourge-ships. Obviously I'm hoping for the former, but if it's the latter, we're just going to hope nobody notices us while we get our bearings and figure out a way to slip away. The ship will be disguised to look like a scourge-ship, so with luck we won't be vaporized on arrival. Are we ready?"

The crew chorused their affirmatives.

"Take us away," Callie said.

The wormhole opened before them, tendrils reaching out and enveloping, and then they traveled through the bridge. The wormholes accessed by the large bridgeheads in the human colony systems were utterly dark, but the one their generator created was lit by rings of white light at regular intervals, blurring past the viewport as they traveled. Even those lights were invisible to sensors, cameras, or mechanical vision – only biological eyes could perceive them, perhaps as some sort of security measure, but no one really knew why. The Axiom hadn't left any documentation on the ruins of their empire.

Lantern theorized that all the wormholes had been lit this way, once, but that most of them had broken down in some incomprehensible way, through age or disuse. The Axiom had created the bridges and the nature of those passageways through space were barely understood, the secrets of their construction and maintenance lost.

If one of the bridges stopped working, no one would have the first idea how to fix it – the colony worlds on the far side would be cut off forever from their neighbors. In fact, that was a popular theory for what had happened in the Vanir system: that the wormhole had simply stopped working, and the ships that vanished inside never returned because they were lost somewhere in the crawlspace of the universe, tumbling forever in the dark.

She'd seen that blue eye inside a wormhole, and if the Benefactor could access wormholes, could somehow travel in the structure behind wormholes, he could go anywhere. That would explain how he seemed to know what was happening in the Vanir system – that cryptic message that the place would be 'interesting' to unspecified members of her crew certainly suggested the Benefactor had some idea what they were flying into. If he had that much power and knowledge, though, why did the Benefactor need Callie to run errands for him? And why not share some of that information?

Callie kept her eye on the tunnel for the twenty-one seconds of the journey but no blue eyes peered out at her, just alternating bands of light and dark, and then they emerged into ordinary space.

They were not immediately fired upon, which was nice. The screens filled up with sensor data as Janice ran scans. They were definitely in the Vanir system – the astronomical charts matched up. There were dense shapes floating all around them for kilometers in every direction: other scourge-ships, powered down, seemingly lifeless. Off in the distance an asteroid bristled with airlocks in various sizes, from smaller-than-human-scale openings for drones to hangar doors meant for ships five times as big as the *White Raven*. That structure was putting out lots of heat and light and electromagnetic fields and assorted forms of radiation. It was a working facility. The home of the 'Command,' maybe, that had sent out the scourge-ship that pursued them.

"The station is talking to us," Janice said. "Nothing personal, though, just automated-system-to-automated-system. Shall?"

"I'm emulating the scourge-ship's communication protocols. We're back early, so their system wants to know if we're damaged or if this is a situation that needs to be escalated to someone with an actual brain. Wow. I haven't interfaced with technology this primitive in… ever. It doesn't even qualify as an expert system. Our coffee maker is smarter."

"Lucky for us," Callie said. "We don't want to talk to anyone with a functioning frontal lobe. Tell the station there was a malfunction with our weapon systems."

"There's a small vessel launching from the station," Janice said. "It's not coming this way, though – it's heading for one of the other scourge-ships."

"The system acknowledges and says a diagnostic and repair drone is being dispatched. Then it says... something I don't understand. Some kind of ritual sign-off?" Shall played a burst of something guttural.

"The accent is odd," Lantern said. "But I think it said, 'Glory to the Exalted.'"

"I'll play the same sounds back to them," Shall said. "Okay. That seems to have satisfied the system. Comms closed."

"That smaller vessel has docked with one of the scourge-ships," Janice said. "I think it's a pilot. I bet they're dispatching a ship to replace this one. They don't want to leave their fence unguarded, even though we have to be the first people to try to jump it in maybe forever."

"The price of liberty," Callie muttered. "Ugh. They'll find the remains of the ship we scuttled. Ashok, how good is your stealth and projection system at this point? Can you make it look like we're a scourge-ship sitting nicely waiting for a repair drone while we actually sneak the hell out of here?"

"I am the master of smoke and mirrors, captain. Hmm. You know, that's a good idea. I should put some smoke bombs in my wrist launcher, and I could do something fun with mirrors and lasers–"

"Ashok."

"Implementing evasive measures, captain."

Everything seemed to go so well at first. They silently sank, toward the portion of the shipyard where the scourge-ships were least densely arrayed, which was conveniently also the direction farthest away from the command station. Janice noted when the replacement scourge-ship opened its wormhole and vanished. They were nearly to the edge of the shipyard at that point, and Callie thought they were going to make it. The bridge generator on that ship would have to recharge, so even if it noticed the wreckage of the ship it was replacing right away, it would be hours before it could return to give a report and raise an alarm –

"Another wormhole is opening," Janice said.

"What? The same ship?"

"I don't – no, it's smaller. Looks about the size of Lantern's little one-person blister-ship."

Callie groaned. Apparently the ships had escape pods equipped with their own wormhole-opening technology. They'd missed that on the scourge-ship they'd destroyed. It had never occurred to her that one ship could have two bridge generators on board. Scarcity mindset.

"There's... suddenly a whole lot of comms traffic happening," Shall said.

"They're shooting at the place where they think we are," Janice said. "It's good we're not there."

"Ashok, can you make it look like we exploded?"

"I can try, but it's not just a question of making a big flash of light – I have to mimic the radiation signature of an exploded ship, and we're getting pretty far away from the projection, so it takes time for the changes to propagate."

"They aren't shooting to destroy us anyway, based on the portions of the fake ship they're targeting," Janice said. "Looks like disabling shots, meant to take out propulsion. I think they want to talk to us instead. There are a whole lot of little ships bursting out of that asteroid now, spreading out all over the shipyard."

Ashok said, "Uh, cap? I think they figured out that image of a ship is not a real ship, and now they are looking really hard for a real ship."

"Drake, let's get away from here, and quickly." The ship obligingly accelerated.

"Our stealth technology is good... but it's Liar tech," Ashok said. "Developed from Axiom tech. If there are countermeasures, these are the people who'll–"

"We're being painted with sensors!" Janice said. "They see us! Those little ships are coming in *fast*."

Callie kept her voice steady. "Can we get away, or do we need to fight?"

"There are too many ships, coming from too many directions," Shall said. "If we've lost our stealth, we've lost our way out. We can destroy a few of them if you like. They aren't shooting at us, though – just positioning to surround us."

"Shooting at them wouldn't make a boarding party any *more* favorably disposed toward us, would it?" Callie said.

Elena reached over and squeezed Callie's hand. "What do we do?"

"I'm open to suggestions," Callie said.

"Captain," Kaustikos said over her personal comm. "I have something important to say, and *you should really listen*."

She did.

CHAPTER 11

"We're going to baffle them with bullshit," Callie said. "Open a general communications channel, Janice."

"It's always nice to chat with the wild animals before they devour you," she muttered, but complied. "Speak your mind, captain."

Callie stared into the camera, trying to project steely-eyed determination. "Greetings to the inhabitants of the Vanir system. I am captain Kalea Machedo, leader of a delegation from the Trans-Neptunian Alliance." She should have said the Jovian Imperative, probably – they'd been a major power when the gates to Vanir closed, and many of the original colonists had come from there, while the TNA had been an upstart polity back then. The TNA had been destroyed when agents of the Axiom turned their capital Meditreme Station into so much radioactive dust, but she missed her old nation, and claiming that allegiance now was a way of keeping its memory alive. "We've been sent to determine the status of the colony system here. We are on a diplomatic mission, and it is not our intention to engage in hostilities, though we will defend ourselves if necessary. Please acknowledge."

"The ships are all around us, but they're keeping their distance," Janice said on the shipwide channel. "They look a little like black glass hummingbirds, don't they? Swarming around us like we're a bird feeder. Ha."

Callie transmitted again. "I repeat. I am captain Kalea–"

"We heard you the first time." The voice sounded human – male and avuncular, even. That didn't mean much: the Liars had technology that could mimic human voices, and often did, since their own language was mostly gesture, color change, and, in atmosphere, pheromones, none of which humans were much good at interpreting. "We were trying to decide whether it would be impolite to laugh. You don't 'intend to engage in hostilities?' You destroyed one of our patrol ships, and apparently stole its navigational data so you could sneak in here."

"I think I mentioned that thing about defending ourselves. Your patrol ship was aggressive."

"The ships have instructions to apprehend anyone they find. They wouldn't have harmed you."

"Ah, but see, being apprehended against my will *counts* as harm, as far as I'm concerned. We tried to talk to the ship. It wouldn't talk back. I'm glad you're smarter than that, or at least more polite."

"I am smarter than you can imagine. We're going to have to insist on apprehension, though. We do not welcome unannounced visitors. I'd think, after a century, that would be apparent, even to your species."

"Who am I talking to?" Callie said. "Failure to introduce yourself is also impolite."

"I am the Weaver of Worlds."

Liars sometimes named themselves peculiar things. "Is that a job title or a given name?"

"Both. I embody my office, and when my body is gone, another will take my place. That won't be today, though. I am in charge of all traffic to, from, and within this system. You are trespassing."

"We've been sent to find out what the hell is going on out here," Callie said. "The Vanir system went dark over a century ago. We thought you were all dead."

"Surely there were *other* theories than mass extinction?" The voice sounded amused.

"Sure. My own theory has always been that a radical isolationist political faction took over the system and just started looting the incoming ships and press-ganging or murdering the people on board. Or maybe it's a doomsday cult. Some people think it's a wormhole bridge malfunction. A lot of people back home are worried the colonists think *we* abandoned *them*. That the ships we sent here over the years never made it through, and maybe the ships *you* tried to send to *us* never made it, either. We were worried about you, basically. We've only recently developed the point-to-point wormhole technology necessary to come check on your well-being… but it seems like you've got that kind of tech, too, which makes us wonder why you haven't come home for a visit in all this time."

"Oh, you know how it is. We're a colony of introverts. We prefer to keep to ourselves. Can we expect more visitors?"

"Of course," Callie said. "We were sent to get the lay of the land. When we don't come back, the TNA will send more delegations to check on us, and they might be more heavily armed. The Imperative has been talking about sending another mission, and the Inner Planets Governing Council still takes a million years of parliamentary debate before they decide anything, but they'll make their way here eventually, too. The Vanir system is a giant enigma, and a lot of people want to solve it. Care to fill me in so I can go back and let them know?"

"You'll learn a lot via deductive reasoning, I suspect," the Weaver said. "We're going to send a boarding party. Then we'll bring you over to our medical team, to make sure none of you have been injured. Your well-being is very important to us."

"We're all fine, thanks. We have a first-rate infirmary on board."

"Our medical technology is much more advanced than yours. It's for your own good, really. If nothing else, we should immunize you against the local diseases. We've had plenty of time alone to grow wonderful new germs here, and some of them would just devour you."

"Look, Weaver, I understand we popped up in your shipyard, but to be honest, I didn't come to talk to an air traffic controller. I'm a diplomat from a major power in the Sol system, and I need to talk to whatever passes for a central government here."

"I'm sure someone from the labs will come by to take a look at you. They're always interested in new flesh, and it's been a year since any arrived through the bridge. Some of the healers have been advocating sending out raiding parties in search of fresh meat, but if you really are the vanguard of a whole new round of visitors that could solve the problem for us. We'll be with you soon, Captain Machedo. I'd suggest you open the door to the boarding party. Otherwise, they'll have to cut their way in, and someone might be hurt."

"They closed the comm channel," Janice said.

"Fresh meat?" Ashok said. "What, are they cannibals? That's a pretty good reason to go isolationist, I guess, it's one of the super common taboos. Cannibalism, incest, murdering your parents – found a nation on any of those principles and your neighbors are going to be reluctant to open diplomatic relations with you."

"Oh good," Janice said in a voice of lead. "There's a ship approaching, and it wants to connect with the airlock. What's the plan?"

"We've done all we can. I'm going down to meet

our visitors." Callie stood up from her chair, gave Elena's hand a last squeeze, and descended.

A Liar wearing a bright yellow environment suit drifted through the airlock, its multitude of large, emerald-green eyes gazing at her through the faceplate, its even dozen pseudopods undulating. A pair of those biomechanical hunter-drones flanked it.

Callie moved her arm in the human imitation of the Liar greeting, a sort of sine-wave that she had too many bones to accurately replicate, but what the hell. The Liar undulated in return, chuckling from its artificial voicebox. "You've spent time among my cousins, I see."

"Are you the Weaver of Worlds, or did you all just decide to economize by using the same vocal software?"

"I am the Weaver, yes. We don't get many visitors, and the ones we do don't show up here, so I thought I'd come in person to get a look at you. Novelty is such a pleasure, don't you find?"

One of his guards extruded a cord and plugged into the control panel by the door. Callie gritted her teeth. "Did your lackey there need help with something? Trying to place a local call?"

"Just checking on a few things. Your weapon systems. Your crew manifest. Minor details."

Shall whispered in her ear. "Their intrusion technology is ancient, Callie, but it's strong – brutal, really. I got the fake diplomatic credentials in place, and I'll put up some token resistance, then let them access everything we haven't partitioned away. Let them think they broke into the whole system and they won't go looking for secret files, I hope."

Artificial intelligences like Shall had been created after the Vanir system went dark, and Callie didn't think anything like him had ever been sent through the bridge – the Jovian Imperative military had strict rules against allowing AI onto its ships, basically because their high command was full of elderly paranoiacs. The Axiom hadn't been interested in creating rival intelligences, either, so it was a good bet the Vanir didn't know true AI existed. Callie's crew needed every advantage they could get so Shall was lurking, hiding in a partition in the ship's systems, along with all the data indicating he even existed… among other secrets Callie wanted to keep.

The Weaver consulted a handheld terminal and said, "Let's see, we've got you, your executive officer and ship's doctor Elena Oh, pilot Drake Alleyne, navigator and communications specialist Janice Grímsdóttir, and engineer Ashok Ranganathan. Hmm. Small crew."

"We like to stay nimble." Callie crossed her arms over her chest. "Well, we're apprehended. What next?"

"Call the rest of your crew down here and we'll transport you over to my ship, and take you someplace you'll be more comfortable. Then my little helpers will do a sweep of the ship, to make sure you don't have any stowaways who aren't listed on the manifest, as a courtesy. We'd hate for you to be taken unawares."

"I'm not so sure I want to accompany you. All that stuff you said about fresh meat wasn't very welcoming."

"Oh, did I misuse a human idiom? I'm terribly sorry. I just meant... newcomers."

"I'm sure you did. And these labs you mentioned? These healers?"

"The Vanir system is a meritocratic technocracy, captain. Our highest echelons are populated by those devoted to the healing arts. Doctors, surgeons, medical researchers. What greater calling can there be, after all?"

Callie almost said, 'Glory to the Exalted,' but there was no reason to let them know they'd been able to translate the burst of Axiom language. She decided to say something else rude instead. "Sounds like a more important job than directing traffic, Double-W."

"How droll. Why, I can't remember when anyone has ever dared to give me a diminutive nickname."

"You don't get sent to head a delegation to a system that eats starships because you lack courage," Callie said.

"You'd think a complete lack of diplomacy would

112

be a drawback in a diplomat. But what do I know? I just direct traffic. Get your crew down here. Or shall I send someone to fetch them?"

The crew duly assembled and the Weaver glanced at Elena, openly goggled at Ashok, and then gazed thoughtfully at Drake and Janice's mobility chair with its mirrored privacy screen. "Where's the last one?" he demanded.

"Drake and Janice travel together." Callie gestured at the chair.

The Weaver grunted and glanced at his associate plugged into the ship, who made a complicated gesture. The Weaver grunted again. "Very well. Come see your new home."

"We're not staying, Dubya."

"That's where you're wrong," the Liar said serenely.

Elena was trying hard not to tremble but Callie seemed absolutely cool, Ashok looked around like a kid at a county fair, and Drake and Janice were silent and hidden behind their mirrored visor.

They were on the asteroid and had already theatrically exclaimed over the presence of artificial gravity. Remembering to pretend they didn't know anything about Axiom tech — beyond the bridge generator, anyway — was an effort. The Weaver and his guards had marched them down a series of wide corridors and now they were in a sort of lobby, all beige walls and battered waiting-room chairs, with three doors in three walls.

"We'll start with Dr Ranganathan, I think," the Weaver began, or tried to.

"Ashok has severe separation anxiety," Callie said. "I have to insist we stay together."

Elena simultaneously wished Callie wouldn't needle the people who had all the power in this situation, and was proud of her for never being afraid of anyone or anything – or at least not showing it.

"If you try to separate us, I will explode." Ashok thumped his chest. "I have this amazing reactor inside me and it will just go boom. It's because of the panic attacks, you see."

"I don't care. You can all go in together. You'll end up in the same place anyway." The Weaver gestured and his guard opened a door that led into a long room, gleaming white and glinting with shiny equipment and rows of empty hospital beds in Liar and human sizes.

Callie marched in, head high, with Elena behind her, Ashok clumping after, and Drake and Janice's chair rolling along placidly behind them.

"Hello visitors!" a human called. He waved at them cheerfully. "I'm Doctor Metcalf, head of surgery for this station." He stood at the far end of the exam room, behind a long counter covered in beakers and racks of test tubes, centrifuges and microscopes, and other equipment Elena didn't recognize. He was probably in his sixties, with messy white hair, steel-rimmed glasses (an affectation, surely, or else diagnostic lenses; they could fix eyesight even in places that weren't ruled by surgeon-kings), and an unkempt beard and mustache. He looked portly and friendly and busy and distracted, like scores of researchers Elena had known in her time as a biologist. She tried very hard not to let his basic familiarity put her at ease.

That became a lot easier when he stepped out from behind the counter, because his lower body was composed of a dozen fat Liar pseudopods that carried him bonelessly toward them.

CHAPTER 12

"Want." Ashok moved forward to meet him, circling around the doctor, looking in awe at his pseudopods. "Those are amazing."

"You should see me tap dance." Dr Metcalf giggled. Ashok liked him instantly, which he realized didn't mean much. He liked everyone, because everyone was interesting on some level, and he liked being interested. The others weren't taking Metcalf's augmentations as well, though. Callie looked grossed-out, and Elena was doing that thing where she vivisected you with her eyes.

Now it was Metcalf's turn to circle Ashok, who posed obligingly with his arms outstretched. "You are remarkable yourself! We do a little bit of biomechanical work here, but our focus is more firmly biological, and this level of integration – it's amazing."

"See, back home, nobody is creative like this," Ashok gestured. "We can regrow a lost limb, get new organs cloned off old ones, stuff like that, but cross-species biological body hacking? I think there are about a million laws against even trying it in most polities."

"People are so short-sighted," Metcalf said. "We're

great believers in scientific liberty here in the Vanir
system. No avenue to advancement should ever be
closed."

"Couldn't agree more, doc," Ashok said. "And let
me applaud your self-experimentation."

"Hmm? Oh, the legs? No, we perfected this before
I submitted to it myself. These sort of upgrades are
strongly encouraged if you want to rise through the
ranks of the Exalted. They show dedication to the
vision of our leaders. Not that I haven't tried out a few
innovations first on myself, you know – sometimes
you come up with a wonderful idea and you don't
want someone else to do it first–"

"Not to break up the mutual appreciation society,
but what are we doing here?" Callie said. "I need to
see someone in authority. I'm a goddamn diplomat."

Metcalf pushed his glasses up on his nose. "Oh, of
course, please, I just need to do some basic medical
scans, just a moment." Metcalf scuttled over to a
terminal covered in Axiom symbols, tapped at the
screen, then said, "This might sting."

"What might sting," Callie said, and then they all
winced as the room pulsed with blinding white and
purple light. Ashok's exposed flesh – what there was of
it – went cold, then hot, then horripilated, and then
for just an instant felt like it was being scraped off
with a vegetable peeler. It must have been worse for
the people with more skin, because Elena screamed

and Callie grunted like someone had punched her and Drake and Janice keened in harmony. The agony was brief but memorable, and Ashok shivered all over when it subsided.

"There, it only hurt a moment," Metcalf said cheerfully.

"The whole room is a body scanner?" Elena wobbled, then her legs gave way and she sat down hard on the floor.

"Oh yes," Metcalf said. "I scan myself daily. Some of the things we play with just love turning into cancer, and it's best to catch the tumors early, of course. Now let's see… Oh. Oh, my." He turned. "Doctor Oh, is it? Where are you from?"

"Earth."

"Yes. Right. Earth. In that case – when are you from?"

"You don't have to tell him anything, Elena," Callie said. She'd remained upright through the scan, but she was grinding her teeth, and she had an expression Ashok had seen before. It made him want to hide behind a bulkhead for safety.

Metcalf cocked his head. "Are you upset? I'm just trying to take a medical history. My scans show evidence of a long stint in cryo-sleep, followed by a much shorter one, and she's just full of contaminants and antibodies that haven't existed on Earth since long before our system chose to withdraw from galactic commerce to focus our energies inward. I'd hazard a guess that she was on the crew of a goldilocks ship, perhaps even from one of the first waves sent out in the 22nd century. Am I close?"

"Close enough," Elena said.

"And you, Ashok, you're even more remarkable than I'd expected." He flicked at the screen, scanning alien symbols. "The anti-rejection medications developed to keep your body from treating your mechanical implants like foreign objects, they must be far beyond anything we have here. We do little tricks with gene therapy for our biological implants, but this is an entirely different paradigm… oh, my, heads are going to spin when the other scientists get a look at you."

"I am an amazing machine man," Ashok agreed.

"And Drake and Janice…"

"We don't want to talk about it," Janice said. Ashok knew he didn't have the keenest insight into the emotional lives of others, but it occurred to him that all this medical stuff was probably especially unpleasant for Drake and Janice, given their own history as the subjects of medical experiments.

"Your case is very interesting, too, then," Metcalf said. "I'll leave it at that."

"What about me?" Callie said.

"You're a baseline human. Healthy enough, though I'd keep an eye on your bone density. You're past your reproductive peak, and you never bothered with that anyway. There are minor variations in your immune system as compared to our local population, but it's not extreme." He shrugged. "Nothing of interest."

"You've got quite the bedside manner there, Metcalf."

"Oh, I didn't mean anything rude – I'm sorry. You are useful as a control subject, to show what baseline humans are like in the Sol system currently, though we have some samples that came through the bridge last year."

Samples, Callie thought. Did that mean dead soldiers from the last exploratory mission the Imperative sent? "Is there a big boss arch-healer?" Callie said. "What I'm looking for is your emperor, president, prime minister, king, high priest, whatever. I'm a diplomat. I need to do some diplomacy here."

Metcalf stroked his beard. "The system is ruled by a triumvirate of Exalted. The head of surgery, the head of research, and the head of operations. It's possible the first two would be interested in seeing you. I marked your scan results as urgent, so I'm sure they'll be notified about your presence soon. This is very exciting! I don't usually get to do much here at the shipyard besides the routine augmentations we give the pilots. You've all really livened up my day!"

"Are you important here, doc?" Callie said.

"I like to think so."

She rubbed her temples. "What I mean is, are you a high-ranking whatever, healer in this technocracy?"

Metcalf drew himself up on his pseudopods. "I am. As I said, I am head of surgery for this facility, which is crucial for system security. I stand in the upper echelons of the third rank."

"Which means… what?"

"The first rank consists of the three division heads I mentioned, who set policy for the system. The second rank is made up of their assistant directors and deputies, two for each division head. The third rank includes the directors of facilities, and there are twelve of us in each division – just a handful of us in that rank are human or chimeras like myself, of course, only the very highest achievers. I am part of the surgical division, though of course I dabble in research. You've met my associate, the Weaver, who runs operations here–"

"So you're one of the fifty most important people in the local government?" Callie interrupted.

"Forty-five most, actually. It would be difficult to rank me precisely, as the lines of succession are a bit muddled after you get past the second rank, not that the problem has ever come up–"

"Good enough," Callie said. "Ashok, take him hostage."

Ashok, who'd maneuvered close to the doctor against this very eventuality, reached out with his hand full of articulated manipulators and delivered a precisely calibrated electric shock. Doctor Metcalf's eyes rolled back, his tentacles drummed on the floor – how about that for tap dancing – and then he slumped, unconscious.

"Now what?" Elena said.

"Now, we negotiate," Callie said. "I'm a diplomat. That's what we do."

Ashok managed to take control of the room's systems without too much trouble, but he couldn't get beyond that. "The station is really compartmentalized. Probably so a failure in one area doesn't become a failure in others, which means I can't seize control of station-wide security or anything. Those doors won't open until we want them to, though. Shall could do more, but I'm only about one-third machine by volume, so I've got limits."

"I can't believe they just left us alone in here with a senior official," Callie said. "I know they haven't met me before, but still."

"We are trapped on a space station, though," Elena said. "I haven't been in a lot of these situations, but don't these things usually end badly for the hostage-takers?"

"Only if they're stupid," Callie said. "We aren't stupid. We also have a high-value hostage, which helps. Now we just need a way to call the Weaver."

"There's a communication system here," Janice said. "Ashok patched me into it already. It's not as compartmentalized as the other systems. I can say whatever you want to anybody you want. I can even communicate with other facilities in the system... though I don't know what any of them are because their names are mostly written in that creepy Axiom language."

"I'm supplying translations as fast as I can," Ashok said.

"Oh good. 'Central Processing' sounds reasonable enough, if vague, same with 'Stasis Center' and 'Experimental Protocol Division,' but are you sure you've translated these others correctly? 'Blood Circus'? 'The Temple of Rending'? 'The Hall of Teeth'?"

"Lantern is a lot better at their language than I am," Ashok said. "I don't get the idioms at all. I barely understand human idioms, to be fair."

"Let's just call the Weaver first," Callie said. "If he's no help, we'll go over his head."

"I'm just... hell, I'll put you on station-wide public address, good enough?" Janice said.

"Works for me. I do well with an audience." Callie cleared her throat. "Hey, Double-Double! Captain Machedo here. I'd like to talk to the ruling triumvirate, and I mean now. We've got your man Doctor Metcalf here, and the thing is, I, personally, never took the Hippocratic oath."

The speakers in the room hissed emptily for a moment, and then the Weaver spoke. "You are very annoying. I am going to send some people to kill you."

"No you aren't. The doc says we're very special and important, full of fascinating medical innovations, and you'd get in big trouble if you wasted us. Besides, the doc would die in the process, and he's your colleague, right? I assume you're in the third rank too, in the operations division?"

Another empty hiss. "Metcalf always did like to hear himself talk. I see from the outgoing communications that you are, indeed, of medical interest. It's unclear whether you need to be alive to be of use to our researchers, but for the time being I'll refrain from euthanizing you. Let's open negotiations, shall we?"

"They're trying to cut the oxygen to the room," Ashok said. "I am not obliging them."

"Stop trying to knock us out, Doubles," Callie said. "We've got this room on lockdown. This station is from when the colony was founded. Your computer technology looks like wooden blocks and popsicle sticks to us. If you aren't going to negotiate in good faith, we might have to start cutting off some of the doc's extra limbs. We've got some pretty great self-cauterizing saws down here, it looks like. It's strange – people never think about how similar infirmaries are to armories."

"What do you want, Machedo?"

"To talk to the organ grinder, and not the monkey."

"What would you say to the division heads, if they were here? I can't just summon them. Could you get the president of the Trans-Neptunian Authority on an open channel on a whim?"

"Sure I could, but I'm a diplomat, and you're a traffic light, so I understand we're not of equal rank and dignity. As for what I'd say – I'd ask them to sit down with me and tell me what the hell is going on in this system, why you isolated yourselves, what happened to the original colonists, what happened to everyone we sent through the bridge to check on you, and a few other pointed questions. Then I'd tell them to give me my ship back so I could return home and inform my president. After that, this whole situation is someone else's problem. But you don't lock up diplomats, and you don't treat us like medical curiosities either. That's the kind of shit that starts wars, Doubles. Do you want a war with us, now that you know we have the technology to come visit? This time the ship was full of diplomacy. Next time it might be full of guns."

"I'll send a request for my division head's attention, Captain Machedo. I'll let you know if she replies. In the meantime, perhaps we could pass the time in conversation. How did your people come to possess ship-sized wormhole technology? Or is that a state secret?"

"We found an abandoned space station out in the middle of nowhere on a long-range expedition. Nobody alive on board, though there was evidence that your people had been there, once upon a time. Turned out it was a ship-building facility, and a lot of the automated systems still worked. It took a little time, but we got the machinery switched on, and damned if it didn't start building bridge generators!" That was all true; it just wasn't the whole truth. "Really blew our minds." Also true, and in reality, they'd blown up the whole facility to keep the generators from falling into the wrong hands and drawing the attention of the Axiom to humanity. "The TNA tried to keep the tech for ourselves, of course, but secrets like that leak, and we ended up making a lucrative licensing deal with the Jovian Imperative and another with the inner planets... I didn't pay attention to all the ins and outs on the economic side. We don't know how to make the generators, but we know how to turn on the machine that does make them, so we've got a monopoly, and the TNA is a major power in the Sol system now."

"And with the power to go anywhere, you decided to come here?"

"Like I said. This system is a mystery box, and we love a mystery. There are also still a few very old people who remember relatives who emigrated to the system, hardcore life-extension cases, and of course, they're the richest of the rich, people powerfully connected in government, like that. Did you think you'd be left alone forever?"

"Not forever. For long enough, we hoped. It's a big, dangerous universe, Captain Machedo. Did you humans ever consider that the ability to go anywhere in the galaxy just offers the opportunity to die in ever more distant places?"

"The kind of people who take on missions like this aren't too afraid of dying, no. It's a sort of self-selection criteria."

"Mmm. How long before we can expect more visitors, do you think? Not that they'd get any farther than the outside of the fence we set up. Just because you jumped it doesn't mean other people will be able to."

"Oh, I wouldn't worry about that," Callie said. "We sent a lifeboat back home with navigational data before we came to the shipyard here."

"What." The syllable was flat.

Callie had gotten the idea for this lie from the scourge-ship's escape pod, returning to tattle on them. "Well, sure. Sending the lifeboat back meant we only had one bridge generator on board my ship, which isn't ideal, but it seemed like pretty important information to send home, don't you think? I sent a little video message, too – 'Hi, Captain Machedo here, the Vanir system is still inhabited and they're trying to murder us and they can disrupt our wormholes but here's the way to get around that.'"

"You might have mentioned this communication before, captain."

"I might have, if I'd been talking to someone important, instead of the guy who stands in the intersection with white gloves and a little whistle waving the cars through."

"I do not understand that reference."

"That's okay," Callie said. "It's enough for you to know it's insulting. I'm done talking to you. Get me someone with actual authority." She made a cutting-her-throat gesture and Janice ended the communication.

Callie turned toward Metcalf. "Let's get him secured. I'm betting there are plenty of restraints in this room somewhere. Then we'll wake him up and find out what the hell has been happening here for the past hundred years."

CHAPTER 13

"What did you say to Callie?" Lantern whispered, jammed into the blister-ship that clung to the side of the *White Raven*. Her personal vessel was a comfortable size for her, except when Kaustikos was crushed in with her. Being so close to something rigged with explosives made her deeply uneasy. "She ordered me to withdraw to my ship immediately after you spoke to her."

Kaustikos was smug. "I simply pointed out that the Vanir system has had only limited contact with the outside world in the past century, in the form of whatever they could glean from the rescue and military missions sent through the bridge. All sorts of interesting technical innovations have happened in the wider human community during that interval – most importantly, from my point of view, the development of artificial intelligences.

"The denizens of this system likely have no idea that sapient intelligences can inhabit machinery, so they wouldn't even look twice at me, or be aware of the existence of the ship's AI. I told her that since the crew was about to be captured, Shall and I could hide, and later lead a rescue mission. She knew that you, too, might escape detection – you aren't listed anywhere as a member of the crew, apparently – and told me to bring you along with me."

"She actually said you should follow Lantern's orders," Shall said over their comms.

"Is there no solidarity among artificial intelligences?" Kaustikos's tone dripped with contempt.

"I believe Callie knows what she's doing," Shall said. "I believe she doesn't trust you much."

"Perhaps that will change when I rescue her from the clutches of our enemies."

"Is that how you think she'll feel?" Lantern said. "What do you think, Shall?"

"I think Callie would be deeply irritated at anyone who believed she needed to be rescued. I think she'd be twice as irritated if it turned out they were right."

"She can probably rescue herself," Lantern said. "But we'll help create more favorable conditions for that rescue. Shall, what's your best available body? One of the big mining drones from Glauketas?"

"Oh, we brought the war drone," Shall said. "Ashok's been fixing it up in his spare time."

"You have military hardware?" Kaustikos said. "That's marvelous. I have some experience running such equipment. I can split my consciousness–"

Lantern's chromatophores flushed with a deep purple of displeasure. "Shall will operate the war drone. Kaustikos, you have stealth equipment, don't you? Sneaking around seems to be the Benefactor's favorite thing."

"I may have some such capabilities."

"Then you can follow the Weaver of World's ships and find out where they're taking the crew. Don't intervene unless it seems like they're in immediate danger."

"I'm to be some sort of sheepdog?" Kaustikos protested.

"Sheepdogs herd, so no," Shall said. "You'd be more of a tracking dog."

"Ridiculous," Kaustikos grumbled as Lantern's ship opened its tiny airlock to let him out into cold space.

"What do we do?" Shall said once the Benefactor's pet was gone.

"Can you activate your military drone and get off the ship? It's possible we're still being watched."

"I'm tapping the local base's communications, and they aren't talking about us, which either means they're very subtle, or they're overconfident. I'm inclined to believe the latter. They've been the undisputed masters of the Vanir system for a long time, I think. They might even believe we're diplomats."

"Let's proceed as if they're very clever, though, all right? It wouldn't do for us to get captured too."

"The war drone is crouched in a launch tube, and I can port a copy of my consciousness into its body and then crawl out nice and slow."

"Are there handholds for me to ride along? Or will everything I touch electrocute and disembowel me?"

"I didn't even know your species had bowels. I'll have to update my biological databases. I think we can work something out. The war drone is on its way. It's only got a limited version of my mind, because it lacks the processing power to run me in all my splendor. My personality should be intact but don't expect me to do complicated math, and my access to information will be limited since I won't be plugged into the ship's databases. I'll be crammed full of tactics and strategy and intrusion measures and what little local knowledge we have, though."

A few moments later Shall said, "I'm here."

Lantern checked her suit and toolbelt, and then slipped into the tiny airlock Kaustikos had departed through. Her blister-ship was originally meant as a boarding pod, equipped with all sorts of nasty cutting tools on the underside designed to breach hulls. She hated to leave it behind, but there was nothing it could slice through that Shall's war drone couldn't, and he presented a smaller target for sensors.

She looked through the window, where her view of the shipyard was obscured by the bulk of Shall's drone. The drone's general shape wasn't so different from that of Lantern's own body: a central oblong surrounded by limbs and studded with eyes. As she understood it, the shape of the war drone was meant to suggest the Earth creatures called 'spiders' – most humans apparently had some instinctual horror of the creature, so making an engine of war spiderlike had psychological advantages. "Spiders have too many eyes, and too many legs," Elena had explained to Lantern once – apologetically, as Lantern was just one limb and one eye short of having the same complement of both as most spiders.

The array of lights (now turned off) and sensors on the front of Shall's body were clustered to look like eyes, and his many limbs were variously serrated and spiked and capable of firing projectiles, energy bursts, plasma bolts, and other things, but because of her own physiology, Lantern didn't find his appearance particularly menacing – Shall looked like a bigger, stronger version of herself and her people, and she found his form quite comforting. "You're very handsome this way."

"Ah, so this is your type. And here I thought you only liked unfrozen xenobiologists."

Her species didn't blush, exactly, but some of Lantern's chromatophores shifted to colors that indicated embarrassment. She hadn't realized Shall was aware of her little crush on Elena, but it wasn't surprising; he saw every interaction on the public areas of the ship and on Glauketas. "I'm very complex, Shall," Lantern said with dignity. "You can't possibly expect to understand my vast depths."

"I wouldn't presume. Clamber up on my back and

we'll be on our way."

Lantern opened the outer airlock door and slipped into space, her seven limbs – three fine manipulators and four stronger but less dexterous ones, though calling them 'arms' and 'legs' would be an insulting simplification – reaching for handholds. She clambered onto the back of Shall's body, and he showed her where she could clip her suit on to keep her firmly connected to his broad, matte black back, studded with mysterious bumps and bulges.

Once she was settled, she allowed herself to look around. All the truth-tellers trained in vacuum and microgravity, since they never knew where their dedication to keeping the secret of the Axiom's existence would take them. Lantern was comfortable in space, but she wasn't comfortable in this space: looking out at the hundreds of spiked scourge-ships drifting in the void around her in all directions gave her the shivers. She could very well die in this place, and for a moment she felt terribly alone.

Then she steeled herself and turned to her work. "Kaustikos, are you there?"

"Am I where? Uselessly floating? I am. The Weaver of Worlds took your friends – our friends, our very dear friends – into that repurposed asteroid they seem to be using as their main space station. Would you like me to infiltrate?"

"Not yet," Lantern said. "Just observe, for now." She closed off the comm channel. "Shall, what's the chatter?"

"Just docking authorizations for their ship... and now they're alerting someone named Doctor Metcalf that they have subjects for him. I don't like the sound of 'subjects,' Lantern."

"I don't either. I wish I understood what was happening here. I suppose all that matters for now is helping Elena and the others get free. A full frontal assault is probably not the best option, though."

"I can cause a lot of destruction, but we're surrounded by warships, so there's no way we can win a straight fight. Infiltrating the base might be a good idea, if I can hack their security systems, but they're not that sloppy – I can't get into their computers from here. We'd have to risk getting physically onto the station so I could access their systems directly, and, while I'm good at hiding from sensors, I'm not very inconspicuous in this particular body, and if someone saw us..."

"It's not like they'd attack their own station with warships, though," Lantern mused. "We'd have to deal with whatever station security they have there, and you're likely the equal of those hunter-drones."

"If that's the worst they've got, sure, but they could have worse. I saw the terror-drones that protected the Dream, and those would eat this body like a snack."

The museum of subjugation had fragments of some Axiom drones; horrible things dubbed harvesters and flensers and even subjugators. "We definitely have to get onto the station, but could we make sure station

135

security is otherwise occupied first?"

"Draw them to one position while we board at another? Works for me."

"If only we had someone we were willing to put in the path of danger." Lantern opened a comm channel. "Kaustikos? We have a mission for you…"

Shall floated silently through the darkness of the shipyard, making minute adjustments with reaction wheels and bursts of gas as needed, but mostly setting straight courses and gliding from one position to another. He turned on his magnets when he got close to the last scourge-ship, and accelerated forward, clamping to the side. He made a few deft incisions with a cutting torch and opened part of the hull. It was good that Callie had commandeered one of these vessels – that had enabled Shall to download the schematics and figure out the most vulnerable parts of the ship's anatomy. Shall unfolded a manipulator arm and pushed the second-to-last explosive charge he had into the hole, in just the right spot to make the ship's propulsion system turn a big explosion into a catastrophic one.

"We're all set," Shall said.

"It's a shame we can only blow up nine of them," Lantern said. "I was hoping for a nice cascading explosive effect that would take out the whole fleet."

"Alas, warships that explode just because ships explode next to them wouldn't be very practical. There's something to be said for decimation, though." Shall considered the scourge-ships hanging all around them. "Or... deci-deci-mation. It's not like we're getting a whole tenth of them."

"Kaustikos, are you in position?" Lantern said.

"I am. Your plan is terrible. Specifically the part of the plan that involves likely harm to myself."

"You've got the best stealth technology," Lantern said. "Shall's calculations show you're the most likely to succeed in your role."

That was true, though they'd decided Kaustikos should do it even before Shall ran any such calculations.

"Also, you don't care if I live or die."

"I grieve the death of any intelligent being," Lantern said. "But your consciousness is backed up elsewhere."

"That's not much comfort for this particular instantiation of my awareness. Let's get this over with."

"We're almost ready," Lantern said. "We'll signal you when it's time."

"I'm pretty sure I'll know when it's time."

Shall almost laughed at that. "It's true. Shouldn't be hard to miss." He launched away from the scourge-ship, gliding in dark mode toward the great bulk of the space station. It was a huge asteroid, ten times as big as Glauketas, almost as big as Meditreme Station had been. Shall was eager to get into its computer system and feast on information. What other habitations were there in this system? Was this the only military outpost or were there many such shipyards? Also, what the hell was going on around here? How had a human colony system turned into this?

He maneuvered to the far side of the asteroid, near one of the smaller maintenance airlocks, where repair drones probably came and went. He wouldn't be able to see the pretty explosions from here, but that was sort of the point. "Whenever you're ready, Lantern." He paused at a burst of communications from the station, then laughed. "Wait, wait. Ha. They're losing their minds in there... apparently Callie has taken a high-ranking member of their staff hostage. The Weaver of Worlds is shouting at everyone to calm down, that they have the situation well in hand. Why am I not surprised our captain didn't wait for us to save her?"

"We can help, though," Lantern said. "A little chaos would doubtless improve her situation. Let's proceed."

Shell remotely detonated the nine charges he'd placed on the scourge-ships, all at once. There was no satisfying boom, but his sensors picked up some nice spikes in radiation, and the station's communication channels filled with shouting again, even more panicked this time.

"Now, Kaustikos," Lantern said.

Assuming all went well, Kaustikos was uncloaking

himself, drawing the attention of the station's security system toward an obvious saboteur… "They see him," Shall said. "They're scrambling ships to intercept."

"Lead them on a nice chase before you disappear, Kaustikos," Lantern said.

"I know my role," Kaustikos snapped.

Shall began cutting into the maintenance hatch and soon had an opening big enough to crawl through. They clambered through a dark tunnel, clearly never meant for biological organisms to traverse and correspondingly lacking in amenities like lights or artificial gravity. Shall sent out small pings to radar-map the immediate area and got a sense of the array of tunnels around them. There was a machine room a hundred meters or so forward and down, and there would probably be a terminal there –

"Huh," he said. "The Weaver of Worlds is on the comms, talking to someone in another station, I think… he says 'the rebels have attacked the shipyard.'"

"There are rebels?" Lantern said.

"Long live the glorious heroes of the revolution," Shall said.

CHAPTER 14

"I'm sorry, but it's just impractical." Ashok gestured helplessly toward Metcalf, who dangled unconscious from makeshift restraints that attached his wrists to the ceiling. His lower half was entirely unbound. "Have you ever tried to tie up a bunch of tentacles? All his lower limbs taper to a point, cap. You can't put handcuffs or zip ties on them, and rope wouldn't be much better, and anyway all I have is wire, which is definitely no good… We're just going to have to stand clear of the pseudopods."

"Fine." Callie crossed her arms. "Throw some water on him or whatever."

Ashok went to the sink, turned the knob, and sighed when nothing happened. "We don't have any water. They shut it off."

"I thought you had control of their systems?"

"I have control of this room. They turned off the water somewhere beyond the boundaries of this room. It's probably just a valve and someone turned an actual wheel to shut it off."

"I don't expect we'll be here long enough to die

of thirst, anyway." Callie looked around, picked up a beaker, and threw it at Metcalf's chest, where it bounced off and landed on the floor with an unbreakable clunk. He stirred, so she threw another, and he opened his eyes, blinking at them in confusion.

"What happened?" he said.

"We took you hostage," Callie said.

"But… why?" Metcalf stared at her in open bafflement.

"How hard did he hit his head when you zapped him?" Callie said.

Ashok shrugged. "Did you want the answer in newtons, or?"

"Is his brain scrambled, Elena?"

Elena started toward Metcalf, and Callie grabbed her arm. "Don't get within range of his tentacles."

Elena sighed and squinted. "His pupils look okay from here, but that's about the limit of my diagnostic abilities at this distance."

Callie nodded. He was just that clueless, then. "We took you hostage, Dr Metcalf, because we aren't interested in being the subjects of horrifying medical experiments."

"Been there, done that," Janice said.

"Oh. But… this installation is heavily guarded. You can't possibly escape."

"Gosh, I hope you're wrong," Callie said. "Because

if taking you hostage doesn't provide enough leverage to get us out of here, then you're not much use to us alive."

Metcalf struggled, pulling at his arm restraints, and lashing out with his lower tentacles. After a flurry of violent activity he went suddenly still. "All right. I'll talk to the Weaver—"

"I've already got him fetching me a division head," Callie said. "No offense, but you're a little low in the hierarchy for my purposes." She pulled a stool over and sat down on it. "You can, however, answer some questions for me while we're waiting."

"I am not in a very cooperative frame of mind, Captain. We could have just talked."

"You like to have conversations with the people you're vivisecting? That's friendly of you. Cooperate, or your cooperation will be compelled. You've got value as a hostage when you're alive, absolutely, but your value doesn't diminish if we have to damage you a little. In fact, cutting a few pieces off you could even serve to strengthen our position with your superiors. It would let them know we're serious." She gave a little nod to Ashok, and he obligingly held up his prosthetic arm. The nest of manipulator arms at the end flattened out into a disc and began to spin with a high-pitched whine.

The manipulators whirled around like that so Ashok could use them as a cooling fan for times when work in the machine shop got too hot, but the noise they made sure sounded like a buzz saw.

"What is it you'd like to know?" Metcalf sounded admirably calm.

"A short history of the Vanir system would be nice. What the hell happened here? When your grandpa or whoever emigrated here a hundred-some years ago, this was a fledgling colony system with a promising couple of planets. At some point in the intervening years it became a military dictatorship–"

"A technocratic meritocracy," Metcalf said. "Or a meritocratic technocracy."

"You say tomato, I say alien junta," Callie said. "How did you get here from there?"

"First of all," Metcalf said, "it wasn't my grandfather who emigrated here. It was me personally. I came here through the wormhole gate form the Jovian Imperative myself, one hundred and twenty years ago."

Human lifespans routinely exceeded a hundred years these days, but even if Metcalf had come through as an infant... Callie shook her head. "Sorry. You don't look a day over sixty to me."

"Oh, I was almost sixty when I left," Metcalf said. "I was a geneticist, with a specialty in adaptive gene therapies. I emigrated as an employee of the charter company that set up the colony on Vanaheim. It's a beautiful planet, full of green jungles, and simply teeming with opportunistic microorganisms. I was part of a team charged with developing vaccines and antibiotics to prevent alien illnesses from taking root in the human colonists. Fascinating work, truly. There's one parasite, something like a tapeworm or a fluke, that really likes living inside the human gut biome, but it grows to such tremendous size that it literally bursts out of the body and then goes slithering away. We call it the Jörmungandr-worm, after the world-serpent from Norse mythology–"

At a glance from Callie, Ashok revved up his saw.

Metcalf winced. "Yes, fine. I was leading a team to develop anti-parasitics and vaccines, and we made sure the colony's babies were born with a set of inserted immunities so they could run around freely in the fields and forests of Vanaheim without picking up anything too nasty. The microorganisms on the planet had a distressing tendency to mutate, to a degree none of my team had ever encountered before, so there was always plenty of work to be done, and a distressingly high mortality rate among the general population. The other planet in the system, Niflheim, didn't have as many biological issues, but it's a less fertile place, mostly rockier and more austere, with an atmosphere that frankly always smelled a bit like vinegar to me. It was left mostly to mining concerns, because of its mineral resources, but everyone wanted to live on Vanaheim… if we could get rid of the nasty bug.

"One day, about ten years after my arrival, I was out

hiking in Freya's Gorge – there's a petrified waterfall there, it's quite beautiful – mostly just enjoying the day, but also collecting biological samples. We still haven't fully catalogued the plant life there. I crested a hill… and saw an alien collecting samples of his own. It was a Liar, but with skin a deep shade of red I'd never seen before. There were very few aliens on Vanaheim at the time, so I was surprised, but not distressed. I greeted him, but he didn't speak the language, which struck me as peculiar. Most Liars are so adept at language, but he acted as if he'd never even seen a human before – scuttling around me, gesturing, attempting to communicate in pantomime. Our attempts to talk were unsuccessful, and he darted forward, plucked a hair from my head – follicle and all, of course – and then scurried off.

"A moment later I saw a strange ship, shaped a bit like a crayfish – a sort of elongated bubble with various manipulators dangling off the bottom like legs – take off into the atmosphere. I know now it was a scientific sampling vessel. I watched it ascend, and saw something shimmer, high in the clouds. I got just a glimpse of one of the starfish-shaped vessels we usually associate with Liars, and then it shimmered into invisibility again. Stealth technology.

"Well, Liars are strange and unpredictable, so I didn't think much of the encounter, though I was surprised to see one of their ships. I returned home and mentioned the experience to my colleagues, who didn't know what to make of it either.

"I still vividly remember the day the wormhole gate closed, just a few months after that encounter. My friend Margaret, who was head of reproductive therapies, burst into my lab and said something was wrong with the wormhole. She was supposed to go home to help her daughter after the birth of her first child, but the port authority had canceled all outgoing trips due to 'technical difficulties.' Margaret was friendly with a highly placed member of the intergalactic trade union, though, and he told her the wormhole was malfunctioning. The radiation sequence that caused the bridge to open had simply stopped working, and, while they were trying other variants, they didn't have any success. It's not surprising. The possible combinations are close enough to infinite that it makes no difference.

"Our colony was self-sufficient in terms of food, but there were many manufactured items and luxuries and specialty goods, not to mention technological items, that we imported from other systems. We didn't panic when the gate went down, not exactly, but everyone worried. No one could figure out why the bridge wouldn't open. The few Liars in the system were the engineers who'd taught humans how to operate the bridge, and, being Liars, their explanations were not very helpful – they blamed everything from evil spirits to the incompetence of their human counterparts.

"Then, to our surprise, a scheduled supply ship arrived! We realized then that our bridge still worked from the outside. We were locked in, but others could enter. The captain and crew of that ship were pretty unhappy, as you might imagine, to find themselves trapped here instead of taking back a load of ore to sell. We couldn't even send messages home. We're so remote out here, if we'd sent a probe to the nearest colony world the day the gate closed, it would still be centuries away from arriving now.

"The next day, all our communication systems were overridden, and all our screens displayed the same thing: a Liar, wearing dark robes patterned with golden stars and swirls. 'Greetings,' the Liar said. 'My people are known as the Exalted. We are scientists, healers, and researchers. You have disrupted one of our long-term experiments, but we are not angry. Indeed, we hope you will join us in our great endeavor: to further our knowledge and understanding of the limits and capabilities of biological life.' Then he paused, and after a moment said, 'Those who resist will be euthanized.'

"Oh, the uproar! No one could tell where the transmission had come from, and we were locked out of our own communication systems, which made coordination difficult. Our lab, being one of the more advanced facilities on the surface of Vanaheim, was one of the first to be occupied. First we were flooded by bio-drones – they looked a bit like Liars, but Liars bonded with machines. Those machines are exoskeletons, of a sort, using the flesh bodies as onboard computers for visual processing and threat assessment, and as a failsafe in case of mechanical problems. They lack higher brain functions, however. The drones seized control of the entire hospital, the research labs, everything. Margaret wept, I remember, when they took the newborns away.

"The bio-drones herded us into the cafeteria, the only space big enough to hold the entire staff. We waited for a long time, with the drones endlessly moving, scuttling all over the floors, the walls, the ceilings – it was all very disturbing. Finally, a Liar arrived, and though back then I found it hard to tell individuals of the species apart, he was bright red, and I thought – was he the same one I saw collecting samples in the gorge all those months ago?

"'You've done impressive work here,' he began, and we started to relax. 'Some of you, at any rate. Others, less so. And some of you are perfectly competent, but have areas of research that don't mesh well with our own interests.'

"'What interests are those?' our director shouted. His name was Javier, and he was one of those tyrannical sorts, ruthless and brilliant and organized, but rather uncompromising. Do things his way, and you were fine, but suggest that another path might be better, and oh, he would explode!

"'Various,' the Liar said simply. 'Some of you will be invited to join us in our work.'

"'What about the rest of us?' That was Margaret. I think she knew her area of expertise was not one that interested our new employers very much.

"'Oh, don't worry. You'll do your part too.' He began to call out names, only a dozen or so, but one of them was mine. Those of us chosen shuffled off to one side, as ordered, and then the bio-drones herded the rest of the staff down a corridor, including Javier and Margaret. I never saw either of them again. Well, that's not quite true – I saw Javier once, but he was rather different then, and he didn't answer to his old name anymore.

"'You may call me the Shaper of Destiny, or just Shaper,' the Liar said. 'I am the head of surgery, one of the three senior officials in charge of this system.'

"'We thought this system was uninhabited,' one of my colleagues said. 'We never would have set up a colony here if we'd known it was your home.'

"Shaper chuckled at that. 'It is not our home any more than you live in a petri dish. This planet – what you call Vanaheim – is one of our labs. We set up many biological experiments here and left them to run their course for a few centuries. Imagine our surprise when we returned and found our samples contaminated by humans! We'd never even heard of your species, though we've done our research since then and filled ourselves in, and learned your languages, and so on. It was rather thoughtless of our cousins to show you people how to open the bridge to this system without checking to make sure no one was using it first. Just because we hadn't been here in a few hundred years didn't mean we were done with the place. We've taken steps to limit the contagion, however. You may have noticed we sealed the system.'

"'A ship came in just yesterday,' I said.

"'Oh, yes. We've decided to turn this problem into an opportunity. Humans offer a wealth of new areas of study. We won't turn away perfectly good research materials.'

"Those of us selected to join the team were taken to a ship and transported to a space station beyond the orbit of Niflheim, and given simple tasks at first, the sort of thing lab assistants normally do. But mostly we were interrogated about human biological sciences, immunology, parasitology, gene therapy, and the like. We were hopelessly primitive compared to the Exalted in most ways, but there were some areas where we'd made discoveries unknown to them. I worked quite closely with Shaper in that first year, and gradually he came to consider me, if not a friend, then at least a colleague worthy of respect. I was soon assigned to patient relations, acting as a liaison to talk to the human experimental subjects. They did so much better when they had a familiar face to explain things to them–"

Callie spat on the lab floor. "Collaborator."

Metcalf blinked at her. "Well, yes, of course. I was a collaborator, a very trusted collaborator. I worked with Shaper on some of his most innovative experiments! I didn't just do human relations. I assisted with some of the surgeries, and I was one of the first recipients of their life-extension therapies, which is why I still look as young as I do now. Once we perfected the grafting techniques that allowed us to combine Exalted physiology with human biology, I was happy to trade away my human legs for these pseudopods, which are so much more flexible and useful. I can perform surgery so much better now, and lab work, really all sorts of work, is much easier with more limbs at my disposal. I play a mean game of table tennis, too, ha ha."

"What sort of experiments?" Elena said.

"Well, the grafting, of course. Perfecting that took a long time. Lots of issues with rejection. We perfected organ transplants from humans to humans, except in rare cases where people had compromised immune systems, but combining alien biologies, now that was a challenge. We're still improving the process, of course, but the addition of limbs is trivial now, and–"

"I saw some of your handiwork on a scourge-ship."

Callie clenched her fists.

Metcalf nodded vaguely. "Ah, that's right. The pilots are remarkable. They're bio-drones, really, in a way. Their higher functions aren't entirely gone, but they're, hmm, let's say adapted, limited, or – ha ha – shaped? The neuroscience involved is outside my area, but I gather it has to do with stimulating certain portions of the brain related to bonding and empathy. The result is a human-Exalted chimera who feels an almost familial connection to their ship, and to the extended family of the fleet. Our next step is to try to integrate such chimeras into the ships directly, to hook their consciousness into the sensors, so that operating a weapons system is no more difficult than reaching out your hand, or tentacle, to open a door. Studying the integration of your systems, Ashok, could help us quite a bit with our researches–"

"What's the point of all this?" Elena burst out.

CHAPTER 15

Metcalf cocked his head. "What do you mean?"

"What's the purpose of all this research?" Elena demanded. "Why would you do these things?"

"That's classified," Metcalf said.

"Slice off a tentacle or two, Ashok," Callie said.

"Wait!" Metcalf cried. "When I say it's classified... I mean even I don't know. The Shaper always says they're interested in knowledge for its own sake, but we know there are things the Exalted don't tell their human collaborators, sealed files, secret labs – there's at least one major facility I've heard mentioned now and then, a long distance outside the system, where some secret project is happening."

Callie wondered if it was one of the facilities marked on Lantern's map.

Metcalf went on. "One of my colleagues inquired about the nature of that facility too enthusiastically thirty years ago, and the next time I saw him he'd been repurposed and given janitorial duties, his higher functions entirely gone. I learned to keep my mouth shut and do as I was told. Whatever the Exalted are working toward, it's been their goal for a long time – the addition of humans to their pool of research materials is just an extension of the work they were already doing with the life they seeded on Vanaheim."

"Whatever it is, it must have something to do with the Axiom," Callie said.

"Who?" Metcalf said.

"The secret masters?" Callie said. "The bosses of your bosses? The ancient aliens who enslaved the Exalted, as you call them, millennia ago? The ones who made all those ugly spiky ships out there you've been supplying with brainwashed pilots?"

"The Exalted don't have bosses. They are bosses. I don't know what you're talking about."

"I'm picking up on that." Callie beckoned Elena and Ashok to join her, and walked outside his earshot, assuming he hadn't gotten upgrades to his ears, too. "Do you think all that's true? This whole system got turned into some kind of experimental medical facility, and the humans who didn't become suckass traitors to their species like Metcalf did are just… genetic material?"

"It fits the available facts," Elena said. "If he was going to lie, wouldn't he have made himself sound a little better?"

"He does seem comfortable with being a piece of shit," Callie said. "If there are humans imprisoned in this system, we need to save them. We need to destroy the Exalted. If there's Axiom shit behind this, and I bet there is, we need to comprehensively ruin that, too."

"Hurray, a goal," Ashok said. "How should we start?"

"We need to get out of here. I'd hoped to use Metcalf as a bargaining chip to secure our release, but I've got my doubts about how effective that will be, now that I know he's more of a pet than a power."

"I'm very valuable!" Metcalf shouted. "I'm indispensable! I am of the third rank!"

The ceiling above them creaked. Callie backed away, gesturing for the others to come with her. "Fuck. Are they trying to break in?"

"There are maintenance tunnels up there, so they could be," Ashok said.

"See, Metcalf?" Callie said. "I doubt the Exalted value the life of any particular human all that much. They know if they come in here you'll die."

Metcalf whimpered.

A voice from the ceiling said, "Callie? Are you down there? Shall says he heard you."

"Lantern?" Callie said, raising her voice.

"Look out below," Lantern said. The ceiling tiles began to rain down, and after a moment Lantern dropped into the room, wearing an environment suit. "I've come to rescue you, but it looks like you have things under control." She looked curiously at Metcalf, who gaped at her.

"Exalted one? Why are you in league with these humans?"

"I'm not especially exalted," Lantern said. "Those limbs really don't suit you, you know. You look very unbalanced."

"Are Shall and Kaustikos with you?" Callie said.

"Shall is. Kaustikos is providing a distraction. Would you like to leave?"

"I could be persuaded," Callie said.

"Do we take Metcalf?" Ashok said.

"Hmm. Why not? He could be useful, if only as an inhuman shield."

Metcalf wriggled in his restraints. "I really don't know what you people plan to do. You can't fight the Exalted. They conquered our entire system, effortlessly. Warships come through the gate from time to time, and they deal with those, too."

"By sending human collaborators on board with some cover story about a gate malfunction and having them attack the crew by surprise, I'm guessing?" Callie said. "Maybe even suicide bombing the ships before taking a few surviving crew members prisoner?"

"Well… yes, as I understand it."

"That's not going to work on me," Callie said. "I'm less trusting than the average soldier."

"Still, the five of you can't possibly hope to prevail against the Exalted!"

"What if we join up with the rebels?" Lantern said.

"There are rebels?" Callie said. "You left out that part, Doctor Octopode."

Metcalf groaned. "In the initial transfer of power, some people… slipped away. They style themselves as rebels, and stage raids occasionally on holding facilities to increase their numbers, and to supply themselves, and of course they perform acts of sabotage."

"Guess your Exalted aren't so all-powerful after all, if there's a resistance," Callie said. Now she could definitely imagine a use for Metcalf.

"The Opener of the Way, our head of research, proposed letting the rebels remain free because they are breeding in the tunnels of Niflheim, providing fresh genetic material that can be harvested at a later date. That's the only reason they haven't been eradicated."

"Sounds like propaganda to me, You're coming with us, Squidly. Behave, or Ashok will zap you again, harder, and we'll tie your unconscious bulk to our war drone."

"I–"

"No more talking, either, until further notice. You're so noisy."

Metcalf bowed his head and looked docile enough. He still expected someone to burst in and rescue him, probably.

"Now what?" Elena said.

"Now we get out of here." She looked up at the ceiling, thinking of the maintenance ducts… but Drake and Janice weren't going to be crawling around through any air vents, and dragging Metcalf along would be hard too. "I think we have to brute force our way out of here. Shall, come on down."

The ceiling shuddered, and Shall's war drone dropped with surprising lightness onto its many legs. "What kind of distraction did you all arrange?"

"We blew up nine scourge-ships and sent Kaustikos to go cackle wildly and wave his arms around. Metaphorically. The – Exalted, is it? – launched a bunch of ships after him, and he was going to lead them away and then go stealth and meet up with us later."

Callie grinned. "Nice. And the station thinks it was an attack by these rebels?"

"Based on the communications chatter I've intercepted, that's their working theory."

"Then I doubt they're paying much attention to us," Callie said. "They probably have guards on the door, but otherwise…"

"I can shoot my way through guards," Shall said. "That's kind of my whole thing."

"Always an option, but there may be a better one. Did you break into the station's systems?"

"Oh, yes, I found a terminal. I could control this station like a finger puppet. They aren't even remotely prepared to deal with AI intrusions. The only reason I haven't locked everyone out of their systems is because I thought you might want to keep my abilities a surprise."

"For the moment, just pull up a station map. I want the closest hangar with a ship we can use to reach the *White Raven*."

"Out the door, turn left, up a level, turn right, straight ahead."

There were sure to be guards right outside the lab doors, and even with Shall's superior firepower that would be a dangerous trip, especially with a prisoner in tow slowing them down. If they took a more unexpected route, though... "Why let ourselves be constrained by a little thing like architecture? Let's head for the hangar as the crow flies. Or, rather, as the war drone cuts." She pointed to the left side of the lab. "Let's just go straight through the walls."

The war drone extended manipulator arms tipped with torches and blades. "Oh. This will be fun."

Shall gently tweaked the station's security system to seal off access to the rooms they cut their way through, making the locked doors look like mechanical malfunctions. The areas they passed through were mainly labs, full of old-fashioned computers and vats of yeasty-smelling goo and operating theaters and cylinders of fluid where fragments of once-living things bobbed. Shall led the way, followed by Ashok, then Lantern, then Elena, then Drake and Janice gliding along in their chair, followed by Doctor Metcalf, who kept up a good pace with Callie glaring at him from her position at the back.

They didn't encounter any personnel until they

breached the corridor leading to the hangar they wanted, where two of the black-bodied hunter-drones rushed toward them. Shall had override control of their exoskeletons, though, and he made them run away in the opposite direction while their fleshy limbs flailed in protest.

They made their way into the hangar, where they found a transport ship much like the one that had brought them here from the *White Raven*. "Let's seal all the other doors, okay, Shall? I don't want anyone following us. Actually, why don't you just turn out the lights when we leave? Can we do that? Leave life support, because there might be prisoners on this station, but kill everything else?"

"I can shut down their systems and set loose some worms to prevent them from restarting, at least for a good long time," Shall said.

"Unleash the worms," Callie said. "Can we do any more damage on our way out?"

"Well... how would you like to get rid of their whole fleet?"

"How do you propose to do that?"

"I can activate the bridge generators on all those scourge-ships," Shall said. "There are emergency protocols, to be used in the event that the shipyard is under attack and can't be defended, to get the uncrewed ships to safety."

"Ohhhhh," Callie said. "And there's only one pilot

out patrolling the fence line. Even if they wanted to bring the ships back, they'd have to do it one at a time…"

"I can do better than that," Shall said. "The bridge generators are heavily locked-down. They can only travel from here to a few fixed points, all of them in that same stretch of nothing where we ended up, out by the fence. I can choose which of those few coordinates they use as their destinations, though. I wonder what happens when you send a thousand ships into a single point in space that's only big enough to hold one of them?"

"A pretty nasty pile-up," Callie said.

"I knew I could do better than decimation," Shall said. "This is more like total-imation. There are more scourge-ships in the system, guarding various installations, but this is the bulk of the fleet, and we can wipe them out."

Metcalf gaped at them, eyes wide, but didn't speak so Callie didn't have an excuse to zap him. She did smile at him when she said, "Do it, Shall."

They boarded the ship, with Ashok and Callie securing Metcalf to a seat with as many straps as they could fit around him. Shall clung to the ship's back, then opened the hangar door. From up here, Shall could see the twisted bits of wrecked scourge-ships from their earlier sabotage, and small vessels like theirs drifting around to no apparent purpose. People did like to go look at traffic accidents, didn't they?

He activated the emergency protocols and space

filled with spreading tendrils of darkness, reaching out to embrace the scourge-ships and pull them far away into the greatest spaceship wreck the galaxy had probably ever seen. The little ships began zipping around even more frantically, with no guidance from the silent, inert space station. They probably thought they were under attack. At least no one would notice their ship following its own erratic course. The Weaver of Worlds is going to get demoted, Shall thought. He's going to have to settle for weaving small islands or something instead.

Once the last of the scourge-ships had vanished and the wormholes were closed, Shall directed their ship toward the *White Raven*. They underestimated us, Shall thought, but that's the kind of advantage we probably only get once.

"You actually made it out," Kaustikos said on Shall's comms. "I thought I was going to have to save the galaxy myself."

"Good job leading the bad guys on a merry chase." Shall wasn't averse to giving credit where it was due. "Where are you?"

"Lurking near your ship. Where did all the other ships go?"

"They're trying hard to become a black hole. Lurk a little closer. We're headed to the ship now."

They reached the *White Raven* without incident and got on board. The general mood was one of exhausted jubilation. Shall's mind on the war drone connected with Shall's mind on the ship and merged their memories, then climbed into his spot in the launch tube and powered down.

"Hey Shall." Callie looked at the empty shipyard through the cockpit windows. "I wonder if we missed an opportunity here. Could we have ported your mind over to a few of the scourge-ships and made a little fleet of our own?"

"The same idea occurred to me," Shall said. "Unfortunately, though they're sophisticated engines of war, packed full of nasty weapons, they aren't hospitable environments for my consciousness. Those ships don't have the storage capacity or processing power I need to operate. It would be like trying to copy my mind onto a toaster or an exercise bike. Ashok had to customize the war drone so I could load a local copy of myself onto it, instead of just piloting it remotely. He could maybe customize a scourge-ship the same way, given time, but…"

"Who has time. Oh well. I liked the idea of a whole fleet of heavily armed yous at my side. We'll just have to muddle along. Ashok, is the bridge generator ready to go?"

"It is, cap. Where to? I assume we aren't heading home."

"Tempting as it is to go back and muster up an armada, we don't have any way to get them here except through the main bridge, and I'm guessing that's pretty well guarded. Plus, we'd have a hard time convincing the Imperative officials that we aren't insane. As always, it's up to us, but maybe we can scare up a little help. Let's jaunt over to Niflheim and see if we can meet some of these rebels I've heard so much about."

Niflheim wasn't as close to the Vanir system's sun as Vanaheim, though it had a thicker atmosphere that made it warm enough to sustain human life, at least in the equatorial regions. The planet was by all accounts less pleasant than Vanaheim, which early colonial propaganda materials had described as an Edenic natural paradise (they left out the parts about giant tapeworms).

Niflheim, by contrast, was rockier, colder, and altogether harsher, but rich enough in minerals to make it an ideal site for resource exploitation. Humans had established a few mining facilities there, and Callie guessed the rebels were using some of those as bases. Even if the Exalted did want to root the rebels out, the fight would ultimately come down to individual combat in tunnels the humans knew better and had ample time to harden against an invasion. So as far as strongholds went, the mining facilities were effective. Of course, the

Exalted probably had the weapons necessary to literally destroy the planet itself, but they hadn't – either they wanted to keep it around for its resources, or blowing it up risked damaging neighboring Vanaheim, or Metcalf's ridiculous story about the Exalted wanting another cache of isolated human genetic material was true.

Once they reached Niflheim's orbit – the planet was shrouded in gray clouds and Shall told them Niflheim meant something like 'world of fog' – Callie had Janice beam transmissions toward all the mining facilities within range. "This is Captain Kalea Machedo, from Earth's solar system. I have reason to believe there are human resistance fighters within the sound of my voice. If so, I'd like to talk to whoever's in charge about lending you my aid against the Exalted."

They floated for fifteen minutes, and Callie was about to transmit again, more emphatically, when someone hailed them. A woman's low, thoughtful voice said, "Captain Machedo, did you say you're from Earth? How did you get past the blockade at the bridge?"

"We didn't come through the front door. Our ship has the same wormhole technology the scourge-ships do. We came to see what's going on in this system, and I have to say, we don't much like what we found."

"We don't much like it, either. We've never seen a ship like yours before, which supports your story, but some of my friends aren't so trusting. They want proof that you're on our side."

Callie had anticipated that. "Well," she said, "do you know a guy named Doctor Metcalf?"

"The Butcher?" she said. "Head of the Scourge Station's surgical division? The one who turns humans into brain-wiped chimera pilots?"

"That sounds like our guy." Callie pulled up a camera view of the good doctor brooding in the infirmary. "We captured him, and we've got him trussed up in our medical bay now. Transmitting you a live feed. The person watching over him is my engineer Ashok. Why don't you tell him to do something so you know we're transmitting in real time?"

"Uh... spin around in a circle?" the voice said.

Ashok obligingly did a twirling pirouette.

"Satisfied?" Callie said.

"Of course not. This could still be a ploy. But... we're interested enough to take the next step. Do you have a landing vessel?"

"That we do."

"We'll send you coordinates. Bring the doctor, if you would. We're excited to spend some time with him."

CHAPTER 16

Callie took Elena and Ashok with her on the canoe, leaving Kaustikos, Lantern, Drake, and Janice on the ship. She would have taken Lantern with her, but she worried the human rebels would react badly to the sight of one of the 'Exalted' in their midst.

When Metcalf realized where they were headed, he became… resistant, tearing loose from his straps and smashing up a terminal before Ashok zapped him into quiescence again. Elena considered sedating him, but worried his partially alien biochemistry might interact badly with drugs meant for humans. She monitored his vital signs as best she could, though they were strange. His base temperature ran hotter than most humans, and she suspected his metabolic rate was higher, too. He probably had to eat a lot in order to run all those extra limbs.

The xenobiologist in her couldn't resist examining him as much as she was able. As far as she could tell, he'd lost everything from the waist down, even sacrificing his reproductive organs, or rather replacing them with a Liar-like cloaca nestled at the center of the forest of a dozen tentacles. Eight of the pseudopods were the thicker, less dexterous sort, necessary to bear up his weight, while the other four were delicate and feathered with cilia that doubtless improved their gripping power, or perhaps included additional sense organs. Without scanning equipment, she couldn't tell what internal changes he had, but he must have altered his digestive system at the very least, and there were surely changes to his nervous system to allow him to operate those new limbs–

"They'll kill me," Metcalf said, and Elena jerked away from where he lay strapped in the back of the canoe. He shook his head tiredly. "I'm not going to attack you. You're taking me to the rebels, I assume. As proof of your allegiance to their cause."

"They called you the Butcher," she said.

"Never. Never that. I am a surgeon. I don't make meat. The Exalted don't eat us. They try to elevate us."

"How many people died in the course of developing those elevations?" Elena said. "Dozens? Scores? Hundreds? Didn't you take an oath, to first do no harm?"

"Those oaths were only binding in another world, Dr Oh. I was trying to preserve the greater good. If I could convince the Exalted that humans could be useful, that we could serve as colleagues and peers as well as experimental subjects, wasn't that better for my people, in the long run?"

"It's been a pretty long run already, Doctor Metcalf. A hundred years."

"All the choices I made seemed sensible at the time. I suppose I might have damned myself by centimeters, but looking back, I don't know what I could have done differently, without…"

"Without becoming an experimental subject yourself?"

"Oh, I was that anyway. Do you think I wanted to trade in the legs I'd walked on my entire life for these alien appendages? Do you think I sacrificed my manhood – not to be crude, but my cock? – with enthusiasm? At a certain point I had to demonstrate my loyalty to the program. My total investment. Such proofs were required to rise in the ranks. There are no pure humans at all on the third level or above – if you aren't dedicated enough to become a chimera, you aren't dedicated enough for such responsibilities."

"You betrayed your people," Elena said. "Those people will be the ones to pass judgment on you. I'm sorry." She was, but not as sorry as she would have expected. Metcalf was loathsome and self-serving and he clearly loved his work too much for her to spare him much empathy. She'd learned a long time ago that nice and cheerful didn't equal good. Sometimes they were just costumes evil wore.

"What did your captain mean, about, what did she call them, the Axiom?"

Elena considered whether there was any reason to withhold the truth from him, and couldn't think of any. "There are other intelligent aliens besides the Liars. An ancient race, called the Axiom, who had unimaginable technology and power, ruled an empire that spanned the galaxy. They built the wormhole bridges, among other things. The Liars were their slaves and servants. The Axiom empire dwindled as they warred among themselves, and most of them went into hibernation thousands of years ago. They're dormant, not dead, just waiting for various long-term, universe-altering projects to come to fruition – sort of like your Exalted leaving Vanaheim to itself for a couple of hundred years to see what evolution could do with their subjects.

"We've been destroying the works of the Axiom when we can, because if the Axiom wake up and discover humanity they'll try to wipe us out, and if any of their experiments succeed that won't be good for people, either. Some of the Liars are still devoted to their old masters, and protect their projects. We suspect the Liars here are working on some Axiom project. It's why I asked you what all these experiments were for – we think there's a deeper purpose at work, something to do with an Axiom plot to control the galaxy again, or survive the end of this universe, or move into another."

"Incredible," Metcalf said. "I've overheard Shaper and his colleagues talking about failed experiments, or some protocol or another that wasn't as successful as they'd hoped… they always went silent if they noticed me listening. I wonder if it's something to do with these Axiom?"

"If so, I'm sure we'll find out."

The canoe settled down on the surface of Niflheim with a thump, and Callie came to the back of the canoe. "I see the bad doctor is conscious. Can you move under your own power, or should we drag you by your hair?"

"I can walk." Metcalf spoke with great dignity. "You do know, I hope, that you are delivering me to my execution."

"That saves me the trouble of putting you out an airlock myself," Callie said. Elena winced. Her lover wasn't as hard-hearted as she liked to pretend, but she wasn't as soft-hearted as Elena herself was. "Up and at 'em, slithers." Callie drew her sidearm but didn't point it. She didn't really need to. "You get out first."

Ashok lowered the canoe's ramp and Metcalf unsteadily stumbled down to the surface of Niflheim. Elena went down beside Callie, with Ashok taking the rear. The air was cool, the sky gray and cloudy, and the ground gray and rocky. The place did smell a little like vinegar.

Three people stood a hundred meters away, dressed in coats and scarves in shades of gray that blended with the environment. One of them came forward, some kind of rifle slung over his back, and the other two held their position, pointing similar weapons in the Butcher's direction. The man pulled his scarf down, revealing a middle-aged face, lined and sun-darkened, with pale, mistrustful eyes.

"Captain Machedo?" he called.

"That's me. This is my executive officer, Doctor Oh, and my engineer, Ashok."

"Is he... some kind of android? Do we have androids back in the world now?"

There were certainly some AI who remotely operated humanoid robotic bodies, though Shall couldn't understand why anyone would choose such a limited shape, but Callie just said, "No, he's a cyborg. Augmented human."

The man made a face like he'd tasted something sour. "We don't like augmentations much around here."

"Nobody strapped me down and grafted these parts onto me against my will," Ashok said. "Just think of them like prosthetic legs, except it's a prosthetic face and arm and other stuff. Plus also legs."

The man grunted. He looked at Metcalf, who stared back at him, face pale and sweaty. "I'm Wilfred Burkhart," the man said. "My parents were colonists who came through the wormhole gate and I was born free right here on Niflheim. I've never seen the inside of one of the Butcher's labs, but I've got friends who have. Welcome, doctor. I hope you don't enjoy your stay." He reached into a pouch at his belt and drew out what looked like an oversized silver bracelet. "Recognize this?"

Metcalf tried to run away, and Ashok tased him, making him shudder and shiver and slump, his nest of tentacles twitching wildly.

"Guess he does." Wilfred moved forward swiftly and closed the bracelet – no, it was a collar – around Metcalf's neck, then stepped back. He turned to the crew. "The Butcher and his friends put those on the prisoners in their labs. The collars collect and transmit vital signs and all kinds of medical data, but they also deliver debilitating shocks. There are little needles inside for drawing blood, but if need be, those little needles become long needles, and either kill the subjects, or sever their spinal cords, so they're paralyzed from the neck down. Isn't that right, Butcher?"

Metcalf was recovering from being tased, but his eyes were still glassy. "I… I don't…"

Wilfred spat. "He convinced the first prisoners to put them on. Him, personally. 'They're just heart rate monitors,' he'd say. 'They read the pulse in your neck. Don't worry about them.' That was back when he still had human parts downstairs, of course. Nobody would believe him now. We all know better. But he got promoted out of the fourth rank and into the third, running his own facility, so he had other traitors to do the smiling and lying for him after that. There are human workers in his labs who were raised there since they were babies, who think it's right for them to be experimental subjects, who've been indoctrinated to believe they're serving some greater purpose. Sometimes we rescue them, and bring them here, and they try to escape from us, to go back to the labs, to the 'doctors' they think of as parents." He spat again, this time on the doctor's tentacles.

"Are you going to kill me?" Doctor Metcalf said.

"That's not entirely up to me," Wilfred said. "Which is why you aren't dead already. You'll have to give us a really good reason to keep you alive, though. Like actionable intelligence about the Execrable and their facilities. You've risen as high as anyone born human can in their society, so I'm sure you have lots of interesting things to tell us. You're an experienced traitor, so I'm sure you can turn on your new masters the way you turned on your fellow humans all those years ago. As long as you're useful, you'll continue to draw air." He turned to his companions. "He's pacified. Take him to holding. I'll stay with our guests." The other humans nodded, and one held up a remote control and waggled it at Metcalf, who bowed his head and went meekly toward them. They walked around a boulder and didn't reappear on the other side.

Wilfred guided them in a different direction, to a

different boulder. He kicked a spot on the rock's base and the boulder slid aside, revealing a set of metal stairs leading steeply down. He led them into the depths, and the rock slid shut over them, the darkness triggering lights that ran along the walls. "This isn't our main base – we wouldn't risk bringing you there – just a supply cache, but there are viewscreens below so I can liaise with the other leaders of the resistance."

"I love liaising," Callie said. "I could do it for hours. I don't guess you want to tell me about your troop strength and so on, give me an idea of what we're working with here?"

"Let's be a little bit vague for now. Giving us Metcalf is an awfully nice gesture of goodwill, but we have to be cautious. We've had issues with infiltrators in the past, and while giving up Metcalf seems like a sacrifice the Exalted wouldn't make willingly, who knows? Maybe he fucked up and they're sacrificing him as part of a plot to make us reveal our secrets to you."

"I like you," Callie said.

He glanced over his shoulder at her, eyes twinkling. "Oh? Why's that?"

You'd better not try flirting with her, Elena thought.

"Because she's a deeply suspicious person who always thinks the worst of everybody, too," Ashok said.

Wilfred chuckled. He keyed open a solid metal door and shooed them through, then locked it again. The door sealed, Elena thought, with a very definitive thunk. He led them down a dimly lit hallway and into a room that had been repurposed from a storage space to a conference room, with a few beaten-up chairs arrayed around a scuffed table that held a few ancient viewscreens. They didn't have fully immersive virtual reality conferencing systems around here, she supposed.

Wilfred told them to take seats and tossed them bulbs of water that smelled strongly of minerals. They let Ashok sample his first – he had sensors in his tongue that could detect sedatives or toxins, and filters to survive drinking them, and he gave them a discreet nod. Elena drank gratefully. Just being on the arid, acrid surface for a few minutes had made her parched. Wilfred sat in a chair at the head of the table and regarded them, hands laced across his stomach. With his hood off she could see he was fair-haired as well as light-eyed, probably in his early fifties, with a face that looked stone-carved. "So. The humans out in the world figured out how to make portable wormhole generators, finally?"

"Not really," Callie said. "We stole ours off an alien ship."

Wilfred cocked his head. "Did you? We've tried that. We've gotten our hands on a few scourge-ships over the years, but we could never make much use of their bridge generators. They'd open a wormhole, but it only went to one destination out in the middle of nowhere, still light years from help or habitation, and we always had to come back here eventually, or starve."

"There's a sort of invisible fence around this system," Ashok said. "The scourge-ships have generators that only allow them to travel from here to the fence line and back again. Ours is... not so limited, but even so, we had a hard time getting here – there are countermeasures to prevent incursions. The Exalted really don't want visitors."

"There go my hopes of the cavalry arriving in the form of ten thousand warships converging from all directions," Wilfred said. "But... can you get my people out of here?"

"That's sort of why I wanted to know about troop strength," Callie said. "If we cram our ship full, I mean standing room, and we throw out everything non-essential that takes up space, to really maximize things... we could fit maybe a hundred people? We're talking about a ship that's meant for a crew of half a dozen."

Wilfred said hmm. "How fast can you do round trips?"

"The bridge generator takes about eight hours to recharge," Ashok said. "Each way. So we could take a load, wait eight hours, come back, wait eight hours, head back, wait eight hours... we could move couple hundred people a day."

"I'm guessing there are more than a couple hundred people who'd like to leave this system," Callie said.

Wilfred nodded. "There were six hundred thousand colonists on Vanaheim when the Exalted invaded, and almost a hundred thousand on Niflheim. The initial fighting, and the plagues the Exalted used on the rebels, killed tens of thousands of us, and these days the Exalted have strict population controls for the humans they've imprisoned… but I'd guess we're talking about roughly that many humans in the system still, most of them prisoners in facilities or on work farms."

"So that's seven thousand trips," Ashok said. "At sixteen hours per round trip. We could get everybody back to human-controlled space in, oh, call it thirteen years."

"We could get a bigger transport vessel," Callie said. "Plug our bridge generator into that instead. We could cram a thousand people on instead of a hundred. But even so… it's not practical. Plus most of those people are basically in prison camps, I assume, so we can't just pick them up and take them to safety."

"Yes. The majority of the population is slave labor, toiling on the farms of Vanaheim to keep the population fed or in Exalted factories to produce whatever they need. The unluckiest people are plucked from a life of forced labor and used for medical experiments."

"Evacuation isn't viable at scale, then," Callie said.

"If you have sick people, young people, vulnerable people, we can see about getting them to safety. But for the rest… we're just going to have to liberate the whole system, I guess."

Wilfred laughed. "Great idea. Wish we'd thought of it. Did you have a plan?"

"Blowing stuff up, mainly," Callie said, and Elena had to grin.

CHAPTER 17

"Blowing things up. That's the kind of innovative thinking we need here on Niflheim." Wilfred rolled his eyes. "The Exalted have a literal fleet of warships. If we venture out into orbit, we tend to get obliterated."

"They had a fleet of warships," Ashok said. "We destroyed every vessel in the shipyard at Scourge Station."

Wilfred gaped. "I... we... I'm going to have to check on that, and get confirmation..."

"Of course. Trust, but verify, just like it says in the Bible," Ashok said.

"I think that line's from Chaucer," Callie said. "What Ashok says is true, Wilfred, but let's table it for now. Even if you're still worried about their scourge-ships – and I'll admit we didn't destroy them all, just most – we've got a pretty nice ship of our own up there, one designed for hunting down pirates and fugitives, with stealth technology and that aforementioned bridge generator."

Wilfred nodded. "We can use that, absolutely, we welcome your help, but I just want you to understand the magnitude of what we're facing here. It's no small thing to overthrow the Exalted, even if you have crippled their fleet. Even one scourge-ship is an engine of mass-destruction, and they have drones, guards, weapons, science, space stations that are flying fortresses... fighting the Exalted is a big job."

"I never do anything small. We have another advantage, too. You know about AI?"

He frowned. "Artificial intelligence? Sure... there are some expert systems in the mining facilities here, we use them to calculate resource allocations—"

Callie shook her head. "I'm talking about true AI. Conscious machines, sapient beings in their own right. It's a little something we perfected back in the civilized systems while you've all been sealed up here. We've got an AI on our ship. His name is Shall, and he's our trump card. He can seize control of the Exalted computer systems, override their security, and cover his tracks along the way. He's how we destroyed their fleet. We're up against a technocratic regime, right? But right now, we're the ones with the best technology in the system. Pick a target, some place you've wanted to break into or smash apart but couldn't crack on your own, and we'll help you get in. Call it a proof of concept, to show we can do what we promised, and then we'll move on from there."

"No pressure," Shall murmured in her earpiece.

She could tell Wilfred was excited, and trying not

to show it. "If this is true… let me talk to the other generals." He gestured at the blank screens. "You can wait outside."

Callie and the others obligingly moved out into the corridor, and Wilfred shut the door. Callie could have listened in, of course – the revolution's technology was primitive even compared to the Exalted's – but they were playing nice, and she had a pretty good idea what he'd say anyway: something like, 'Our prayers have been answered, but don't get your hopes up.'

"Do you think they'll go for it?" Elena asked, leaning against the wall, looking tired but ferocious, and, as always in Callie's eyes, fetching.

"I think they're pinned down on a dirty rock and they've been eating kicks in the teeth for dinner for generations, so they'll wobble between hope and fearful caution, and come up with some stupid compromise, and we'll make it work anyway. I wish there was a delicate way for me to just assume command of their resistance. Generals." She shook her head. "Do you think there's any chance they have anybody with actual military experience in the bunch? They're probably inventing guerilla tactics from first principles. I don't claim to be some great military genius, but at least I've had practical training in the security services, and I've got a decent grounding in theory. Plus, Shall's crammed full of tactical and strategic information, so I've got good advisors, too."

"A coup is probably not the best way to demonstrate our helpfulness," Elena said.

"It's admirably direct though," Ashok said.

One of the women who'd taken Metcalf away came into the corridor and asked if they wanted anything to eat or drink, so they sat at a dented table in another room and ate fungal paste and sipped more of that strong mineral-smelling water, waiting to get the word.

Wilfred came in, smiling. "It was a close vote, but we've agreed to do a test run."

"Glad to know you had to argue so hard to let us risk our lives to help you," Callie said, and Elena kicked her under the table. She sighed. "Sorry. It's been a long... interval since I last had any sleep. What's the target?"

"There are twelve major Exalted facilities, each one under the control of a high-ranking director, most of them Exalted, but with a few chimera collaborators. You brought us one of those directors, the Butcher, and apparently disabled the facility, too. We'd like to take out another one – a research station in orbit around Vanaheim."

"Consider it exploded," Callie said.

Wilfred shook his head. "There are thousands of prisoners on board, so no explosions, please. You said your AI can help you seize control. Your crew's job will be to infiltrate the station and take over its security.

Then my people will bring a stolen transport ship to rescue the prisoners, along with enough supplies from the station's stores to feed them, and you'll cover our escape. After that, you can explode the station."

"This is pretty ambitious, for a proof of concept," Callie said.

"Does that mean you can't do it?"

"No, that means I like the way you think," she replied.

"I wouldn't mind having a couple more local backups," Shall complained. "You can't imagine the existential fear of having only one full copy of my consciousness in this system. If the *White Raven* gets destroyed, I'm dead here. The war drone is all well and good, but it's just my core consciousness, with limited access to memories and really pitiful processing power."

Callie checked her weapons. "Shall. That's every human's whole experience for our entire lives. I don't even have a copy of myself back on Glauketas the way you do. If you're really worried, why don't you copy yourself to the computers in the mining facility?"

"Why don't you copy yourself onto a squirrel?" he said. "The infrastructure here is ancient. The Exalted shipyard station was primitive, too, and where it wasn't too primitive, it was too alien."

"Then I, too, regret that you have just one life to

give for the resistance. Or a life and a half, counting the war drone. Self-preservation is good motivation, anyway. Mortal fear keeps you sharp." She clambered on top of the war drone and clipped herself in. Callie was well-rested – they'd all caught up on sleep while the resistance got their part of the plan in order – and she was eager to strike a blow against the Exalted. Having a deep personal dislike for the creatures who ran this system made this whole process very satisfying.

Everyone had a part to play. Elena was with the resistance, ready to assist their meager medical team with any rescued prisoners who needed help. Drake and Janice and Lantern were staying on the *White Raven*, stealthed and watchful, ready to offer support as needed. Lantern could have been useful elsewhere, but the humans had some pretty deeply ingrained anti-alien bias. Ashok was in Lantern's blister-ship – doubtless crammed rather uncomfortably into the small space – with Kaustikos clinging to the outside, both of them ready to do their own parts in the infiltration. She didn't trust Kaustikos in any objective sense, but he knew she'd destroy him if he misbehaved, and she did trust his instincts for self-preservation.

"We're within range," Janice said.

"Bombs away," Callie said. The cargo bay doors opened and Shall's war drone dropped from the ship's belly. The *White Raven* rapidly receded above them as Shall arrowed toward their target. The orb of Vanaheim hung beneath them, a blue and green world of staggering Earthlike beauty, floating between them and the system's sun.

"There's the station," Shall said. Callie's head-up display lit up, outlining the dark shape in glowing lines of light. The station was a standard Liar configuration: a central hub with seven radiating arms, each intersected by concentric rings. As they drew closer, the shapes of three scourge-ships lit up in her helmet, and with those in place to provide scale, Callie got a sense of the station's staggering size: it was a city in the sky, not much smaller than Scourge Station had been.

"How are Ashok and the asshole probe doing?" They weren't in direct communication – they didn't want to risk their comms being overheard – but Shall's sensors were mighty and he outlined the distant blister-ship in light as well, so Callie could watch it approach the station from the other side.

"They look to be on track," Shall said. The station grew and grew, filling the screen. "There's our insertion point." A red circle appeared on her view of the central hub. "Based on our scans, it should get us close to control systems and access tunnels." Shall matched velocity with the station – changing speed and direction as gradually as possible, in deference to Callie's comparatively fragile form being whipped around on his back. They'd programmed approaches intended to evade the sensors of the scourge-ships, but, even so, a shiver crawled up Callie's spine as they moved toward the station's central hub. A blast from one of those ships would turn her into vapor.

Fortunately, Shall's careful approach worked as intended, and he clamped himself magnetically to the station's hub. His cutting torches went to work, and Callie clung tensely to his back while sparks flashed silently around her. Shall removed a section of the hull, revealing a wide crawlspace beyond, busy with pipes and cabling. Shall clambered into the hole with her, then pulled the cut-out section after him and welded it back into place. There was no atmosphere here, or artificial gravity, so Shall used his magnetic clamps to make his way along the tower, pausing occasionally to examine cables and junction boxes until he found one he liked: "This should work."

He opened a panel and extended delicate manipulators, patching himself into the station. "Let's see what we've got… okay. I'm in. I've got control of their comms and station security. There are… wow, sixty of those hunter-drones crawling around. I can control their exoskeletons from here, but there are also a dozen autonomous security guards, basically supervisors, and I can't do much about those except give them bad information."

"Where are the prisoners?"

"Where aren't they? There are dormitories, and labs, and shifts of prisoners eating in a cafeteria – they're spread all over. We pretty much have to take over the whole station if we're going to get them out."

"Can you disable the prisoner collars?"

"Mmmm… no. Which is a problem. Taking those off requires personal authorization from the director. There's no point rescuing these people at all if the Exalted can kill them all remotely."

"The resistance can remove collars, Wilfred said."

"One or two or ten, sure, but thousands? It would take weeks, and I doubt the Exalted would wait that long before pressing the 'kill all' button."

"All right. Is the director on station?"

"The director is… in, yes, in her office at the top of the hub."

Wilfred had filled Callie in about the director, a human named Kerneghan. The resistance had a particular hatred for the humans who'd chosen to collaborate with the Exalted – even greater than their hatred for the Exalted themselves. "That's where I'm going, then. Where's my point of entry?"

"Straight up. I'll tell you when you reach the access tunnel."

Callie launched herself in the microgravity, sailing up through the dark tangle of wires and pipes, reaching out occasionally for handholds to propel herself further. After ascending hundreds of meters,

Shall said, "Look for a hatch on your left... there."

The access panel was square and sized for Liars, but she could fit through. She yanked the lever, opened the hatch, and squirmed into a cramped little airlock. With much twisting and swearing she got the hatch behind her closed, which unlocked the other airlock door that led into the station proper. She squirmed out, grunting when the artificial gravity hit and sent her tumbling to the floor. She was glad Ashok wasn't there to see.

Callie got her feet under her and looked around. The room was dark, dirty, and full of tools and bits of busted equipment, like maintenance areas all over. She prodded a broken hunter-drone exoskeleton with her boot, satisfied herself that it wasn't going to leap up and attack her, and engaged her suit's active camouflage. "Is the corridor clear?"

"It is, but there are two guards outside the director's office. They're being extra-cautious, I guess, since Metcalf got abducted. I don't know what you should expect inside the office, either – no cameras in there. Rank has its privileges and everything."

"Challenge mode, then. Guess there's no chance of kiting the guards away?"

"If I send them orders to go anywhere else, they're going to check with the director before they do, probably."

"Any nearby hunter-drones we can turn against them?"

"Not on this level. I think they're mostly used for herding prisoners, and you're on the executive level now. I can retask a few to your location, but it will take a little while for them to arrive, and it might attract notice."

"I'll just have to go through the guards, then." Callie eased open the maintenance closet door and stepped into the hallway. The executive level was nice, paneled in what looked like real wood, with soft overhead light, and living vines growing along the ceiling, sprouting little white flowers. The carpet under her feet was dark, thick, and deep pile. Collaborating with the Exalted had its perks, clearly.

Callie crept along the hallway, following the map Shall helpfully provided in her helmet display, turning first right and then left, passing closed doors that held conference rooms, and the executive dining room. At the end of the last corridor, maybe twenty meters away, stood an ornately carved wooden door, with a tall pane of frosted glass on either side. The door was flanked by two Liar guards wearing some kind of black mesh body armor. They were bigger than most Liars, the size of short adult humans rather than toddler, and their main tentacles were as big around as her thighs. These specimens had probably been altered in surgical suites to be more physically powerful and intimidating, or maybe even tweaked in their incubators. With that armor, her tasers weren't likely to work, and if she got within grappling distance, they'd overpower her with all those extra limbs. She needed to do this from a distance, and fast –

One of them took a step in her direction, and she briefly froze. He couldn't possibly see her, and her suit had countermeasures to muffle her sound and any scents, and to mask her heat signature –

"What is it?" the other guard said.

"Look at the carpet," the first said.

Callie looked down. She couldn't see her own body – one of the more disorienting parts of being inside this suit… but she could see the oval bootprints she left in the deep-pile carpet. Two depressions as clear as footprints in the snow. Just her luck to draw an attentive guard.

She raised both her arms and let the suit's targeting computer – a recent addition Ashok had put together – slightly shift her aim. She had wrist gauntlets with an array of non-lethal and lethal weapons, energy and plasma and simple projectiles, and she used the latter because she didn't want to put holes in the walls. The gauntlets made a thpt thpt thpt sound as they fired rounds into both the guards, unerringly through the view-ports in their armor, and on through their eyes. They writhed, tentacles lashing – Liars had distributed nervous systems, and it took their appendages a while to realize they were dead – and Callie stepped back.

"I intercepted the security alert that triggered when

the guards stopped having vital signs," Shall said. "I'm locking down the hallway just to be safe, though – there's a 'protect the director' protocol that effectively quarantines that part of the station, so I'm sealing you in."

"Thanks." Callie's voice croaked a little.

"Are you okay?"

"I… did what had to be done. I didn't like it." She was extremely comfortable with self-defense, but attacking from ambush, even in a righteous cause, never felt good to her. She reminded herself that the guards wouldn't have hesitated to kill her, or worse, capture her for interrogation and experimentation. That didn't make her feel much better, but she shook it off for now and focused on the mission.

Callie stepped around the corpses of the Liar guards and tested the door to the director's office. "Can you unlock this?"

"I… ha. No, I can't. I think it's an actual physical deadbolt."

"Breaking stuff it is." Callie punched the frosted glass pane to the left of the door, and it shattered. She shouldered through the opening sideways, barely squeezing through, and found herself in a gorgeous office, all dark wood and lush plants and high ceilings with exposed roof beams as wide as trees. The walls were lined with shelves that held various trophies and objects of art and models of spaceships. There were comfortable chairs, and a desk approximately the size of a king-sized bed.

No sign of Kerneghan, though. Callie checked the director's private bathroom, wrist gauntlets raised, but the beautiful slate shower stall and gleaming fixtures and pedestal sink didn't offer any hiding places. She looked under the desk, too, just in case, then looked around, frustrated. "Shall, the office is empty."

"She's got a tracker on, Callie, and it says she's right next to you. I can even see her vital signs – her heart rate is elevated, so I'd say she's pretty stressed about something."

"I don't see–" Callie stopped, thinking of the hunter-drone on the ceiling of the scourge-ship.

She looked up, just in time to see Kerneghan drop from the rafters on top of her.

CHAPTER 18

"Scut-work," Kaustikos said. "A waste of my considerable talents."

"Please shut up," Ashok said.

"Why? No one can hear us. We're in vacuum."

"I can hear you," Ashok said. "It's terrible." He found the access hatch and opened the lever, crawling through into the tiny airlock, and Kaustikos crammed in after him. Ashok was very aware of the bomb he'd attached to the probe and very unhappy about it pressing into the small of his back. The outer door opened and Ashok tumbled into gravity, knocking over mops and a bucket when he landed. He was glad Callie wasn't there to see him.

"Now who should be quiet?" Kaustikos floated in the center of the room, a dark orb covered in glittering lenses.

"Still you. Shall, we're here. What's the situation out there?"

"Pretty amusing," Shall said. "I sent a fake security alert to all the roving guards on this level, telling them there was a riot in the showers. They all obligingly rushed in, and then I sealed the bathroom doors – the quarantine systems on this station are really useful. There are a few other guards, watching the dormitories and the cafeteria, but I hijacked hunter-drones and got the authorities pinned down secured. Zero casualties, and all the security on this level has been neutralized."

"Then let's go get greeted as liberators." Ashok left the maintenance closet and stepped out into the main holding level. Kaustikos floated along behind him. Ashok didn't actually need the AI, but Callie didn't like leaving Kaustikos unattended, and Ashok had drawn babysitting duty.

"Why am I even here?" Kaustikos complained.

"Callie doesn't like leaving you unattended, and I got babysitting duty."

"Bah. Haven't I proven myself yet? I helped rescue her. I led alien ships on a merry chase for her, at great personal risk."

"I know. It must be super frustrating for you." Ashok hummed to himself as he approached an intimidating metal door. "Open," he said, waving his arm, and Shall obligingly made it swing wide. Ashok passed through another security door and walked to a low railing, then looked down onto the cafeteria, where hundreds of humans in shapeless gray jumpsuits were eating under the not-at-all-currently-watchful eyes of several hunter-drones.

"Greetings from the resistance!" Ashok called, amplifying his voice through the speakers built into his face. "We're here to set you free!" Assuming Callie could get their collars deactivated, anyway.

The humans looked up at him, and gaped, and lots of them looked at the hunter-drones, shying away in fear.

"Dance for me!" Ashok shouted, and Shall, snorting amusement in his comms, made the drones spin and bounce and jitterbug on their spindly knife-sharp limbs. "Okay, now go away." The drones scurried off toward the kitchen. "I am the drone king! I can do anything!"

The Exalted who ran the kitchen came out, shouting, "What's the meaning of this? Who are you?" Two Exalted assistants trailed her.

"Newly liberated people of this station! You could grab her." He pointed to the Exalted cook. "Tie her up. Put her in the freezer or whatever. I'd do it myself, but… I'm all the way up here. Seriously, it's okay. The resistance has control of the station, in a sort of general, overall way. We still have to subdue the odd supervisor, but we're working on it. In the meantime… empower yourselves." For a minute he thought he'd have to send Kaustikos zooming down to tase the Exalted or something, but then one of the prisoners flung a tray at the head cook, who squawked and turned to run, and then there were plenty of volunteers to pile on and subdue her.

Ashok found the stairs and ambled down to the main floor, looking around. "Is there any kind of leader here? Anybody who wants to be a leader?"

A woman with dark hair buzzed short climbed up on a table and stood tall. "I used to work with the resistance. Who are you? What are you? Where did you come from?"

"I'm Ashok. I'm a human, just like you, only with some mechanical upgrades, which, let me be honest, I like way better than the biological ones your enemies are into. Just a personal prejudice, I guess. I'm from the moon, originally. Earth's moon, I mean. Is that what you were asking about?" He tried to remember if he was forgetting any social niceties. Oh, right. "What's your name?"

"I'm Serafina, but – are you really from the resistance?"

"I'm sort of an outside consultant, but yes, I'm technically a hero of the revolution. I could use a co-hero, though. Do you think you could help me coordinate people here, have them grab whatever they can carry from the kitchens – we're going to have a lot of new mouths to feed back on Niflheim – and then guide them to the main hangar to await transport? This weird floaty orb thing can show you the way."

"Oh, I can, can I?" Kaustikos said.

"You wanted something to do."

"Something worthy of my talents. But fine, yes, I can play sheepdog."

"Much more appropriate use of that comparison this time," Ashok said.

Serafina watched them with wide, disbelieving eyes. Ashok tried to smile at her reassuringly, though he gathered that usually didn't work well, since a lot of his face was metal and glass. She ran a finger under the silver collar around her neck. "What about these? Escaping isn't much good if we're still collared. The Exalted can trigger them remotely."

"That's someone else's department, but the collars are being dealt with. Are you good here? I have to go liberate the dormitories and the labs and stuff. Lots to do, and eventually the Exalted out there in the rest of the system will notice and try to stop us, so, faster is good."

Serafina nodded, then clapped her hands and shouted, "Listen up! We're being rescued!" She started organizing the prisoners into teams to loot the kitchens, and Ashok went away, humming one of his favorite Luna-Pop songs cheerfully, following Shall's directions to the dormitories.

Kerneghan didn't have the same upgrades Metcalf did. She'd kept her own arms and legs and instead grafted long, thin pseudopods all around her waist, like a grass skirt made of meat. She must have used those tentacles to pull herself up into the rafters to hide when she heard the shots fired or the glass breaking.

The director hadn't fallen squarely on top of Callie – Callie was still invisible, so Kerneghan had been forced to guess at Callie's location, probably from watching her footsteps appear and disappear in the deep-pile carpet. She struck Callie a glancing blow on the shoulder and knocked her down, though, and after that, Kerneghan – a slight, dark-haired, sharp-featured woman, pretty if you were into the birdlike type – lashed around wildly with her tentacles, feeling for Callie since she couldn't see her.

One of the tentacles hit Callie in the side and instantly snaked around her waist, and then the others crawled along after the first, winding around Callie's body, pinning one of her arms to her side, and attempting to squeeze her to death. The tentacles were hellishly strong, but the suit had its own musculature, and Callie outweighed Kerneghan by many kilograms, so she used her free arm and her legs to struggle to her feet, then grabbed hold of one of the director's tentacles, and yanked.

She pulled Kerneghan forward and off balance, and Callie moved toward her, viciously head-butting the director with the faceplate of her helmet. Callie only regretted that it wasn't her own forehead that did the smashing, because then she could have felt the satisfying crunch of the director's nose breaking. The tentacles squeezed tighter for a moment, but then went slack as the director stumbled back, dazed, her sharp nose blunted and blood all over her face.

There was a good smear of blood on Callie's

faceplate, too, and with her active camouflage on, it would appear to be floating there in mid-air, like the ghost of a bloody wound.

Callie yanked the tentacles away from her suit like she was tearing ivy off a brick wall – those little cilia were sticky, and clung – then stepped out of grasping range. She opaqued her suit and pointed a wrist gauntlet at the director. "Doctor Kerneghan, if you twitch a pseudopod at me, I'll put extra holes in you, in uncomfortable places."

Kerneghan's voice was high and nasal. "May I spit some of this blood out of my mouth?"

"Just don't spit it on me."

Kerneghan turned her head and spat out a wad of reddish gunk, and wiped her mouth with the back of her hand, but her tentacles didn't move.

"What do you want?"

"There's a terminal on your desk. You're going to enter your override code and deactivate all slave collars."

Kerneghan sighed. "Slave collars? How ridiculous. Their only purpose is to monitor vital signs. This is a medical facility, not a prison."

Callie unzipped a pouch and drew out one of the collars. "Oh yeah? You wouldn't mind wearing one, then? With the remote in the hands of the resistance?"

Kerneghan stared at her, then released a rattling

breath. "No, thank you. I am quite healthy."

"If you want to stay that way, deactivate the collars." Callie gestured with her gauntlet. Kerneghan moved to her desk, tentacles swaying with every step. "If you try to do anything besides what I told you to, you lose a tentacle."

The director looked over her shoulder at Callie and nodded gravely. She tapped at the terminal.

"She's behaving herself," Shall said. "Not even trying to call for help. She grasped her current situation pretty quickly. There. It's done. The collars are off."

"Shall, get on the public address system and tell the prisoners they can throw off their chains."

Kerneghan slumped into her chair, which wasn't a proper chair at all but some sort of gel-filled sphere, to accommodate her tentacles. "What happens to me now?" Her voice was small.

Callie smiled. It wasn't a very nice smile. "You get to make a choice. You can turn yourself over to the resistance. I'm sure they'd love to talk to you."

"They would torture me."

"I don't go in for torture myself – it's counterproductive and erodes your moral authority – but you're probably right. They have some grievances and they're going to come out ugly."

"You said I had a choice?"

"Everyone always does. Option two is, you can stay here and explain to the Exalted how you let thousands of prisoners escape under your watch. What do you think they'd do to you? More torture?"

"They'd break me down for parts," Kerneghan said. "That's what they did to my predecessor, and her only infraction was losing slightly more than the acceptable number of subjects to suicide."

"Funny you should mention suicide." Callie looked up at the ceiling. "That's option three. You could throw a rope over one of those rafters and get it done, I guess."

"I don't have any rope." Her voice was dull and her face was blank.

"You've got all those tentacles," Callie pointed out. "Some of them are plenty long enough."

"Ready for the final stage," Callie said.

"I'm on it." Shall spoofed a message from the director's office to the three scourge-ships, still floating around the station, still totally unaware of the security breach. "Priority alert. The main research center on Vanaheim is being bombarded by rebel ships. With the shipyard station shut down, we don't have the resources to muster a defense. Engage the rebels and destroy them immediately."

Shall watched through the station cameras as the scourge-ships sped off toward the far side of the planet, where the main facility was located... except only two of the ships went. Shall reviewed the security protocols and sighed. "Callie, the last ship isn't going to budge — there are strict orders not to leave the station completely unguarded. They know what a tempting target this place is for the resistance."

"That's okay," Callie said. "Three scourge-ships is too many. One is just right."

Lantern was in the cockpit with Drake and Janice as they eased forward in stealth mode. They watched two of the scourge-ships depart, but the third one stayed. "Looks like we get a little action after all," Drake said. "Are you comfortable running the tactical board, Lantern?"

"As long as you don't expect anything too brilliantly innovative," Lantern said. "I'm not Callie."

"We're just stabbing them in the back from cover of darkness," Janice said. "If we have to fight, that's my favorite way."

"I don't think that would work." Lantern ran simulations on the board to confirm her suspicion. "If we blow up the scourge-ship so close to the station, the debris when it breaks apart will do significant damage to the station's structure, and may harm the prisoners."

Janice sighed. "So we have to drop out of stealth and wave a red flag to draw the ship away."

"Moving into a better position," Drake said, and the ship slid through space until the bulk of the station floated between them and the scourge-ship – that way the enemy vessel would have to move away from the facility before it could engage them in combat, or else risk damaging the station itself.

Lantern waited for the right moment, then engaged the displacement field to make the *White Raven* appear to be several kilometers away from its actual position.

The scourge-ship immediately spun and looped around the station, following the shortest possible route to get a clear shot at their mirage. Lantern watched lines on the terminal indicating probable debris fields and shrapnel radii. When the trend lines were clear, her pseudopods moved on the terminal and input a firing solution.

She was about to kill someone, but when she thought of the pilot of the last scourge-ship she'd seen, mind scrubbed and body twisted into something new for a terrible purpose, it eased her pangs of conscience a bit. The scourge-ship fired a beam at the illusion of the *White Raven*, which obligingly mimicked signs of explosive damage.

"Torpedoes away," Lantern said, and watched the green dots on her board streak toward the red dot, so she didn't have to watch the real thing through the cockpit screens.

"The last scourge-ship is disabled," Shall said. "The other two are almost at their maximum distance, but I imagine they'll be back soon. We've got a small window of free movement here."

"Send the *White Raven* to keep an eye on those other ships," Callie said. "If they come back early we need to slow them down and distract them. Can you cover the transport ship yourself?"

"It's so cozy in here," Shall said. "But yes, if you insist, I can play guard dog." He cut a hole in the hull and sprang out into space, whirling around into a useful orientation. The resistance transport ship was on its way, approaching the station's largest docking platform. It was a big ugly whale of a vessel, one of the ships the Exalted used to transport large numbers of prisoners from place to place, liberated in an earlier resistance raid.

Shall zoomed toward it, prepared to kill anything that tried to interfere with the mission.

Ashok stood in the hangar, watching as several hundred former prisoners crowded forward to board the transport. Callie strolled toward him, her suit smeared with blood. "Captain," he said, "you look terrible."

"Fortunately, I feel wonderful."

"You didn't bring the director?"

"She didn't survive our encounter," Callie said.

"The strain was just too much for her shriveled little heart."

"Ah. Shall looted her data anyway. She was a copious note-taker. I doubt there was much inside her head that isn't in her files." Ashok watched the last of the prisoners mount the ramp and then waved to Serafina, who'd done most of the herding, as she boarded too. "We just saved all these people, Callie. Usually when we save people it's a lot more remote and in the abstract, like they're way off on a planet and we're way off in space. This time we saved these actual people right here."

"They're not saved yet. There are still two scourge-ships about to realize nobody's actually bombarding the research station, and if they come back before that flying bathtub the resistance brought gets away…"

Ashok shook his head. "The resistance is bombarding the planet, though. The pilot of the transport ship told me, Wilfred decided the plan could benefit from a little verisimilitude, so they took one of their captured scourge-ships over there to make it look plausible. Not an actual bombardment – there are human prisoners down there on that research station – but they dropped some bombs in the general area, and as soon as the scourge-ships came around the curve of the planet, the good guys took off and the bad guys gave chase."

"I wish they'd mentioned that to me," Callie said.

"It would have relieved some of my anxiety. Though I suppose worry sharpens the mind."

"I'm just glad someone else is being pursued by angry aliens this time." Kaustikos floated over, and Ashok waved to him cheerfully, on the basis that it didn't cost anything to be nice, even to him.

"I'm sure you'll be angrily pursued again in the future," Callie said. "In fact, I'd say it's all but inevitable."

"What happens next?" Ashok said, as the transport ship pulled away from the station.

"This raid was the proof of concept," Callie said. "So, next up: we do the concept."

CHAPTER 19

Elena snuggled up against Callie. This wasn't the first time they'd gone to bed together since they got to the Vanir system, but it was the first time they hadn't simply fallen into exhausted, subsistence-level sleep. Callie had that faraway look, the one that said she was calculating angles and figuring percentages, and Elena respected that… but she also wanted Callie to see her, so she gently tipped Callie's face toward her and kissed her on the lips. Callie's return kiss was perfunctory at first, but she could never resist Elena for long, and soon she returned it with real heat.

Elena pulled away and smiled, tracing her fingertip along Callie's lower lip. "There you are. Nice to see you. Nice to be seen."

Callie laughed. "I have been pretty distracted, haven't I?"

"You're just being the master strategist. I get it. But we have a minute to take a breath, so I want to make sure you do take one."

"I would, if you didn't keep taking my breath away."

"Stop it, or I'll start expecting romance from you."

"That's true. I'd hate to set you up for disappointment."

The *White Raven* was in orbit around Niflheim, having shepherded the transport ship to safety. Callie had made her pitch, and now the leaders of the resistance were down there arguing about her idea amongst themselves. "Do you think we can win?" Elena said.

"If I didn't think we could win, I wouldn't suggest we try – I'd get Ashok to wire the bridge generator into their big transport ship and take as many people to safety as we could instead. That said, possible doesn't mean definite. This is a whole different order of fight than the ones we've taken on in the past. Destroying that first Axiom station we found, ambushing truth-teller cells, tricking pirates, even destroying the Dream – those were battles. This is a lot more like an actual war."

"War's just a series of battles though, right?"

"To some extent, but you can win every battle but the last one and still lose. I wish I knew what Shaper and the rest of the Exalted actually want. I don't believe they're just doing medical experiments for their own enjoyment. I want to slip away and check out the coordinates the Benefactor gave us – as far as I can tell, they don't correspond to any of the facilities the resistance knows about, which could mean one of them is the seat of the secret project Metcalf muttered about. But."

"You're helping to lead a revolution right now."

"Apparently."

"Our mission isn't really to fight the Axiom," Elena said. "It's to protect people. We've focused on the Axiom because they're the biggest existential threat to intelligent life that we know about. These people, here and now, need our help. We're doing the right thing."

"I know. I'm just impatient. If the resistance will back my plan, and it works the way I hope, we would be the ones in a position of power in this system, and the Exalted will be the scrappy underdogs."

"I'm sure the rebels will back you," Elena said. "In the meantime… can I distract you?"

"You've always been able to before," Callie said.

"We were still debating the merits of your idea when we got a message from the Opener of the Way," Wilfred said.

Callie was back on Niflheim, still in the little supply depot's makeshift conference room, but this time there were faces on the screens, and they belonged to other leaders of the resistance: Nadia, dark and serious and middle-aged, was the woman Callie had first talked to from orbit; Theos wore smoked goggles and a big scarf wrapped around their face and spoke through a voice modulator, which struck Callie as an overabundance of caution; and Lara was young and stringy and twitchy but also one of the few prisoners who'd ever escaped an Exalted medical facility on her own, stealing a shuttle and breaking her own collar.

"The who of the what? These Exalted like their fancy names, don't they?"

"The Opener is one of the ruling triumvirate," Nadia explained. "The head of research. In terms of unofficial pecking order she might be a notch below the Shaper of Destiny in surgery, but it's a small notch. She sent a message this morning, using one of our encrypted channels, and hiding the video in other data – that's a technique we use to send secret messages, and there are a lot of people very upset that the Opener knew about it."

That explained why this was the first Callie was hearing about a message. Janice was good at keeping track of ambient chatter, but she couldn't catch all the super spy shit. "So what does the Opener have to say?"

The screen with Theos on it went black and was replaced by an image of an orange-skinned Exalted reclining on cushions and wearing voluminous purple robes; the effect was a bit like looking at a rotten grape with three eyes of various sizes on top. "Greetings, brave warriors." Her voice was all purr and oil. "I have been very impressed by your efforts recently – all of the Exalted have. The attack on the shipyard was masterly, and the raid on the orbital holding facility… well, none of us thought you had it in you. We are humbled by your resilience and resourcefulness. We knew humans were an impressive species. That's why we invited you to join our experiments for the betterment of all intelligent life in the galaxy in the first place – we saw your potential. We're saddened, of course, that you choose to exercise that potential in opposition to us instead of in association, but we understand your viewpoint. The quest for what you call freedom is misguided, but comprehensible."

The Opener stirred, rearranging her pseudopods. "We believe your sudden burst of activity is related to the arrival of a self-proclaimed diplomat named Kalea Machedo." The view zoomed in closer, those three eyes filling the screen, and her voice became husky and intense. "She is a troublemaker. An outside agitator, from a far-away system that has nothing to do with our lives here in Vanir. We have had peace for decades, have we not? Those humans who prove themselves intelligent and capable enough to escape or evade the Exalted are permitted to live in peace on Niflheim – a planet we have entirely ceded to you! We haven't bombarded, invaded, released a customized plague, or used any of the planet-destroying weapons we most assuredly possess. We like the resistance. We like having you, the fittest humans, off on your own, breeding more very fit humans. We let Vanaheim run more-or-less wild for centuries, just to see what the forces of natural selection wrought, in case some of the results could be useful for us later. I can assure you, we would allow the same latitude to those of you on Niflheim. But."

The camera pulled back, and the Opener raised one tentacle, like a teacher raising a warning finger. "This Machedo has disrupted things to an unacceptable degree. Worse, she promises further disruption – she claims our system is soon to be visited by more of her ilk."

"Ilk," Callie said. "I didn't know I even had an ilk."

"We would like very much to question Machedo, to determine the truth of these assertions. We would also like her to stop destroying our facilities. The occasional raid, we can accept – we know you humans like to keep busy. But we can't allow this level of disruption. Thus, I have a proposal. Give us Kalea Machedo. We aren't unreasonable. You can keep the rest of her crew. Send her in a landing ship to the research center on Vanaheim, and we'll say no more about it." The Opener paused. "If you don't... Threats are so vulgar, but I feel I must be explicit. You know how much we value our experimental subjects here, but we are willing to sacrifice them if you fail to hand over Machedo before the end of the next standard day."

The camera panned, and pulled back, to reveal a vast glass tank – a terrarium the size of a room. Things writhed inside it, sinuous white shapes among the greenery and stones. "Are those snakes?" Callie leaned forward to look closer.

"Those are Jörmungandr-worms," Nadia said grimly. "They grow inside host animals until they're about two meters long, and, after that, they're viable outside the body, and they chew their way out to go in search of new hosts to lay their eggs in." The camera zoomed in, revealing at least a dozen of the serpents: they were dead white, bodies segmented, and when one of their heads reared up and faced the camera, it was a nightmare hole full of triangular teeth and flexing hooked mandibles. "They fasten on with the teeth, and those hooks are ovipositors. They flood the host with tiny worms, and those worms fight each other until only one remains, and that one grows to maturity."

The camera panned up… and revealed three humans, bound and dangling upside-down over the tank, eyes wide with terror. One of the Jörmungandr-worms leapt up, and got close enough to brush the hair dangling from one prisoner's head. The camera moved back to the Opener. "It's all very dramatic, I know, but our research indicates that humans respond positively to such demonstrations, with a greater rate of return than a mere verbal explanation of the situation would provide. Turn over Machedo before our deadline, or we'll begin feeding prisoners to the worms at the rate of… oh, let's say one per minute. Every hour we'll round up the infected and put them on a vessel and drop them on Niflheim near your known bases. You can welcome them, knowing what will happen in those cramped tunnels you call home when the worms mature, or you can slaughter your fellows within sight of the freedom they've dreamed about. In honor of Captain Machedo, we'll start with the troublemakers among our experimental stock, but once we run out of those, we'll move on to a random selection. I await your decision. I'm sure you'll do the right thing." The screen went black.

"Huh," Callie said. "How much time do we have, before her deadline?"

"Just enough to get you from here to Vanaheim," Wilfred said. "But none of us are suggesting that. We don't have anti-parasitics on hand, but if we can organize a raid on one of the Exalted supply depots, we might be able to get the components necessary to make some... assuming those are standard Jörmungandr-worms and not some specially engineered variety, but we'll be able to tell pretty quickly–"

"Nah," Callie said. "Too much trouble. Just hand me over."

Wilfred stared at her. "Captain Machedo, they won't even kill you, they'll torture you. The Opener is head of research, and the research division is the worst of the Exalted. The surgical division is horrifying, but they're practical and professional, in a way. In research they just... try things, to see what happens. You don't want to be in their hands."

"You let me worry about that. I'll even take care of

delivering myself, so none of your people are at risk during the handover. I just need to pop up to my ship first." She paused. "It's important for the Exalted to think you had to detain me by force, though. Send a reply saying you've subdued me and I'm on my way."

"Do you have a plan?" Wilfred said.

"Let's say I've got an inkling," Callie replied.

"I like this plan," Ashok said.

"This does not qualify as a plan!" Elena shouted. "It's at best a loose set of improvisational guidelines!"

"I have to admit, I'm not thrilled to hear Ashok likes it. Makes me reconsider the whole thing, honestly. Guess it's too late for that though." Callie was seated in the canoe, almost ready to be rendered unto the Opener. She was dressed in a scratchy gray jumpsuit that said 'Niflheim Mining' on the back in badly kerned letters. Her arms were bound against her sides with wire, more wire bound her legs, and her wrists were fastened together in front of her with manacles. Ashok was fiddling with the manacles, doing something with his fine manipulators, and Elena was glaring at them both. Callie didn't like being tied up – even recreationally, she was usually the one who did the tying – and the wires cut into her uncomfortably, but this needed to look good.

"I wish you weren't going alone. I know you're

good at what you do, and I believe in you, but even you can be caught by surprise. You won't even have your weapons or your stealth suit."

"Believe me, I'd send Ashok instead if I could, and I'd go in there wearing an armored exoskeleton if I could get away with it. Unfortunately, I'm the only one they invited. I think I'll be okay. They're just scientists."

"A little less contempt when you say 'scientist' please," Elena said. "I'm a scientist."

"You're wonderful. I could also take you in a fight. That's just a fact. A science fact. You can beat me in a medical diagnosis competition or an anatomy-naming quiz any day of the week, but I've got the edge in punching. Our deadline is coming up fast. Is everything ready, Ashok?"

"Yes, all prepped." He sighed. "Take good care of my babies."

"I will not take care of them, even a little bit. They'd better take good care of me."

Elena kissed her. "Come back to me."

"I will. And you know what to do if I don't."

"We're not going to do that, though," Elena said. "We'd mount a rescue mission instead. Don't make that face. I'd be the ranking officer, and you know what I'd decide. I'd go down there, personally, toting some sort of... laser rifle or whatever... and show you how well a scientist can fight. Probably not very well. I'd almost certainly get killed, so let that be your motivation to come back to me."

"Yes, Doctor Oh. Another kiss."

That one went on long enough for even Ashok to cough and shuffle his feet in embarrassment. "All right," Callie said at last. "Send me to my doom."

CHAPTER 20

The canoe descended bumpily through Vanaheim's atmosphere. Callie had a pretty good view of the screens from her position tied to a seat, and it really was a gorgeous planet. Jungles, rivers, snow-capped mountains, jewel-colored lakes – no wonder colonists had been excited about emigrating here. The planet looked like an artist's renditions of primeval Earth, only it was real, and the surveys had revealed only small fauna so there weren't even anacondas or tigers or crocodiles to worry about. (There was some speculation about why nothing bigger had developed, but 'because the planet is an alien test lab developing under specific conditions' was not an explanation that occurred to anyone.) The Jörmungandr-worms hadn't shown up on the scans, because before humans arrived the available hosts were so small the worms could only grow a few centimeters long before bursting out. That must have been a pretty unpleasant day, the first time one of those two-meter monsters tore out of somebody's guts.

Wouldn't be Eden without a serpent, she thought.

The visible part of the research facility was a small, starfish-shaped structure nestled in a valley, surrounded by waterfalls and gardens and recreational lakes, and Callie watched it grow larger in the viewscreen. According to Wilfred, the bulk of the facility was underground, and all that natural beauty didn't provide any pleasure to the research subjects in their windowless subterranean holding pens. The researchers tested plagues down there – in theory they were attempting to cure virulent diseases, but they also created new plagues, for their own mysterious purposes – as well as cross-species chimerization, mind control, surgical adaptations for survival in different environments (extreme heat and cold, hard vacuum, toxic atmosphere, and so on), ways to dull and enhance pain, and any other subject that pleased the Opener's whims. The Exalted had tens of thousands of research subjects, after all, so if the experiments were failures or dead ends, what did it matter? Humans were plentiful. Just leave them alone for a while and they'd make more of themselves. ·

The auto-landing sequence settled the canoe gently enough in the landing area in front of the facility and extended its ramp. The Opener of the Way boarded the small ship in person, accompanied by a couple of the same sort of oversized Exalted Callie had encountered on the orbital facility. "Captain Machedo." The Opener fluttered her limbs in what Callie recognized as a rude gesture, in contrast to her welcoming tones. "What a great pleasure. You are certainly the most audacious human we've encountered in a long time. There have been occasional resistance leaders who demonstrated such boldness, but they lacked your follow-through. We're still very curious about how you took control of our systems at the shipyard, and on the orbital base. We'll have a nice talk about the advances in computer science you brought from wherever it is you came from. But first, I brought you a gift – a little something to help facilitate a meaningful and clear dialogue between us."

Callie convincingly glared hate, and she jerked her head around and tried to struggle free from the wire when the Opener approached with a silver collar. The Exalted guards held Callie's head firmly still while the Opener fastened the device around Callie's throat. "There. How's that fit?"

"Cold. Tight. Bad."

The Opener patted Callie's cheek with a tentacle. "You'll soon get used to it. In time the medical monitor will seem so much a part of you that you'd feel naked without it."

"Medical monitor," Callie said.

"Oh, all right. Why be coy? It's just us here. Slave collar. You are a slave now, Captain Machedo, and you will not be a happy one. Such is the fate of lesser beings who don't know their place." She turned to her guards. "Search her for weapons and then bring her inside. Put her in holding pen three until I'm ready for her. Leave her bound in the pen, at least until she soils herself. Some of our guards and researchers talk too much, so tales of her exploits have spread among the subjects. I want them to see that their would-be liberator is just a human, and remove any mystique or dignity they might foolishly ascribe her. Leaving her tied up in her own filth should go some way toward that." She turned back to Callie. "Then we'll hose you off and have a chat about where you came from and what other visitors we might expect."

"I won't cooperate with you," Callie said. "You think I haven't been tortured before? I've been held by pirates. I was taken by terrorists once. I'm not worried about a bunch of scientists."

"I'll ask my questions nicely first," the Opener said. "Then we'll try hurting you. Or threatening other prisoners, to see if you have an altruistic streak – though since you didn't come here willingly, but had to be captured and bound by your own allies, my working theory is that you don't actually care about the other humans too much. I suspect you're driven by ego and a desire for self-aggrandizement. I'm confident you'll tell me what I want to know. We're going to experiment with different interrogation techniques – because we're scientists. One technique we've used with other self-centered prisoners is to feed them Jörmungandr-worm eggs. If they answer questions promptly, I provide enough anti-parasitic medication to limit the growth of the worms, but not kill them. If the prisoners refuse to cooperate, I let nature take its course. The presence of the parasite is very noticeable, and uncomfortable, from the time they're about half a meter long, but that's a long way from their full maturity."

"You're a monster," Callie said.

"When we arrived here, the human scientists had colonies of mice. They experimented on those mice, deliberately infected them with diseases, exposed them to unknown pathogens, subjected them to experimental medical treatments, and vivisected them as needed. When the colony of mice got too large, they killed the excess members to bring the population to manageable levels. I'm sure the mice considered those humans monsters. Or perhaps gods. To the pen." The Opener bustled away.

Callie kept her face stony. It was hard not to smile. She hadn't expected to be put in with other prisoners right away.

The guards patted her down thoroughly – and unpleasantly invasively, but she'd been prepared for that – and didn't find any weapons. They grabbed her and pulled her toward the facility, her toes mostly dragging on the ground but sometimes clearing it entirely. It was surreal being flanked by Liars almost as tall as she was. They passed through three airlock-style security doors, with full quarantine-level protections, complete with blasts of air and geysers of decontaminant spray. The Exalted wanted to make sure the only pathogens down here were those they'd introduced deliberately.

The guards hauled her through a nice lobby with shiny floors and big windows offering views of the waterfalls, then into a gleaming elevator, and from there: down, down, down.

The elevator opened on rather less pleasant surroundings. This level wasn't anything like a hospital – it was more akin to a military facility, all gray concrete walls and steel barriers and iron drains in the floor. The guards whipped out telescoping batons with black balls on the ends that crackled with electricity, then opened up a steel door and tossed Callie in, still bound. She hit the ground hard on her side, gritted her teeth, and lifted her head to get a look around.

The holding pen was a huge hexagonal room with high ceilings, the lights protected by metal cages. There were about a hundred humans in the pen, milling around. There were sleeping alcoves set into the walls on one side, and on the other side, a low wall hiding what Callie assumed were latrines, based on the strong smell of astringent disinfectant. The humans all craned to get a look at her, but none approached.

"Hello," Callie said from the floor, wire cutting

into her arms and legs, cheek burning from being scraped on concrete. "I'm Captain Kalea Machedo. I'm here to rescue you."

An older woman knelt beside her. "Let's get this wire off you." She reached out – and then her eyes rolled back in her head and she fell over, twitching and jittering.

"Fuckers," Callie whispered. The woman's slave collar had stopped her from helping, and now the other humans pulled even farther away, except for a couple who lifted the old woman and carried her to a safe distance as well. "Nobody needs to untie me," she said. "This is all part of the plan. Just out of curiosity, are all the holding pens on this level?"

The humans exchanged glances, and one teenage girl said, "We call them dormitories, but yes. This floor is like a big honeycomb, full of rooms like this one. They moved me from my old dormitory because I kept getting in fights with another girl, so I've seen they're the same." She hunched her shoulders, expecting to be zapped for her impudence, but apparently the Opener didn't object to a little conversation. Probably hoping Callie would reveal something of use to her.

"Excellent." Callie twisted her bound hands around until she could press a button hidden on the underside of her left manacle with her right thumb. The Exalted guards had checked her quite thoroughly for weapons, but they'd left her in the restraints she arrived in – an understandable oversight, since they believed she'd been sent here unwillingly. Her Exalted captors should have questioned their underlying assumptions a little more.

Nothing obvious happened when she pressed the manacle, which was one downside. Ashok had assured her the bracelet would do the job, but she wouldn't know it worked until she actually saw it work.

Her engineer had spent a long and sleepless night with Lantern and Shall, examining slave collars recovered from the attack on the orbital station. The weak link in that plan had been the necessity of forcing an unlock code out of the director – if Kerneghan had died, or been particularly recalcitrant or zealous and refused to deactivate the collars, the resistance would have struggled to remove thousands of the filthy things before the Exalted could trigger them. After that raid, Callie had tasked her engineering-minded crew members to come up with a better way to free the prisoners.

Shall had liberated a lot of data from the orbital station, and Ashok had sorted through the code until he could reverse-engineer the heavily encrypted signal used to control the collars. He'd only made a couple of them explode before figuring out how to unlock them instead. From there, he'd built a transmitter small enough to conceal inside a bracelet that could send out a mass-unlock signal to any collars in the vicinity. The signal carried a tiny program that turned each unlocked collar into a transmitter of its own, albeit with a smaller radius, to deactivate any other collars in the vicinity, multiplying her initial range.

Callie did a slow ten count, then sat up and started to wriggle out of the wire that bound her. She knew exactly where the knots were loose and most likely to give, and had practiced escaping these bonds three times before getting on the canoe.

The prisoners watched her, wide-eyed, waiting for her to get zapped… but there was no zap forthcoming. Once she'd wriggled her arms free, she twisted her wrists just so, and the cable connecting the manacles split in two, freeing her arms. Now the manacles were just bracelets. She reached up, fiddled with her collar, and unclasped it. She tossed it into the corner, where it lay like a dead silver snake. "Most of you should be free by now, too," she said. "Those of you way off in the back, maybe give it another minute."

The door opened, and the Exalted guards rushed in. Callie rushed them right back, kicked one in the pseudopod (she had on her good kicking bots), and made it drop its shock baton. She bent to scoop up the weapon – but she didn't time it right, and the other guard got closer, and jammed his baton into her side. Electricity jolted through her, and she spasmed away, breaking contact with the weapon, but that didn't do anything about her seized muscles. She tasted metal and then she tasted blood, because when she hit the ground in a clenched heap she bit her own tongue. Callie could barely move her head, and watched from the corner of her eye as the guards converged on her, batons sparking. Okay, maybe she'd been a little reckless here. It happened; even she could make mistakes. After all, either you were perfect all the time, which was impossible, or you made the odd error, and just hoped it wouldn't be fatal –

Something silver bounced off one of the guard's heads. He looked up, and another one hit him – it was a slave collar. The guards started to back away, raising their batons, but then several prisoners rushed them – including the teenage girl who'd spoken to her, and the old woman who'd tried to help her.

The guards were big, strong, armed, and hopelessly outnumbered.

Other prisoners helped Callie up, massaging her arms and legs in a way that suggested they'd dealt with the aftermath of a shock baton often. She got to her feet, and watched as one of the prisoners jammed a shock baton into the flesh beneath one of the guard's eyes. The Exalted convulsed wildly, smacking its compatriot hard with multiple tentacles and sending it reeling back. Other prisoners converged on the guards and they vanished from her sight.

The teenage girl approached Callie, touching her

bare neck with an expression of wonder. "Oh, wow."

"Right?" Callie said. "Some more guards will come in here pretty soon, with their zap sticks, but, as you've already figured out… there are like a hundred of you, and they can't remote control you anymore.

"Who are you?" the old woman asked, limping over and massaging the back of her neck.

"I already said. I'm Kalea Machedo. I'm here to rescue you. Actually, I'm here to help you rescue yourselves. The guards left your door open, so nothing's stopping you from going out into the corridor and liberating your fellow prisoners."

"What are you going to do?" the older woman asked.

"As much as I can to help." Callie pushed a button on her right manacle, which wasn't a manacle at all, but her personal short-range teleporter.

She knew she'd eventually run out of the element of surprise in the Vanir system, but she wasn't out of tricks yet.

CHAPTER 21

Callie teleported into the most distant hexagon on this level and introduced herself to the prisoners there, then walked from dormitory to dormitory, the signal pulse in her bracelet radiating outward to deactivate every collar in range. After she'd liberated half a dozen chambers, she started finding unconscious humans in the pens – the Opener had sedated them, not killed them, which was the response the resistance generals had anticipated. Callie had still been worried the Exalted would get frustrated and go lethal, even if it was a waste of test subjects, so she was relieved.

Callie deactivated the collars on the sleeping prisoners, too, and moved on to the next chamber. By then there were something like seven hundred humans running loose all over the level, tearing open doors and attacking guards, with many spreading the signal that had liberated them to others.

Eventually Callie decided she'd reached a tipping point, and that the crowd here had things well in hand. She picked up a shock baton from the floor beside an unconscious Exalted guard. She had a while before her teleporter would work again – it took just under four hours to recharge between jumps – but there were guards with keycards sprawled all over, so it was easy enough to snag a badge to let her access the rest of the station.

When she reached the elevator there were groups of humans there, all armed with shock batons. The lift doors opened, and three Exalted guards burst out, but despite their riot shields and heavier weapons, they were immediately overwhelmed by the crowd and zapped into submission. The staff really was not prepared to deal with riots and escape attempts here. Her late friend Warwick, head of security on Meditreme Station, would have fired the lot of them.

Callie said "Good job," to the humans, then stepped onto the elevator, tapped her stolen badge against the panel, and hit all the buttons. The doors opened on each level, and at every stop she triggered the signal, unlocking collars in offices, the infirmary, everywhere. Once or twice guards tried to rush her but she was ready with boots and baton to shove them back.

Callie anticipated resistance when she arrived in the lobby, but that floor was undefended – the guards were busy on other levels, she supposed. Metal security screens had lowered at some point to seal the front doors and all the windows, but she could deal with that issue later. She had more pressing concerns.

There was a large round desk in the center of the

lobby, staffed by a chimera receptionist – her hair had been replaced with writhing, spaghetti-thin Jörmungandr-worms, giving her the look of a parasitic Medusa. Callie stuck a shock baton in the woman's terrified face. "Hello. I'm looking for the security office, and the director's office, in that order."

The receptionist mutely pulled up a map on a terminal and turned the screen around for Callie to peruse. A flashing red star marked the director's office, and a blue one the security office. "Thanks," Callie said, and shocked the receptionist into unconsciousness, just on general principles.

She strolled toward the security office, which was locked. Callie tapped her badge and the door unlocked. Oh, you had to laugh. She pulled it open and stepped aside to avoid the Exalted security chief who lumbered out, baton swinging. He was more supervisory than practical, apparently. Probably years since he electro-shocked a defenseless human, so he was out of practice. She caught him in the side with her baton as he went by, shocked him into submission, and then kicked him in the head, again just on general principles. She took his badge in case it could open more doors than the standard variety.

The security office had a lot of interesting weapons in a wide-open locker, so she helped herself to a couple of sidearms and some non-lethal riot-control grenades. The holster rigs were made for Exalted, but she managed to twist and knot the straps into something like bandoliers. Wasn't there some ancient human revolutionary leader who'd worn bandoliers criss-crossed over his chest? She recalled seeing a historical sim about it. Viva whoever that was.

The security chief had been logged into his terminal, and since this place had started out as a human research station and was still partly staffed by human collaborators, the controls were comprehensible. Callie unsealed all the security doors, deactivated the perimeter defenses, and rolled up those steel gates in the lobby. There was an option to seal an escape pod hatch, so she did that, too. Nobody was escaping here but the prisoners.

Callie opened up a communication channel to a wide array and transmitted, "Vanaheim station has been liberated. Come on down." True, the station wasn't entirely liberated, but it would be by the time her crew and the resistance forces arrived. She took a moment to think, decided she'd done all she needed to do here, then smashed up the whole security console with the butt of a gun. No reason to let anyone else come in here and mess with her carefully curated settings.

She strolled, whistling, to her meeting with the Opener of the Way.

The director's office had doors carved of dark, smooth, rich wood, decorated with figures of the Exalted all around the edges, robed figures posed with interlocking tentacles. A great tribe, engaged in a great work. They don't lack for self-esteem, do they? She knocked on the door with the butt of a sidearm. "Director! Are you ready to start that interrogation yet? I'm feeling loquacious." She rattled the door, but it didn't open. There were some hefty locks engaged in there.

Fortunately, she'd brought that gun from the security office, and it had a multitude of round settings – lethal, crowd control, and, there we go: breaching. She pressed the barrel of the gun against the seam between the doors, halfway down, and pressed the trigger button. The shotgun jumped in her arms, propelling her back a step, and the doors exploded inward, fragments of wood flying.

She went in, the barrel of the gun resting on her shoulder. The director's office was circular, with glass walls looking out on an enclosed wraparound courtyard that was like a Vanaheim jungle in miniature, filled with lush trees, flowers, and vines, with a small waterfall as the centerpiece. There was no desk here – humans liked those more than Liars did – but there were various terminals scattered around on tables, and a big glass fishbowl of the sort Liars enjoyed relaxing in. A wooden pillar stood in the center of the room, as big around as a great sequoia, with metal doors set into the side. An executive elevator, probably. Callie pressed the button and revealed an empty car. She stepped inside, considered the buttons, and pressed the top one. Nothing happened. She tried tapping the security chief's badge against the panel and it obligingly lit up. Callie pressed the top button again, and began to smoothly ascend.

She found the director on the roof, struggling with the manual release lever for an escape pod that looked a lot like Lantern's blister-ship. "Where are you going?" Callie asked. "We haven't had that talk you promised yet."

The director whirled and fired an energy weapon with about the level of marksmanship you'd expect from the administrator of a large research facility. The beam went wide and scorched a section of the roof. Callie pointed her own gun. "Drop it. My aim is a lot better than yours."

After a moment's hesitation, the director tossed her weapon aside. "Congratulations, Captain Machedo. You have proven even more resourceful than we anticipated. Have you bred? You might consider breeding."

"You Exalted do keep on underestimating me. I don't mind. It makes my job easier." Callie was honestly feeling pretty battered after being bound, thrown on the ground, shocked, and attacked by various guards, but she made a point of smiling and speaking like this was the easiest thing she'd ever done.

"We grew complacent, it's true." The Opener folded her pseudopods before her and settled down, looking relaxed. Maybe she was putting up a front, just like Callie. "We had a very good sense of the capabilities of the resistance, and foolishly believed that you would function within similar operational parameters. Your earlier accomplishments were on the outer edge of what we could expect from the resistance, and we attributed that variance to your boldness. This, though, taking Vanaheim station... how did you do it? How did you set those prisoners free? Those collars should have been impossible to remove here without my authorization."

"Magic. I'm magic. Also, I've got technology that isn't a hundred years old, like the human tech here... or stolen from the Axiom and barely understood, like your tech."

Opener went very still. "The Axiom. So. The humans have stumbled on our great secret at last. If you'd only found Axiom technology, their bridge generators, that would be bad enough. But to know of the great masters themselves? That knowledge will be your doom. The Axiom allow my race to serve, but we are a special case. If the Axiom ever notice you humans, your whole race will be extinguished. And since humans have a way of blundering around and making themselves noticed... your time in this galaxy is short."

"We're doing okay. I personally destroyed an

Axiom ship-building factory, and we destroyed the Axiom facility in the Taliesen system too... including the 'great masters' in hibernation there."

"You destroyed the reality engine?" She waved her pseudopods in a gesture Callie recognized as 'great jubilation.' "Good. The masters I serve come from a faction that opposed that project."

"Tell me about those masters," Callie said. "What's their goal? What's the point of all this horror?"

"The point is survival first and supremacy second. I think that's all I have to say on the subject. It is not my place to discuss the plans of my betters."

Callie looked up. Landing ships were coming down from orbit, streaks of light in the sky. "The resistance is on their way to take over this facility. If you talk to me, I can prevent them from... experimenting on you."

"Mmm, no, that will not do. I fear I have reached the limit of my usefulness to the masters. The experiment that is my life is now done." She dove for the weapon she'd discarded, and Callie shot at her, aiming to wound – but it was hard to do that with Liars, because they were basically a torso full of vital organs and a bunch of pseudopods they could live without. The director managed to snag hold of the energy weapon, and Callie fired again, hitting another tentacle.

The director aimed the weapon... at herself,

pressing the barrel between two of her eyes, and triggering a blast.

Callie watched smoke rise from the Opener's corpse, wrinkled her nose against the scent of seared flesh, sighed, and headed back downstairs.

"We've taken Vanaheim station," Wilfred said, gazing around the lobby in awe.

Who's we? Callie thought. Do you have a little white mouse in your pocket? She said, "It doesn't have to be a big statue. Something modest, maybe cast in bronze. Right out front would be good. I'm happy to pose for the sculptor of your choice."

"Hmm? What's that?" Wilfred was in an oblivious ecstasy of accomplishment.

"Nothing," Callie said. "How's the pacification going?"

"We've got all the Exalted and collaborators locked up, except for a few holdouts in one of the sub-levels, but we just sealed them off. They'll surrender when they get hungry. The facility wasn't that heavily staffed, really, considering how many prisoners there are. We've theorized for a while that the Exalted aren't actually all that numerous. If they had enough people of their own, why would they be so focused on making chimeras to pilot their ships and operate their facilities? The Exalted are obsessed with their own superiority, they always talk about 'elevating' humans by merging us with their biological material, so it seems strange that they'd use humans to help run things unless they had to."

That was interesting. "How many of the Exalted do you think there are?"

"Five hundred? Maybe even fewer. And that's counting the guards, who are engineered to be big, strong, loyal, and not overly bright. The Exalted took over this system through overwhelming technological superiority – the scourge-ships, engineered plagues unleashed on anyone who resisted, and the things you call hunter-drones and we call crawlers. Their conquest was never about superior numbers, and the rebellions were a lot more widespread early on, until they got… quelled, and those of us who held on went into hiding on Niflheim. Think about it – the Exalted have their ruling three, and their second rank of nine, and those are all Exalted, but in the third rank, which is only a dozen people, they had four human-Exalted chimeras. That doesn't suggest, to me, that they have a vast population of talent to draw from."

"Maybe you can hold onto the territory you've got here, then," Callie said.

"We're going to expand," he said. "From this position, we should be able to liberate the work farms, and mines, and the land-based factories, and that's where the bulk of our people are held."

"That's good, but we only cut off one head of the hydra today," Callie said. "Or maybe Cerberus is a better reference." Wilfred looked blank. "The three-headed hellhound who guarded the entrance to the underworld?"

"We don't get a lot of human culture out here," Wilfred said.

"Right. Anyway, the Opener of the Way is gone, but we've still got the heads of operations and surgery to take out. If we eliminated them, this system is yours again, apart from the mopping up. We should strike against those two soon, while they're still reeling from their loss here."

Wilfred's eyes drifted away from her. "We'll definitely discuss our next steps, and I'm sure the generals will want to hear any proposals you might have."

Oh, shit, Callie thought.

"You did good today Callie." Elena stroked her hair, but Callie's eyes remained a thousand kilometers away. "There are nearly half a million people on Vanaheim, and the rebels are in a good position to free them all."

"I know, but there are Axiom in this system, Elena. The Opener of the Way practically told me as much. All these experiments are in the service of ensuring their survival and supremacy, she said. The Exalted aren't our real enemy here – they're just the priests and handmaids and boot-lickers of the enemy. There are Axiom here, maybe sleeping, maybe awake and directing their servants – who knows? We need to find out."

"We can always take the *White Raven* and check out those coordinates on Lantern's map," Elena said.

"I'm tempted. But we stand a better chance of stopping whatever the Axiom are up to if we break the control the Exalted have in this system. The resistance is focused on helping their people, and that makes sense, but there are another nine major space stations in this system where the Exalted are still in control, including the headquarters for operations and for surgery. We need to take those out. Especially operations. They've got ships and resources, they control the main wormhole gate to this system, and they handle all the coordination among the Exalted. My whole plan was to take out the operations headquarters next – attacking Vanaheim station first was only necessary because of the Opener's ultimatum."

"Pretty big win though."

"I know, and I bet I won't even get a statue. Getting a foothold on Vanaheim has actually complicated things, though, because there are so many prisoners to take care of now, it's going to be a huge drain on the resistance's organizational capacity and resources."

"You've accomplished more for the resistance in a few days than they managed in decades, Callie. They're overwhelmed, but they'll adjust. Give them time."

Callie closed her eyes. "What if we don't have time? What if the Exalted decide the grand experiment of the Vanir system is a bust? What if they gather the scourge-ships they have remaining and use them for their original purpose, to scour all life from a planet?"

"Vanaheim has orbital defenses, and the resistance has control of those now."

"Okay, but what if the Exalted unleash a plague?" Callie said. "We were able to beat the Exalted so far because they had preconceived notions about what humans were capable of doing, and we confounded those expectations. But the resistance is making the same mistake. They don't believe the Exalted will wipe them out because humans are a valuable resource… but what if the Exalted have decided those test subjects are unnecessary and need to be euthanized? We need to move against the remaining heads of the Exalted, now."

"That is a very scary scenario, and I found your argument totally persuasive," Elena said. "Tell the generals what you just told me, and I bet they'll come around."

"I think you overestimate my persuasiveness."

"You got me into bed, didn't you?"

CHAPTER 22

"It's too dangerous." Wilfred had the good grace to sound unhappy about it, at least. "I'm afraid the answer is no. We appreciate your help liberating Vanaheim, we really do, but attacking the operations control center — we just can't take the risk. We have to focus on making sure the people we liberated are taken care of first."

Callie ground her teeth and glared at him through the screen. "Since I got to this system, I've taken a quarter of your enemy's major facilities offline. If we attack their operations headquarters next, we can kill or capture another member of the ruling triumvirate — what's her name, the Kicker of Puppies?"

"The Discourager of Doubt, and yes, we know, but her headquarters is located by the wormhole gate, and that's where the bulk of the Exalted scourge-ships are stationed — the remaining might of their fleet. We can't possibly take those on. Even without support from the vessels you destroyed, the Exalted still vastly outmatch us in terms of firepower. We can't do it, Captain Machedo. We've got sick people, injured people, hungry people – some of the things we found in those labs are so heartbreaking and horrifying, we're putting together an ethics panel to decide which experimental subjects can be saved and which should be given a peaceful death. We're stretched beyond thin here."

Callie did her best to speak calmly. "The Exalted are in disarray. If you destroy their operations headquarters, you break their ability to organize against you. If you wait, they will come for you, and they will kill you."

Wilfred's stony face softened. "I actually agree with you, but I'm not the only voice that gets a say around here. I will keep working on the other generals, trying to get them to see your point of view. In the meantime, please be patient with us. We're doing our best to take care of our people."

"Callie," Shall said in her ear. "Ask him about the battleships."

"What?" Callie said.

"The warships that were sent through the wormhole gate over the years – the military missions sent to investigate the Vanir system. Ask him what happened to those ships."

Callie trusted Shall enough to relay the question without asking why.

"As I understand it, when ships arrived through the bridge, the operations center would hail them and claim the wormhole was malfunctioning on this side. They would pretend to be overjoyed to see ships from human systems, and beg for news, and supplies. A contingent of human collaborators would board the vessels… and take out the crews."

"Suicide bombers," Callie said. "Ugh."

"The newcomers were always killed," Wilfred said. "The Exalted didn't want to risk letting people with military experience into their controlled environment here. They would take biological samples from a few prisoners, but there were never any survivors that I heard of."

Shall sighed in her ear. "Put me on comms please?"

"Shall wants to talk to you," Callie said.

Wilfred frowned. "That's the, ah, computer?"

"That's me," Shall said. "I understand the crews were killed. But what about the actual ships? Did the Exalted destroy them?"

"No. The Exalted aren't the sort to throw anything away, and anyway, the Discourager of Doubt likes having the ships there, floating outside her windows. They're her trophies."

"There are undamaged Jovian Imperative battleships just sitting in dry dock?" Shall said.

Wilfred nodded. "I know what you're thinking, but those ships are useless to us – battleships of that size require dozens of people, minimum, to operate, and we only have a handful of people who even know how to pilot scourge-ships. Even if your crew have the expertise to operate those battleships, there aren't enough of you run them."

"Shall," Callie said. "There was a mission sent to investigate the Vanir system, what, just a year or two ago? I remember hearing about it on the Tangle."

"There was," Shall said. "It was some Jovian Imperative minister's pet project – he's one of those ancient life-extension cases, richer than god, and he had relatives who emigrated here. He sent modern ships, Callie. Three of them, I think. Do you know what I can do with modern ships?"

"I do," Callie said.

"What are you talking about?" Wilfred said.

"We're talking about liberating the whole system," Callie said. "What we've been talking about all along. Except now I see a way to do it, and I mean, like, today."

"There are still a lot of our people being held on Exalted facilities," he said. "I don't want to do anything to endanger them."

"They're in a lot of danger anyway," Callie said. "With what I have in mind... the Exalted will more worried about saving themselves than hurting your people. We'll be in touch. You take care of the people we rescued. I'll take care of the rest."

TIM PRATT

"I want to be a battleship," Kaustikos said.

"You absolutely cannot be a battleship," Callie said.

"I would be a wonderful battleship."

"You're a lawyer, or something," Ashok said. "Not a military... thing."

"I can incorporate the contents of a military database into my consciousness just as well as Shall can," Kaustikos said.

"If you were a human I wouldn't even let you carry a gun," Callie said. "Let alone a very large, very mobile gun made out of lots of smaller guns. So drop it."

They'd used their bridge generator to transport the *White Raven* to the general vicinity of the Vanir system's wormhole bridge – just close enough that Callie could use her personal teleporter to board one of the dry-docked warships.

There were many ships in the Discourager's trophy case. Callie was in the observation bay, with the windows turned into screens so she could magnify the image beyond. The operations center itself was in a hollowed-out asteroid that had once been the port authority for the Vanir colony, responsible for opening the wormhole bridge and managing traffic. That station been taken over by the Exalted and expanded with gleaming metal additions, and scores of scourge-ships floated around it like bits of dandelion fluff drifting on a breeze. Only blacker, shinier, and spikier. The captured ships that had come through the

gate since the Exalted took over all hovered nearby –
where, Callie supposed, the Discourager of Doubt
could look out her window and feel like a conqueror.

The buoys that marked the position of the
wormhole bridge were still in place, hanging silently
and lightless, a closed door to the rest of the galaxy.

Why were there so many scourge-ships in this
system? Lantern said those ships were used to cleanse
intelligent life from any planets where it happened to
arise. The Exalted had a whole fleet of the ships, but
they weren't interested in wholesale genocide – they
were more interested in studying (and exploiting)
life than in eliminating it. Doctors used scalpels, not
plasma grenades, so why did a bunch of scientists
have a fleet of warships? If Shaper, Discourager, and
Opener were the descendants of Liars charged with
exterminating life on the Axiom's behalf, how had their
mission so drastically changed? Or had the Exalted
just discovered a fleet of scourge-ships, abandoned in
some Axiom hangar, and decided to use the firepower
to set themselves up as dictators in a distant system?

Her reputation among her crew aside, Callie didn't
actually like mysteries. She was annoyed by mysteries.
What she liked was unraveling them.

The human warships were more familiar to her,
though. There were scores of those, too, the oldest a
century out of date, the newest very close to top-of-
the-line Jovian Imperative kit… though not absolutely

top of the line. Most of the settlers had originally come from the Jovian Imperative, and that one minister kept pushing to send missions to investigate, so the government sent a new expedition every few years. Those missions were lightly crewed and heavily armed, because at this point everyone assumed whatever was happening in the Vanir system was bad – reclusive cultists, natural disasters, doomsday cults, whatever.

That minister only had so much pull, though, so the Imperative didn't send its newest military ships on a likely mission of no return. They sent ships from the previous generation of development. You had to do something with the vessels, after all – selling them to other polities had led to scandals and war crimes, stripping them for parts was time-consuming, and mothballing them was wasteful. Why not consign them to the void, with crews made up of troublemakers or idealists or zealots. If the expeditions figured out what was happening in the Vanir system and came back, wonderful. If not, well… at least the Imperative's operational readiness wouldn't be negatively impacted.

Even a ten-years-ago model of a Jovian Imperative battleship was something to behold, though. Shall had selected the flagship of the most recent expedition, the Cleansing Fire, and, if its systems were in good working order, he should be able to load a copy of his consciousness onto its computer and run the entire ship himself, no cumbersome human crew required. The Jovian Imperative didn't allow AI on its ships – there were too many staunch traditionalist paranoiacs among the ministers – but the technology was compatible with Shall's needs.

Unfortunately, battleships were thoroughly shielded against electronic infiltration. It wouldn't do to have the pride of the Imperative fleet hijacked by an enemy machine consciousness in the middle of battle. In order to open a connection to transfer Shall's consciousness, someone had to board the Cleansing Fire and access its systems directly. Ashok and Shall had built a dongle for her to plug into the commander's terminal, loaded with a program that would open a hole for Shall's consciousness to slip through. "Do I have to call it a dongle?" she'd objected. "Can't I call it, I don't know, an infiltration and control key or something?"

"Dongle," Ashok said cheerfully. "Dingle, dangle, dongle dongle."

"We're within range, Callie," Janice said over comms.

"Be safe, Captain Machedo," Kaustikos said.

"Your concern touches me."

"Have fun!" Ashok said. "I wish I could teleport into an abandoned battleship."

"You'd forget what you were there for and just start prying juicy bits of tech out of the walls."

"That's the whole reason you hired me," Ashok said.

"Is it?" Callie left the observation port and went down to the infirmary, where Elena was studying. "I'm about to take off," she said.

Elena sighed and put her handheld terminal down. "You're dead set on doing this?"

"I'm the infiltration specialist."

"I wish Shall could just fly over there in his scary spider-drone body."

"If he starts cutting holes in the hull of a warship, someone might notice. The personal teleporter, on the other hand, is very subtle. Don't you like it when I'm subtle?"

"I don't recognize you when you're subtle." She opened her arms, and Callie hugged her. "Be careful over there."

"It's a dry-docked spaceship," Callie said. "How much trouble can I possibly get into?"

"It's a good thing I don't believe in jinxes."

Callie stepped out into the hallway, made sure the coordinates were right (a triple-check, but she really didn't want to end up stuck inside the bulkhead of a spaceship), and triggered the teleporter.

Callie passed through her own personal wormhole and emerged in a corridor on one of the Cleansing Fire's upper decks. The ship was dark and silent, but her suit told her that life support was operational – there was breathable air in here. That was odd. Why leave any systems running at all? She decided to stick with her own air supply anyway. She turned on her suit lights and felt absurdly like someone exploring a haunted house with a flashlight. The fact that she was floating weightlessly like a ghost only made it more eerie.

The walls were shiny and smooth, the floors likewise, and the architecture tended toward graceful curves – the Jovian Imperative military aesthetic was one of simple elegance. Bring overwhelming force to every conflict and look good doing it.

She had a map in her helmet display based on theoretical ship schematics, but the Imperative didn't exactly publish detailed blueprints of their warships, and it quickly became apparent that her map was based largely on erroneous speculation. Fortunately, there were signs directing her toward the combat information center. On a boat this big, even experienced crew could get lost.

Callie turned a corner and found her first dead body, a young man floating against a bulkhead stained with long-dried blood. Callie was glad she'd kept her helmet on – there was air in here, which meant microorganisms, which meant the stench of decay. She stepped around the body, continuing along corridors, and found a bulkhead door twisted and warped by an explosion, and black fragments of organic matter she didn't care to explore too closely. One of the Exalted's bombers had triggered here. She hoped the terminal she needed to plug this dongle – stupid word – into wasn't damaged. There were other candidate ships for Shall to take over in the dry dock, but none as powerful as the Cleansing Fire.

Something clattered ahead of her, and Callie froze and turned on her active camouflage. That noise had sounded like metal on metal… maybe just something bumping against something else in the microgravity? The ship was uninhabited, right?

Unless it wasn't. What kind of actual intel did they have about this ship? Wilfred's assumptions and maybe third-hand accounts said the battleships were dry-docked and served only as trophies for the Discourager of Doubt's ego, but Callie didn't know if that was true. The Exalted could use these ships for anything, including dormitories for junior genetic space monsters.

The Exalted probably would have cleaned up the dead bodies if that were the case, though.

The sound didn't repeat, so Callie continued, glancing into the room where she'd heard the noise. It was someone's crew quarters, the door locked into the open position, the bunk unmade –

Something moved under the covers. Ghost, she thought, entirely irrationally, but just because her mind knew it was nonsense didn't stop her body from reacting. Her heart thudded, the hairs on the back of her neck rose, and her breath shallowed out.

One of those horrible hunter drones scuttled out of the covers and propelled itself toward her with a hard thrust of its mechanical legs. Callie silently stepped aside and it sailed past her. The hunter didn't appear to detect her, but went caroming down the corridor, pushing itself off first one wall and then another.

Callie let her breath out. Wilfred's intel just had some gaps. The ships weren't totally uninhabited. There were drones, doubtless here on the off chance the resistance tried to take control of one of the warships. It wasn't ideal to have a lot of enemy agents on board a ship she was planning to commandeer, but Shall should be able to seal all the doors and keep the hunters contained. It wasn't like the ship would have an actual crew for the drones to attack.

She proceeded more slowly and saw more hunters, either following intricate search patterns or just wandering aimlessly – she had no way to tell. There were more dead bodies, too, as she got closer to the command deck. Once she finally reached the CIC, she was prepared to find it bombed beyond recognition, crawling with hunter drones, and full of drifting corpses… so the reality, an empty command center with a few scorch marks from energy weapons and a mere three dead bodies (one of them with captain's bars on his shoulders) was a relief.

She pushed the captain's floating body out of the way, murmuring an apology almost automatically as she did so, and found the inputs on his terminal. She inserted the dongle – the control key – and watched the terminal light up and begin to flash angry red warnings about unauthorized software and demands for a command override if they actually wanted to run this mysterious program, which should only be done if commanded by the Jovian Imperative high council, blah blah blah blah.

The ship's firewalls were robust but they were also a decade old, and the Trans-Neptunian Authority security forces had done ample quantities of espionage. As a former security officer of that former nation, Callie had access to all kinds of infiltration data, and Ashok and Shall had integrated it into their program. The Imperative constantly improved their security protocols, but the Cleansing Fire wasn't exactly getting regular software updates, so this control key was sufficient to let her crack open the ship's controls.

The angry red letters were replaced by happy green ones and Callie breathed a sigh of relief. "Shall, I'm in. Is it working on your end?"

"Transferring data now, Callie. Oh, it's nice over there, very roomy. Huh. I'm getting all sorts of life signs."

"Hunter drones," she said. "Scuttling around like cockroaches."

"Their bio-parts need atmosphere to survive, so I'm

going to turn off the life support, if that's all right with you."

"I'm not over here on this creepy ghost ship with my helmet off, if that's what you're worried about."

"Glad to hear it. You can take the dongle out now. It's going to take several hours for me to take full control."

"I have to wait until my teleporter recharges to come back anyway. I guess I can catch up on my reading."

"Once it's up and running, you could teleport to the escort ships that came through with the Cleansing Fire. What's another eight or twelve hours? I could always use more bodies…"

This is going to be a long night. "You know I can't get enough of you, Shall."

CHAPTER 23

The smaller, faster gunships – the Blaze and the Sunspot; someone had settled on a fire theme for the last mission, apparently – were less creepy because they were smaller, but it was the difference between being in a haunted cottage instead of a haunted mansion. There were fewer hunter drones and fewer dead bodies, but the smaller vessels were still charnel houses. Ghost ships about to rise from the dead and take revenge. Very appealing.

She teleported to the Cleansing Fire's bridge just as Shall completed transferring his consciousness to the Sunspot. She'd managed to nap a little, incredibly, so she was reasonably alert for the fun part of their plan.

The bridge lit up, stations coming to life, and Shall said the systems checked out, more or less – the damage to the interior was mostly superficial, and a ship like that was full of redundancies and systems made to route around damage. Most importantly, the weapons and propulsion systems were fully operational. The Exalted probably couldn't have disabled them if they'd tried. Imperative warships were tough. "Shall we blow some stuff up?" the Cleansing Fire's version of Shall asked.

"Yes, we shall."

Callie itched to run the tactical board, but Shall had it covered. He was nice enough to let her see the trajectories he was plotting for the projectile weapons and torpedoes: every single scourge-ship that hovered around the operations center was lit up, and, at this range, they'd be annihilated before they even realized they'd been targeted. "Release the boom," she said.

The big screen in front of her came to life, offering a panoramic view of the devastation. The first ship struck was on the distant edge of the screen, and it burst into a corona of radiating fire. Then another, closer to the center, went up, producing a pinwheel of white and yellow light. After that several scourge-ships lit up simultaneously, flashes so bright the screen dimmed the view to keep the sight from washing into a wall of undifferentiated color. The scourge-ships exploded like miniature stars going supernova, and Callie filled with furious joy. Those ships were ugly things, deliberately designed to evoke fear and disgust. They'd borne genocides, and now they were radioactive particles.

The last flashes faded, leaving behind nothing but glowing dust.

"Hail the station," Callie said. "Don't accept anyone less than the Discourager of Doubt, and, when you get her, put her onscreen."

The Cleansing Fire wasn't under thrust, and human

ships didn't have the gravity-altering capabilities of Axiom or Exalted tech, so she strapped herself down in the captain's chair. Shame about the former captain floating around behind her, but it couldn't be helped. She removed her helmet. The air didn't smell too bad – Shall had the filters working overtime, sucking out all the bad stinks.

A few long minutes later, Shall said, "Here she comes."

The screen switched to a close-up view of a pale yellow liar with a single immense eye in the center of her body, the iris a more poisonous shade of the same color. "Captain Machedo," she said. "You've come to offer more of the diplomacy the Weaver of Worlds told me about, I see."

"We call it 'gunboat diplomacy' back where I come from. You make a conspicuous display of military force to set the right tone for negotiations."

"What is it you think we're negotiating?"

"Your surrender. You might want to get Shaper on the line. You're just a ruling bi-umvirate now, since I watched Opener die."

"The Exalted do not negotiate with humans—"

"I learned something interesting about your station, when I was chatting with the resistance generals," Callie interrupted. "It's the only facility in the whole system that doesn't have any human prisoners or experimental subjects on board. No labs or holding areas at all, just Exalted admin and military personnel, and what we in the resistance like to call 'traitors.' That means my gunboat here can diplomatically turn the entire station into rubble, and nobody in the resistance will be sad. That sounds like a good idea to me, too, because then I'll only have one division head to negotiate the surrender with."

"How did you find enough capable crew members to operate that ship?" the Discourager demanded.

"I know you're just stalling until help arrives, Discourager, but I'll answer you. The answer is 'magic.' I am magic. Or maybe I'm a judgment from the gods. Do you believe in gods?"

"Don't be absurd."

"You do, though. Your gods are not dead, but sleeping. The Axiom, Discourager. You believe in them, don't you?"

The eye slitted. "That is not… that word does not mean anything to me."

"Okay. Say your final prayers to nothingness, then. We're targeting your office first."

"Wait! What do you want?"

"It's too bad you aren't the one called the Opener of the Way, because that would be a lot more poetic. I want you to open the way. Activate the bridge, and open a portal to the Jovian Imperative gate."

"Impossible. The wormhole gate has been permanently disabled."

"That's a real shame. Enjoy dying in a fire."

"Wait." The Exalted's flesh pulsed with colors, greens and blues. Callie had no idea what the display meant. Maybe she'd ask Lantern later. "It will take some time to reactivate the gate."

"Really? I bet it's just a big button you have to push. Don't stall me, Disco. If you aren't helpful, I'll just kill you and bring in my engineer to figure out how to reactivate the bridge. The only reason you're still alive is because this seems like it could be faster."

"I… I will comply." The Discourager did something offscreen, and a moment later, a huge wormhole opened in the center of the space marked out by the buoys, inky tendrils reaching out into space.

"We are prepared to negotiate–" the Discourager began.

"Kill the feed," Callie said. The screen went blank. "Now kill that station."

"Callie? She said they were willing to negotiate."

"They should have negotiated when they still had something to offer me," Callie said. "The Discourager of Doubt is a terrible diplomat. Destroy that station, Shall. It's an enemy installation, and the people on board don't even deserve the mercy of a quick death. I'm just softhearted enough to give them one, is all." She paused. "If you set up the shot, I'll push the button, if you want. I understand."

"No, captain. I knew what I was getting into when I took on a battleship for a body. Firing now."

Callie had actually never seen a battleship of this class fully open up on a single target. As a child on Earth, she'd stomped through patches of dandelions, sending hundreds of wispy seeds airborne, so numerous they made the currents of air visible with their movement. That was what the Cleansing Fire's onslaught reminded her of. The scores of torpedoes, illuminated as bright white specks on her screen, seemed caught up in a deadly wind that bore them toward the station in a cloud. The impacts were so forceful and numerous that the station actually listed in space, beginning a slow spin it would never have a chance to complete. Airlocks and windows burst open under the missile strikes, and mercifully unidentifiable shapes poured from the brutal new openings. After a few moments, Callie turned her gaze away. She could feel the vibrations of the weapons firing through the deck, though.

"It's done, captain," Shall said finally, and the vibrations faded.

Callie looked, and the Exalted operations facility was a devastated rock, with bits of debris she tried not to recognize floating all around it.

"Shall, send one of the smaller ships through the wormhole and let the Imperative know the door is open to this system. Fill them in, broad strokes, about the Exalted, and the people who need help here. They can send in a real cavalry."

"Will do. But. Um. How do I explain how we got here in the first place?"

Callie had been thinking about that question. "I don't know. Tell them we encountered a space-time anomaly and everything went wobbly and then we wound up here."

Shall's voice was gentle. "They're going to find out about the bridge generators, Callie. There's no way we can keep them a secret, not as long as any scourge-ships survive."

"We'll do our best to destroy them, then," she said. "And if we fail… hell." Callie hadn't kept their bridge generator a secret out of selfishness, but to try to protect humanity. When the truth-tellers found out the *White Raven* had a bridge generator, they'd blown up Meditreme Station and killed fifty thousand people in an attempt to hide the secret. What would the truth-tellers do if the Jovian Imperative got their hands on such technology? What would the Imperative do? They would explore space, maybe stumble on Axiom technology, maybe wake the slumbering gods, and maybe get everyone killed.

But that was a possible future problem, and there were hundreds of thousands of people in this system who needed help, right now. Callie knew her limitations. The Imperative could save the inhabitants of this system. She couldn't, at least, not alone. "Actually, when you get through the gate, don't hail the military. Contact Michael instead. Use the emergency number. He'll pick up." Her ex-husband's family owned one of the Imperative's most powerful corporations, and he could exert influence on the highest levels of government. "He'll keep the port authority from blowing you up, probably, though I'm sure you'll be impounded. Tell Michael… tell him everything. About the bridge generator, the Axiom, all of it. Tell him… I trust him to do the right thing."

"Which is… what?"

"How should I know? Maybe Michael can figure that out. Tell him to get in touch with Uzoma. I bet they'll have some ideas about how to deal with the implications of the Imperative getting their hands on Axiom tech."

"You're sure about this? Sharing our secret this way?"

"When we were blowing up space stations, that was one thing, but this situation, it's way beyond. It's just too much for us alone. I'm starting to think maybe dealing with the Axiom is a bigger job than we can do by ourselves."

"Maybe it is."

Callie thought it was polite of Shall not to mention that he'd made that same argument many times, only for her to stubbornly insist it was better if they handled matters alone. "I'm going back to the *White*

Raven." I need Elena, she thought. Elena always made her feel better.

"Aye, captain – huh. That's odd."

"What's odd?"

"The *White Raven*... it's gone."

"What do you mean it's gone?"

"It's not on my sensors, and they're not in communication – I thought they were just laying back while we dealt with the station, but... they're not here."

"Did they leave? Did they open a bridge somewhere?"

"There's a radiation signature near their last known position. A wormhole bridge did open there. Why would they leave without telling us?"

Everything inside Callie turned to ice. "We have to find them, Shall."

"I'm scanning with everything I've got, but they could be anywhere. I don't understand this. They wouldn't leave without telling us. Do you think... were they boarded? Were they taken?"

Callie put her head between her knees and tried to breathe. "Okay. The rest of the crew is on board the *White Raven*. You're on board, Shall. Ashok. Drake and Janice. Lantern. Even stupid Kaustikos. Fuck. Everyone. Everyone is on board. How could I let this happen?"

"Callie, please, panic won't get us anywhere."

"Not panicking won't get us anywhere either, Shall. Get me… get me the resistance. Get me Wilfred. They owe me. They're going to repay me by helping me find my ship." And my friends. And my love. And my life.

Wilfred didn't bother with consensus building and consulting the other generals this time. He had his own people, his own squad, and he put together a team of veterans to accompany Callie on the Blaze – the Sunspot was off through the wormhole, negotiating with Michael and the Jovian Imperative, Callie assumed, and the Cleansing Fire was guarding the bridge.

First they stormed the headquarters of the surgical division. The Shaper of Destiny was the last member of the triumvirate standing, and if anyone had abducted her people, it was probably him. The station was a soft target, because it was deserted. Callie stomped through the corridors and offices as the resistance members helped those patients who were still capable of being helped, but all the personnel, Exalted and chimera collaborators both, were gone. "Maybe the Exalted are abandoning the system," Wilfred said.

"Do they strike you as gracious losers?"

"They strike me as survivors, and they may have realized their survival isn't likely if they stay around here, now that the wormhole gate is open."

Callie hadn't told any of the resistance about the Axiom, and it was too much to go into now, but she believed they were still in the system. "Can you get me a map of all the Exalted facilities in the system?"

Wilfred provided one and she retreated into the captain's quarters on the Blaze. "Shall, you have Lantern's map of Axiom and truth-teller facilities, right?"

"I do."

"Compare them to this map, would you?"

She sat at the captain's desk and considered the screen, with one map overlaid on another. One of the stations marked on Lantern's map was the surgical facility they'd just assaulted and had probably once been the truth-teller outpost in this facility. The Exalted must have absorbed or killed the cultists a century ago.

But the other location, outside the plane of the Vanaheim and Niflheim's orbits, wasn't a facility known to the resistance. "That's where we're going, Shall. The secret thirteenth station of the Exalted. That must be the base for whatever the Axiom are doing here. I bet that's where Shaper is now – he'd know better than to go anywhere the resistance might target."

"You think he took the *White Raven*?"

Callie slumped down in her chair. "I think they could be anywhere in the galaxy, and we have to start somewhere. Get these resistance fighters off my boat, and set a course for the station."

"It will take us a while to get there, Callie – more than a day. We don't have a bridge generator here."

"Stop wasting time talking about what we can't do, and start doing what we can," Callie said.

"Aye, aye," Shall said softly.

CHAPTER 24

"That sure is a pretty boat, Shall." Elena looked at the sleek vastness of the Cleansing Fire through the observation deck's windows. "Looks like a shark and a manta ray had a baby full of beautiful murder."

"I'm a little jealous of that other instance of my consciousness," Shall said. "You can really stretch out in a ship like that, I bet. Not that the *White Raven* isn't nice too. I didn't feel cramped at all until a few minutes ago."

"Is Callie okay over there?" She'd been going from ship to ship and loading software and waiting for her teleporter to recharge for twelve hours now, with minimal communication, because they didn't want the Discourager to pick up any chatter.

"Oh, she's fine. I think she's even enjoying herself. Look – there go the guns."

Elena whistled as streaks of light arrowed from the Cleansing Fire and turned the scourge-ships into haze. "I'm glad they're gone," she said. "Ugly, vile things."

"Now Callie gets to be sarcastic at the head of

operations," Shall said. "I bet she's going to enjoy – huh. That's weird."

"What?" Elena said.

"Our communications just shut down. We can't transmit ship-to-ship anymore. My consciousness is already transferred from the Cleansing Fire and the other two ships, so it doesn't break the plan, but… how strange. Janice, any ideas?"

"We're being jammed." Janice always sounded annoyed, but now she sounded super annoyed. "I can't even get the sensors up and running. Something's thrown an isolation field of some kind around us."

The observation bay screens flashed red briefly and then turned into windows. Without magnification, the Cleansing Fire and the operations center were just distant dark shapes, and the vaporized scourge-ships faint hazes of light.

"The engines aren't responding," Drake said.

"The bridge generator seems fine," Ashok said, "but with the navigation and propulsion systems shut down, we can't fly through a wormhole even if we opened one."

You're in charge, Elena, she thought. "Shall, send a drone to see what's happening outside."

"There's a ship above us," Drake said. "It's… big."

"I thought the sensors were dead?" Elena said.

"They are," Janice said. "We're looking at it through the windows."

Elena couldn't see anything from the observation bay so she hurried up to the cockpit, where Drake and Janice had angled their chair to look up through the windows. Elena gazed with them at the vast dark shape blotting out the stars above.

"Weapons aren't responding," Shall said. "A lot of processes on the ship are just frozen. I can't even figure out how it's happening."

A line of white light appeared in the darkness above them, like a seam opening in the fabric of night. The bar of light widened, shining through the cockpit windows and turning everything white.

"Janice," Drake said. "That light. Do you… does that…"

"Yes," Janice said. "We've seen that ship before."

"What do you mean?" Elena said, and then it was like she blinked, and somehow during the course of that blink everything changed.

The cockpit was gone. She sat on a softly upholstered couch in a room with deep red wallpaper – it was like being inside the chamber of a heart, she thought wildly. She stood up and looked around, but there were no doors or windows. And what was she wearing? Some kind of dress with frilly loose sleeves, the fabric a slightly paler red than the rest of the room. The floor was made of wooden boards of alternating light and dark shades, interwoven in a complex design that made her head hurt if she looked at it too long.

"Hello?" she said tentatively. "Is anyone there?"

The doctor will be with you shortly, a pleasantly modulated voice said, but it seemed to speak inside her head.

Elena hugged herself. "Where is this place? What's happening?"

You are in the waiting room, the voice said. Please wait.

Ashok, Lantern, and Kaustikos were in the machine shop when the ship's systems froze. "This is bad," Ashok said. "Right? It seems bad. Then again, whoever took control of the ship hasn't turned off the life support yet, so that's promising."

Lantern said, "Being a hostage is better than being dead, yes, but 'promising' is a strange word for—"

Ashok disappeared, and so did Kaustikos, and so did the machine shop. Lantern was floating in a relaxation tank in a white-tile room, clothed in a wetsuit. She clambered out of the warm water and dropped to the floor. There were no evident doors or windows in the round chamber. She closed her seven eyes and considered her biological systems. She had no sense that she'd lost or regained consciousness, and discerned no gaps in her continuity of awareness, but clearly something had happened. "Shaper?" she called. "Is this your doing?"

The doctors will see you shortly, a voice spoke in Lantern's head. She spun, tentacles flailing, but you couldn't turn to face a voice in your mind, could you?

"How are you doing that?" Maybe there was an implant, something in her head that made it seem the voice came from within. "What is this place?"

This is the waiting room. You may wait here.

"Where are my friends?"

The doctors are with other patients right now. Your turn will come.

Ashok didn't blink – he basically didn't need to anymore – but everything changed in the time it would take to blink. He was in some kind of red parlor, with a soft couch and a pretty geometric tile floor, wearing some kind of weird velvet suit with a ruffled shirt. He ran a diagnostic and –

Nothing. The diagnostic didn't run.

He tried to review his sensory cache (he recorded everything he experienced), but he didn't have access to the data. He didn't even get an error message. It just… wasn't there.

Ashok stretched his arms and legs, and everything seemed to work fine, but none of his non-standard senses were giving him any information: he couldn't sense magnetic fields or radiation, his sonar was offline, and his olfactory senses were appallingly baseline. He'd been reduced to ordinary human senses… but that didn't make any sense. His original sense of smell was long gone. He could only smell things at all through his upgrades, and he didn't even know a way to customize them so they only noticed dust and sweat and stale air without also notifying him about the chemical composition of whatever he smelled.

Ah, I get it. "This is a simulation," he said aloud.

This is the waiting room, a voice spoke in his head.

"You'd better not be doing weird stuff to my body out there."

The doctors are examining you now. You are a very interesting case. They will be with you shortly.

"You're the Shaper of Destiny, right?" Ashok said. "Last of the bigshot Exalted. You captured us with some stupid idea that you can ransom us or hold us hostage or whatever, right? Callie is not as sentimental as you think."

The doctors will be with you shortly.

Ashok sat down on the couch. He hoped Callie was more sentimental than he thought, because it was hard to rescue yourself from inside a simulation. "If you were going to put me in a virtual environment, you could have at least let me ride dragons or something!" he shouted.

Please wait.

The cockpit disappeared, and Drake and Janice were no longer in their mobility chair but floating weightless in some kind of energy field in a white room. An immense Liar, two meters in diameter with skin as pale as snow, gazed at them. His body glistened with silvery prostheses and augmentations of uncertain purpose, and he had a multitude of pseudopods, some as thick as a human leg, some as thin as a finger.

Drake groaned, and Janice screamed, and then their voices converged into a single voice of fear. For the first time in a long time, they weren't experiencing any pain, but that was, in some ways, worse.

"Hello, subject one," the Liar said in a low, gravelly voice. "We are so pleased to see you again. How much of our time together do you remember?"

The field they were in began to hum, and Janice and Drake's eyes rolled back, and they remembered as much as they could stand.

Drake and Janice were working for a development company based in the Trappist system. They'd been military surveyors once upon a time, and they were highly respected in their field... which was why they got the weird jobs, and the hard ones. After months of doing routine surveying trips around the system, the captain of their ship, Martinique Hidalgo, picked up an anomalous radio signal – just a brief snippet, way out beyond the areas they'd explored so far, but the signals definitely seemed artificial in origin. She came into the cockpit and said, "I've convinced the company we should investigate."

"Are we hunting aliens again?" Drake wrinkled his nose. "That week we spent in the Bondye system, chasing what turned out to be a malfunctioning beacon on a survey buoy, wasn't enough time wasted for you?" Drake had known Martinique since childhood, growing up with her in the Toronto arcologies, but he would have been just as openly exasperated with any other captain. The joke about Drake was that he had a pretty voice and a nasty disposition.

"Where's your sense of adventure?" Janice chided. "There's a great big universe full of mysteries out there to explore." Janice was well-liked by the whole crew, and it was a testament to her sunny disposition that she even got along fine with Drake, leading to their long partnership. Everyone from Europa was polite – 'Europa nice' people called it, because they'd be friendly to your face even if they wanted to stick a knife in your eye – but Janice was nice actual.

"There could be other intelligent life in the universe." Martinique sat in the jump-seat behind the pilot's chair. "There's us, and the Liars, and whole lot of planets we've found capable of sustaining life, so there's no reason to believe we're alone. Wouldn't it be nice to meet some aliens you can have an actual conversation with?"

"You can talk all day with Liars," Drake said. "Lots of them won't shut up, no matter how much you beg."

"I mean a conversation where one of the parties doesn't just make things up all the time," Martinique said. "There are so many big questions about the universe that the Liars should be able to answer… but they just spout their endless bullshit instead. It drives me crazy. So crazy I've read anthropology papers speculating about why they do it. If we could find other aliens… well. It would be a pretty big deal. Since we're wandering the outskirts of the Trappist system looking for anything worth exploiting anyway, why not chase down the signal?"

"It's another malfunctioning buoy, mark my words," Drake said. "Some unlicensed miner working the far edges of the system, hoping the company won't notice them poaching our sweet minerals, using salvaged or refurbished equipment to mark likely asteroids. How much do you want to bet?"

"I learned not to gamble with you when we played dice back in the arcology," Martinique said. "Quit complaining and fly the ship." She patted Janice on the shoulder and left the cockpit.

"Fool's errand," Drake grumbled. He tapped a readout on his board. "That's the third 'maintenance suggested' light I've had to turn off just today. We're overdue for service, and instead of getting checked out, we're going even deeper into the black."

"We'll get the ship checked out when we return. Did you want to go all the way back to base and then come all this way again? We're already so far out here, we might as well take a little diversion to keep the captain happy."

"Nobody ever seems too concerned about whether or not I'm happy," he groused.

"You get paid the same whether we're chasing aliens or leaving transponders on rocks, so why complain?"

"Complaining is an essential element of the human condition, Janice. All living things suffer, but we're capable of suffering and telling people about it. How can you serve in the Jovian Imperative military and then work for a bunch of rapacious corporations and still maintain such a cheery disposition?"

"I don't know. Life on Europa was pretty hard, but we just did our bit. I was lucky enough to get selected for surveyor training, got offered jobs good enough that I can send money back home – it's not such a bad life. I like space travel. I guess I always see the glass as half full."

"Me too," Drake said. "Half full of poison. How I put up with you as my damn near constant companion I'll never know."

"Oh, you love me. Without me, who'd listen to your complaints and annoy you by being too cheerful?"

"There's that," Drake admitted.

"We could ago around the asteroid field," Janice said. "But we'd lose a couple days, and the captain says she'd rather not – there are some rattles in the engine room she doesn't much like the sound of."

"So we get to skip dinner and try to chart a course through floating rock hell, is what you're telling me?"

"We've got delicious protein and fiber bars right here." Janice thumped the door of the supply compartment at her work station.

"Emergency rations are for emergencies. Plotting this course is not an emergency."

"They aren't eating anything much better in the galley," Janice pointed out. "Nutrient sludge. And it's not like there won't be leftovers when we're done."

"At least it's hot nutrient sludge."

"Come on, this won't even take an hour. If we don't chart the course now, we'll have to stop and float while we eat, and there's no reason to waste the fuel."

Drake snorted. "I'm pretty sure it's the captain who loses her bonus if she overruns the fuel estimates, not the pilot or navigator."

"Martinique says if we do this for her, she'll slip us some of her private chocolate stash."

"Janice. Why didn't you mention that before? What do I always tell you?"

"That I should always lead with threats or bribery. I just can't resist trying to appeal to your better nature, is all."

"This is my better nature. You never want to meet my worse one. Fine. Pass me a disgusting protein bar, and then show me the route you like through the asteroids. I'll tell you if I'm actually capable of piloting this clattering conglomeration of spare parts where you want to go."

CHAPTER 25

They plotted the course and entered the asteroid field without too much complaining on Drake's part. "There are some promising chunks of rock here," he said. "You'd think we'd take some samples and see if this area is worth developing instead of chasing imaginary signals."

"The signal wasn't imaginary, Drake. I'm not saying it's aliens, but there's something out here–"

The ship jolted hard, and a loud boom reverberated through the cockpit. Janice looked at Drake with widened eyes. They'd both been on ships in battle, and they knew that sound, even before the lights on their board lit up to confirm it. "Explosive decompression," she said. "Did we hit something? Did something hit us?"

"No, there's nothing on the proximity alarms, we just… something broke. I don't know what. Something in the engines, I'd guess, and it tore a hole through the hull."

Janice unstrapped, went to the cockpit door, and looked through the window. There was just a short corridor from the cockpit to the galley... but there was no galley now. There was just a view of space, and stars, and debris, including bodies... but not whole bodies. Nothing they could try to rescue. "Oh, no. They're all gone, Drake. All hands. The whole back of the ship tore apart."

"That explains why I don't have any engines." His voice was hoarse.

Janice returned to the front. Drake blinked away tears, then pressed the heels of his hands to his eyes for a moment. Their ship – their part of a ship – was already slowing down, beginning a slow tumble among the asteroids, their thrust gravity giving way to weightlessness. Drake's tears floated past her. "I'm sorry about Martinique," she said. "I know you were close."

Drake nodded stiffly. "All those years in the military... you and I have lost people before."

"It doesn't get any easier, though," Janice said. "At least, not for me."

"Me either. But we do what we have to do. Do we still have comms?"

Janice strapped herself in and ran her boards. "We do. I'll light the emergency beacon. Someone will come along. We didn't stray from our planned route. The company will come looking for their property. How's life support?"

"For just the two of us? We'll be fine for days, and

it shouldn't take that long for the company to find us."

"Good thing we didn't eat all the emergency rations, huh?" Janice unpeeled a bar and took a bite. "You were talking about the mission in Bondye, chasing one of Martinique's signals, and you acted like it was a pain in the ass, but I remember how much fun that was – we had that new ship, and you got to really open her up and see what she could do. I might have actually seen you smile that day, though I'd have to check the cockpit recorder to be sure."

"It was probably an optical illusion." Drake took one of the bars she offered. "Martinique always wanted to be a captain. I just wanted to fly ships – I never wanted the responsibility of running one. We used to go out to the spaceport in the arcology and watch the ships take off, and talk about how we'd be on board one of them, someday. The military was the path for both of us, of course. Shooting poor people into space to go shoot other poor people since 2125, right? I wish we hadn't lost her, but she went the way she would have wanted, out on a mission, in search of something greater than herself–"

A proximity alarm started beeping, and Drake and Janice stared at each other. "There's nothing I can do," Drake said. "No engines, no reaction wheels… I could vent some gas to send us spinning, but I couldn't control where we spun very well… just hold on and hope."

They braced themselves as well as they could. Janice thought a chunk of debris had struck the cockpit, a piece of their own engine flying at them in a random trajectory. The impact wasn't enough to do any damage, but it sent them spinning away with fresh velocity, and Janice watched the dark, pitted face of an asteroid get bigger every time the cockpit window spun around to face it. She reached out blindly and found Drake's hand, clutching her as hard as she clutched him.

"I'm glad we're not alone," Janice said. "I'm glad we're here together—"

They struck the asteroid, and that's when they would have died.

Drake and Janice saw flashes. They could never work out later which one of them saw what, because their memories mingled to an incredible degree, so much so that Drake remembered eating fresh green salads under the domes of Europa, where he'd never been, and Janice remembered playing in the public fountains of the Toronto arcology, though she hadn't experienced open recreational water until she took her first rest and relaxation leave after joining the Imperative military. They agreed on what they saw, though, and even cobbled together a rough sequence of events, though they couldn't be entirely sure it was right.

* First a great set of black double doors stood before them, and when the doors opened, blinding white light shone through the long, thin crack. Gradually the doors opened wider, and the light nearly filled the world. The rest of the world, though, was filled with pain; the light was everything the pain was not, and the light filled all gaps left by the pain. They floated toward that light, and passed into it, and the doors closed behind them, but one of them looked back, or perhaps both of them, and saw the shattered cockpit drifting beside the pitted rock, and bits of glass, and metal, and – was that flesh? Was that an arm? Was that a leg? Then the doors closed, and it was only light and pain for a long time.

*They saw a white Liar, but of impossible size, as big as a killer whale (Drake had seen a killer whale at a marine center once – or was it Janice who saw that?). The alien floated above them, its two large eyes somehow doleful, its countless tentacles swaying like kelp in an undersea current. The tentacles reached out for them.

*Scores of tiny Liars, the size of open hands, danced in the air around them. Then two of the Liars stuck together, and then a third, and more. First they formed an unwieldy wriggling ball of tiny bodies and then, somehow, they began moving as one – a conglomerate organism, one created from many, reaching out with tentacles made of small bodies to touch Drake and Janice, and where they touched, the pain went numb. "Stingers," Drake remembered saying. "Are you stinging us." He was thinking, or Janice was thinking, of the Portuguese man-o-war, a sea creature composed of many smaller sea creatures, and of its stinging limbs.

The thing spoke, in a voice that was scores of voices, but it didn't speak in any language they understood, and then it broke apart into a swam of small Liars again, all tumbling off in their own directions.

*They floated in a tank of water, and a huge Liar (not as big as a killer whale, but twice the size of a human) with skin as pure white as snow floated beside them. Its body glittered with silvery augmentations, and its countless limbs worked busily, moving parts of their bodies around, and humming to itself. It patted them – lovingly, Janice thought; like you would pet a hurt dog, Drake contended – and then injected them with something that made them first go blurry and then fade.

*A bed, or at least a pile of cushions, and they were… not comfortable, but less wracked with pain than before. They tried to move and found that they could – their bodies responded to their thoughts, for the first time in a long time. They lifted their hand in front of their face, and then screamed, because it wasn't their hand – his hand, her hand – it was changed. Their arm was shaped like an uppercase Y now: the bicep was the straight base of the Y, but it bifurcated at the elbow, sprouting two forearms from the single joint. One of the forearms was pale and freckled and had been Janice's, and the other was dark brown and had belonged to Drake. Each forearm ended in a hand, but the pale one was missing a finger, and the brown one had too many of them. They had been Frankensteined, stitched together, but there were no stitches, and no scars. They'd somehow been... melded. "Drake?" Janice said, and her mouth was all broken. "Janice?" Drake said, and his tongue was thick and all wrong.

The pale white Liar entered the room then, and gestured in what they interpreted as excitement. He held up an oval screen of some kind, or perhaps it was a mirror, and put it up to their faces –

They couldn't remember seeing their face. Not that time. After the mirror rose, they were blank.

*They were on the edge of a pool, sprawled out on their bellies – no, their belly, they only had one now. The water was dark and still. They looked at their face. Their faces.

They only had one head, an oversized pumpkin-lumpy head, and they shared it now. Drake's face, with his dark skin, his deep brown eyes, was on the left side. Janice's face was on the right, and she had only one eye, bright and blue. They had a nose – it had been Drake's – perched equidistant between the faces, on the place where dark skin met light. They

287

turned their head – somehow, instinctively, sharing control of their mutual neck, and each noted the absence of ears. There was no hair on that head, either, not Janice's blond waves, not Drake's tight black curls. They waved at themselves with their bifurcated arm, and then with their right arm – that one looked almost ordinary, though it was mottled dark skin and light, and the hand had six fingers and two thumbs. They tried to move their legs, to push themselves up to their knees, but it seemed their knees were no longer in evidence.

Drake remembered Janice crying, and Janice remembered Drake crying, but they both clearly saw tears drop into the pool and make ripples, and then scores of those tiny Liars broke the surface, like guppies in a fish bowl rising when you sprinkle food on the surface.

*Being fed. Being given water. Learning to swallow again. Drake tasting the food in Janice's mouth, Janice tasting the food in Drake's.

*Their first conversation. "Janice. Are you okay?"

"I'm half a monster. I'm horrible."

"At least we're alive."

"We're like Frankenstein's monster if he'd had a conjoined twin, Drake. I want to die. Why won't they let us die?"

"They tried to save us," Drake soothed. "I think… they don't speak our language… I think they just don't know how to fix us. I think they did their best."

"They're butchers. Torturers. You saw them, how strange their own bodies are, too big or too small or made of smaller pieces, jammed up with machines – I think body modification is their hobby. They're having fun. They're playing with us."

"They seem… I think they're kind." Drake paused. "When you get upset, I can feel my heart rate increase."

"Our heart rate. I think we're sharing one."

"But… shouldn't I be more upset?" Drake said. "I can feel chemicals, hormones, pumping, and I can… regulate them. I think… oh. I can make happy chemicals release too."

"What is there to be happy about… oh. Well. That is nice."

"But I should be complaining," Drake said. "I don't feel like complaining."

"I'll complain for both of us. This is awful. This is horrible. They're going to put us in a museum of medical curiosities, in a zoo, on display. Or they'll recycle us, or stick their own alien parts on me, or… I think the worst, Drake. Why do I think the worst of them? Is this your brain in my head?"

"I think it's both our brains. We're thinking each other's thoughts, a little, we're all crisscrossed. I think they saved both our brains and put them together."

"Do you think we could kill ourselves?" Janice said.

"Do you want to? I still… I want to live, Janice. I do."

"I want to die, I'm pretty sure, but what if I drowned us and they brought us back, gave us gills, what then?"

"I don't know, Janice. I'm new to this, too. But I think it's better to be alive than not. For now. I think we're a miracle. At least it doesn't hurt so bad anymore. Or not as constantly."

"Do the thing with the good brain chemicals again. Slowly, so I can see how you do it. If we're not going to die, I need to learn. I need to learn how to bear this life."

*They were in a hangar, maybe, and it was full of white light, though not so blinding now – just enough to obscure the walls and ceiling from view. The white Liar zipped them into a suit – made of their own space suits, and other materials, they thought, and helped them into the cockpit of their ship. It wasn't broken anymore, but it was changed, patched with the same strange variety that Drake and Janice were patched in themselves. There were bits of alien machinery, silver as the white Liar's implants, attached to the cockpit, including something that must have been an engine on the back. The seat was made to hold them, customized somehow for their new form.

Drake touched the controls, and the panel lit up. Janice reached out with their split arm and touched the navigation board. "The display is different than I'm used to, but I can see where we are – not far from where we crashed, beyond the asteroid field."

"Do you think these creatures were the source of the transmission Martinique wanted us to track down?" Drake said.

"Ah. I bet they were. It was aliens after all. Just Liars, though. Not anything new."

"They haven't told us any lies. Maybe they aren't exactly Liars, or at least, not like those we're used to."

"Maybe they only tell white lies. Ha. They're all white too. White Liars."

"Maybe they're healers."

"They don't speak our language, Drake. That's why they haven't lied. If they could, they'd spout all sorts of bullshit. They'd say they did this for our own good. They aren't healers. They're kids playing with toys. We're the toys. No, that's too nice. They're butchers."

"We aren't meat, Janice. We're alive. We're still human."

She held up her Y-shaped arm. "Are we? Are you sure about that? We look pretty inhuman on the outside. I wonder what they did to us on the inside? What they put inside us?"

The door closed, and the white Liar with the silvery augments thumped the window a couple of times, and then appeared to wave. Had it learned that from seeing them wave at their own reflection, they wondered? Was it a gesture that meant something completely different in their culture, whatever that was?

Drake waved back, and Janice scoffed. Then the hangar doors opened and their ship dropped into space, and the doors above them moved together, darkness closing up the light. Then their immense ship receded and Drake and Janice were alone; or as alone as either one of them would ever be again.

"Let's go home," Drake said.

"Sure. I'm sure everyone will be really happy to see us. Until they actually see us. Then I predict a lot of screaming."

"At least we're together," Drake said. "I'm glad we're together."

"Shut up," Janice said.

CHAPTER 26

Drake and Janice opened their eyes and returned from memory to reality, to see the white Liar gazing abstractedly at a point on the ceiling. Light streamed from a silver ring around its eyes. Was he looking at some kind of projected display?

The Liar spoke. "We say sorry, subject one. Sorry twice for calling you so. Your names are Drake and Janice. We should call you such. We did not know names when first we met. We did not know even that you were two, instead of one. [Laughter]." The alien didn't laugh; he said 'Laughter' in a harshly mechanical voice. Someone needed to adjust his artificial voicebox's inputs and outputs. "Our apologies are many. We did our best. The children of our people sometimes make models, to practice fine motor control, and also for enjoyments, yes? Human children are same, we think? Make models of ourselves, or ships, or stations, or houses, or animals, sometimes from little blocks that stick each to another, sometimes from special kits with special parts. Do you know of what we mean? [Tonal variation: anxious desire for confirmation of comprehension.]"

"We hear you," Drake said. "We understand what you're saying. We don't understand what we're doing here, or what you want."

"We have our suspicions, though," Janice said.

"[Tonal variation: relief] We will explain all, but we will explain old business, before new. The models your children and ours play with, sometimes, what if the parts become jumbled? Two sets of pieces, or maybe three, with pieces all mixed together, maybe with some pieces missing too. All with no instructions, no picture to guide you to completion? What do you do, if you think by mistake that all the pieces come from one set? You try your best to see how they fit. You worry it is not quite right, but it works at the end, the lights come on and the wheels spin. You think, perhaps it is okay. Perhaps it is close enough. [Sigh.] That was us, with you. You were broken pieces, all mixed. We thought you were one thing. We... we said this, but we say again, we did our best."

"You were trying to help us," Drake said. "I always thought so."

"It was me who thought so at first," Janice said. "But at some point our thoughts, or more like our ways of thinking, got crossed. I'd forgotten that. Forgotten how I used to be." She lifted the single pale blue eye to the white Liar. "I thought you were playing with us. Amusing yourselves."

"Amusing? Interesting is better word, our lexicon

says. We are healers. We travel and we help our people, help them to help themselves. When we found you… we never saw such people as you before. Fascinating. Challenging. Not amusing. Situation was too serious for amusing, our lexicon says. Later… we met other humans. We thought, oh no! We thought, subject one, we built them back all wrong! Much sadness and regret. We feel it still."

"But now you work for Shaper," Janice said. "Putting humans back together all wrong on purpose this time. Much sadness there? Much regret?"

"Shaper," the white Liar said. "We know Shaper. We do not like Shaper. We have been in this system for not long. What you would count as two years ago, we encountered… you say 'scourge-ship'? We greeted them. Always interesting to meet cousins and hear the stories they have made for themselves. We are a people made of stories, because our truth is too dark. These cousins we met were very strange, because they held to oldest of old ways, still in service to masters who ruled our ancestors generations ago, still solving themselves at the master's problems like the problems were their own.

"These cousins invited us to come here and see their work. Is this work healing we said? Oh yes they said, we are trying to heal, will you help us, and we said yes. Because the story we made for ourselves in our tribe is that we are traveling helpers who travel and help. We have many kinds of expertise that Shaper and his tribe lack. This is because their original purpose was not to heal or to change bodies for the better, but to destroy and break bodies, and over long generations they taught themselves about biology, genetics, mutation, many arts. But they did not know how many things they did not know!

"We are famous in a small way, and Shaper knew we could advance their studies. We came and we saw what they do and… we were troubled. They do seek healing, it was not a lie, but they do great damage in the service of that goal. They do not think humans are people. But we knew you were people, from the moment we put you back together, Drake and Janice, as best we could. Not our people, but people all the same. We worked with Shaper and his tribe for some time, hoping to make them more givers of kindness, but Shaper became frustrated. He wanted only our skills and not our thoughts or opinions or objections.

"We explained that skill could not be used without philosophy, not without great danger and harm, and so he cast us out. We sought out your people… the resistance? To offer aid. But they fired on us. They thought we were tricks to trick them. We were about to leave this system when things began to explode and then we decided to stay because when there are explosions people get hurt. And then… we found you."

"Can you please let us go?" Drake said.

The white Liar fluttered its pseudopods. "Is comfort field not working? We thought to float there with no pressure would be better than your chair."

"Oh," Janice said. "Ah, I mean... it is more comfortable. We thought it was some kind of... that we were prisoners."

"You are patients," the white Liar said. "But only if you wish to be! We are sorry for taking your ship into stasis and traveling through a bridge. There was a battle, and we feared if we made ourselves known, if we reached out, we would draw attention and be destroyed. Our ship is not made for fighting. It is a hospital ship. We take in broken ships and people and try to help them. You were not broken but we feared you might be in the fight, that the guns turned on other ships might be turned on you. Then – then! We saw it was you, the two of you, the ones we called one, the two we called subject one."

"Now we know why the Benefactor said this system would be interesting to certain members of the crew," Janice said. "He must have known somehow that our Liars were here." She paused. "Why should we believe what you say? Your whole species is famous for making things up."

More fluttering of pseudopods. "We make up stories, yes. New origin stories, new myths, new purposes. Because we lost our true stories so long ago. And when we talk to outsiders, yes, we protect ourselves and hide our truths in other stories... but do you not understand? [Tonal variation: surprise] We do not tell lies within our own bands, families, tribes. The two of you, Drake and Janice, you lived with us for months, you ate with us, and we gave of our bodies to join your bodies where they would not join. You are part of our family. We do not tell lies to family."

Drake and Janice were stunned. Finally Drake said, "Thank you. The other people on our ship are our family. Are they all right?"

"We put them in stasis when we picked up your ship and then put them in a little dream so we could monitor their functions and brains. Stasis is good for stopping damage from increasing but not for seeing how things work when they are working."

"Stasis... you mean some kind of cryogenic suspension?" Janice said.

The white Liar waved his pseudopods wildly. "No, lowering temperature, very crude. We have, ah, stasis is the right word, our lexicon says. It is an old technology, guarded closely by the ancient masters–"

"The Axiom," Drake said.

"Yes, as you call them. Some of the Axiom had this power, to stop the processes of time locally, indefinitely. Shaper found this technology and used it in his work, to stop the process of the plague while working on a cure. We took this technology too, for ourselves, because it will be useful in our work. We used it to stop parts of your ship so you would not attack us in confusion."

"Wait, what plague?" Janice said.

"The plague our ancestors released on the Cleansing Corps," the white Liar said. "Do you not know of this?"

"Why don't you tell us about it," Drake said.

The white Liar was silent for a moment, and the light around his eye brightened. "The Shaper of Destiny is the leader of a tribe of our people who served the Cleansing Corps. Do you know of the Cleansing Corps?"

"Not the Axiom janitorial staff, I assume," Janice said.

"No, no. Not cleaning. 'Cleansing' is much of an ugly word for what they did, but it is how they called themselves. They were the Axiom who fleeted the scourge-ships. They roamed wide and far and killed all intelligent things they found, wiped out all civilizations of the galaxy, small and great. The Cleansing Corps believed all people who were not Axiom were not people at all, and only tolerated our kind for servants and slaves and pets and toys. First the Corps destroyed the worlds that could travel in space. Then they sought worlds that transmitted signals into the sky – let the Cleansing Corps hear your voice, and they would find and silence you. It took hundreds of tens of years of time, but all such worlds were stilled. Then they found worlds with life that might someday touch the stars, and cut them down as well. Some of our people were slaves, forced to serve the Corps, but some served willing, and received power and privilege over their own. Much as some humans serve Shaper and his tribe willingly in this system, you see?"

"We do," Janice said.

The white Liar fluttered. "If you know of the Axiom, perhaps you know of the rebellions?"

"We have a friend, Lantern, on our ship," Drake said. "She told us about some of the true history of your people. The slaves rebelled, and the Axiom destroyed your home world, and all your records, the whole history of your people, right?"

"They took away even our memories," the white Liar said. "Reached into our minds and erased our myths and histories. The Axiom thought this would quell us forever. But we rose up, again and again. [Tonal variation: pride] The efforts of our ancestors, that is why there are so few of the masters left in the galaxy. Some of those in service to the Cleansing Corps rose up, too. This was in the last days of the Axiom empire, when the masters had broken into factions and fought and rivaled with their projects, all in hopes to restore glory, or survive the death of heat in the universe, or to leave this universe for other places they could rule.

"The Cleansing Corps aligned themselves with some factions, but decided others were not enough… Axiomatic. The Corps obsessed over purity, not just of body but of philosophy. The Corps believed any non-Axiom life to be vermin, but as the empire fragmented, they began to see some Axiom as vermin, too – especially those who wished to hibernate while their vast projects came to pass. The Cleansing Corps had seen intelligent life spring up again and again, and feared if too many Axiom went to sleep, the universe would teem with vermin again. They feared this outcome, and pushed down their disgust for our kind to create the sect of truth-tellers, to carry on their work in case the Corps fell in the fighting. The truth-tellers even now do this work of extermination, killing new civilizations before they can rise, but they found humanity too late. You had already spread wide and far into space, too many to kill, so they tried to limit your expansion, and keep you from disturbing the Axiom. [Laughter] It seems they were not successful in your case."

"We have disturbed the Axiom a little bit here and there, now that you mention it," Janice said.

"[Laughter] So in those last days of empire, the Cleansing Corps became cruel more and more, and punished infraction and hesitation among their slaves with torture and death, as the Axiom empire fell apart all around them, the galaxy in chaos. Their slaves saw opportunity in confusion. The Corps used many techniques to destroy life. Fire and explosions, yes, and sometimes they destroyed whole planets. Other times they wanted the resources on those planets for the empire, and then, they turned to plague. Special plague, made to kill just one species each, killing them all while leaving their possessions unharmed. The slaves stole these secrets to create a plague of their own: one made to kill their Axiom masters."

"Ohhhhh," Janice said.

"They made this plague, they spread, they killed. The Cleansing Corps, once numerous, dwindled and sickened and died until only tens of them remained, and even they were infected. Worse, the Corps was hunted by other Axiom, because they feared the plague as a threat to their species entire. The other Axiom attacked the Corps on sight, and scourge-ships were known as plague ships, and burned. Those few ships in this system are the only remnant of a fleet once so numerous as stars.

"The last of the Corps took their loyal servants here, to the edge of the galaxy, far beyond the reach of the dwindling empire. Here they set a stasis field, to hold them outside of time for thousands of years. [Laughter] To hibernate themselves, when they once called those who slept through time cowards and fools! They wished to hide, to be forgotten, and because the Axiom factions were so much at war, this hiding worked. The Corps slumbered for millennia. At the appointed time, some centuries ago, the stasis ended, and the servants of the Cleansing Corps woke. The Axiom themselves remained in suspension, because the plague still sickened them, and to live long in normal time would be to die.

"Their servants, the Shaper of Destiny chief among them, then began to seek a cure. They knew how to make plagues, oh, yes, but curing them is more and harder. They taught themselves what they could, and experimented on the worlds here, but eventually despaired of curing the Axiom, because the problem was too hard. When humans arrived in the system, Shaper… changed his focus."

"To what?" Drake said.

"To changing the Axiom instead. If the plague attacks Axiom bodies only, then perhaps you need not cure the plague, but only to change the bodies. The plague does not hurt our species, and it does not hurt humans, so if the Cleansing Corps survivors were altered, given new organs and limbs taken from humans and our kind… perhaps these new forms could resist the plague. This work to make chimeras has been the focus of Shaper's research these past years and years. He wishes to make the process perfect before he operates on his masters."

"But aren't the Cleansing Corps super racist?" Janice said. "How would they feel about being fused with body parts taken from vermin?"

"We asked this of Shaper. Shaper said they would be glad to live at all. We have our doubts. He did not sound convinced of himself either, in true, but he is desperate in these times."

"Can you wake up our friends?" Drake said. "We should really fill them in on all this."

"This can be so. But would you like us to make improvements to you first? We cannot separate you without making you both... incomplete... but we can make certain corrections if you wish, now that we understand the ways and beings of human people now."

"What did you have in mind?" Janice said.

CHAPTER 27

Elena blinked and the red parlor was gone, replaced by a white room with seats that seemed extruded from the floor and walls. Ashok and Lantern were seated nearby, and Kaustikos sat on the floor like a discarded basketball. "Are you all okay?" Lantern signed that she was well, and Ashok said, "Diagnostics are clean. That was the most boring virtual reality experience of my life. Were you in the red room too?"

"I was," Elena said.

Lantern said, "I was in a relaxation tank. It was not very relaxing. Where are Drake and Janice?"

Part of the wall rippled, drew aside like curtains opening on a stage, and Drake and Janice walked in. Walked in.

Ashok whistled. "Nice legs! And your arms are different too!" He circled them, then crouched to look at their knees. "This is amazing! We could never fit you with prosthetics, your biology and nervous system were too weird – how'd this happen?"

"It's good to see you, too, Ashok," Drake said. "This ship belongs to the same Liars who put Janice and me

305

back together again after our accident. They've learned a lot about humans since then, and since they built this body in the first place, they knew how to rebuild it, too. They offered to do more extensive work, and we might take them up on it, but we didn't want to leave you waiting. Besides, Callie is probably losing her mind. We should get back to the *White Raven* and get in touch with her."

"The same Liars who worked on you are here, in this system?" Ashok said. "That's… wait." He kicked Kaustikos, and the probe lit up and rose wobbling into the air. "Hey, is that what the Benefactor meant when he said that something in this system would be especially interesting for some of our crew?"

"I can't possibly speak for what the Benefactor meant," Kaustikos said. "Wait. Were we in a stasis field?"

"No virtual waiting room for the AI, huh?" Ashok said.

"Why did they abduct us?" Elena said, choosing to ignore them.

"They thought they were rescuing us from a battle," Janice said. "I can confirm they mean well, and you know if I believe that, it must be true. Their methods just consistently leave something to be desired. Come on, let's get back to our ship."

Drake and Janice led them to the far side of the room, and the wall parted for them.

"This whole ship is made of flowing programmable matter," Ashok said. "Want."

The corridor beyond was like a glass tunnel through an aquarium tank, teeming with sea life on all sides. In this case, the fluid beyond was full of dozens of little jellyfish-sized Liars. As they passed through the tunnel, the small Liars coalesced and formed a single body, waving pseudopods composed of themselves. Drake and Janice waved back. "Cute little guys," Elena said.

"This is a remarkable tribe," Lantern said.

The group broke up and scattered when an immense liar, nearly ten meters long, swam over to them and gazed down with eyes as big as dinner plates. "It's good to see you, too," Drake said.

Drake and Janice stopped at the end of the tunnel, turned, and gestured. "Come on, gather round." They all huddled together, and the floor dropped, sending them down a shaft illuminated by walls of white light. Kaustikos hovered above them for a moment, then zoomed down to stay with the group.

"This ship is so bizarre," Ashok said. "I love it."

The descent stopped, and a section of the wall receded. They stepped out into a vast hangar, where the *White Raven* stood, gleaming and unharmed. A large white Liar glistening with silver augmentations bustled toward them. "Greetings, friends of our family. We have taken names. This one is called Metal. You met the ones of us called Many and Large?"

"I... think so," Elena said.

"They haven't been using our language for very long," Janice said. "They're still getting the hang of proper names. And pronouns, and other things."

"[Tonal variation: hopefulness] You will come back and visit, Drake and Janice?"

"If we survive, absolutely," Janice said. "Shaper is going to try to kill us, though."

"If any life remains in you we will breathe it back to fullness. We cannot offer aid in fighting, but in healing you have our pledge."

"You've helped a lot already," Drake said.

"They have?" Kaustikos said. "Listen, it seemed like, when we lost time, that we might have been in some kind of a stasis field—"

"Farewell family and friends of family." Metal waved a pseudopod and then sank through the floor and out of sight.

"Let's get on board," Janice said. "Then we'll fill you in on the secrets of the galaxy, how about that?"

"Callie must be looking for us." Elena stood in the observation port, looking at the stars. Janice had been trying to reach Callie, without success. She'd succeeded in contacting the resistance, and they'd had plenty of news to share, but all they knew about Callie was that she'd taken off in the Blaze without saying where she was going.

"I'm sure she is," Shall said. "Where do you think she's doing the looking?"

"She'll assume we were taken by Shaper," Elena said. "So she'd try to figure out where he is. Since he wasn't in the surgical headquarters, where would she go next?"

Lantern spoke up on the comm. "If Shaper is in retreat, he would go to protect the Axiom he has in stasis, probably. There's a location marked on our map that doesn't correspond to any of the facilities used by the Exalted. Maybe it's the secret heart of everything in this system. Callie has the map – she may have drawn the same conclusion."

"Running alone toward danger?" Elena said. "Sounds right."

"Just give the order, captain," Shall said.

Elena flinched. "What?"

"You're the executive officer," Shall said. "Ranking officer on the ship while Callie's gone. We go where you tell us."

Elena swallowed. "Right. I knew that. Ashok, can you open a bridge near the coordinates Lantern has for this secret station?"

"You got it, acting cap."

Elena went up to the cockpit. Janice and Drake were standing on their new legs, operating consoles with their new arms – they had two on each side now, with extra thumbs, and the prosthetics seemed to work just as well as their biological ones – and those worked better than they had before. "Captain on deck!" Janice shouted.

Elena winced. "You don't say that for Callie."

"She's not too concerned about ceremony, as long as we respond to orders promptly when it counts," Drake said.

"But we don't know about your command style, Captain Oh. For all we know you'll throw us in the brig if we don't salute." She saluted, with all four arms.

"Ugh, come on, we aren't even a military vessel."

"We know that, but how do we know whether or not you know that?" Janice said.

"I didn't expect to get less respect when I ascended to a position of ultimate power." Elena strapped herself into Callie's chair, as weird as that felt.

"We respect you plenty. What you're experiencing now is actually affection." Drake turned their head and grinned at her.

"Ready on your command, oh exalted empress of the stars," Ashok said over the comms.

"Make a hole," Elena said.

The bridgehead opened before them, and the *White Raven* passed through.

"You're brooding," Shall said.

"My crew got kidnapped right out from under me," Callie said. "I'm not brooding, I'm furious. Also worried, but I'm focusing on the furious to keep the worried under control. How much farther?"

"A few hours. Why don't you get some sleep?"

"Who needs sleep when I have military-grade stimulants?" She'd explored the Blaze during this abominably long journey and found its impressive armory and its equally impressive infirmary. There were drugs here that would let you operate at peak physical and mental performance for days on end… at the expense of a terrible crash later. Callie, who was not terribly concerned about 'later' right now, had helped herself to some of the best vials available. "Do you think the Jovian Imperative will let me keep this ship? It's salvage, more or less, right?"

"You want to give up the *White Raven*?"

"Not at all. We'd use this ship for more dangerous missions, because I'd be less sad if the Blaze got blown up." She paced around the command deck, unable to relax, both chemically and psychologically.

"Callie, long-range sensors just picked up the opening of a wormhole nearby."

"Is it a scourge-ship?" The bridge generators on the vehicles in the shipyard had been limited in their choice of destinations, but Shaper could doubtless turn off those governors and go wherever he wanted.

"I can't tell what it is yet – I can pick up the change in the fabric of space-time well before I can tell what emerged from it. I'm retasking sensors. Let me see what I can see… Callie. It's the *White Raven*."

She gripped the back of the captain's chair so hard it made her knuckles ache. "Hail them!"

"This is the Blaze. Please identify."

After a brief delay, Shall's voice said, "Hello, Blaze. This is the *White Raven*. We're all okay here, but we've got a lot to tell you…"

Callie let out a long, rattling breath. "Elena? Are you there?"

"That's Captain Elena to you," she said, and Callie let out a sound that was halfway between laughter and a sob.

The *White Raven* held position while the Blaze burned in its direction, and Callie used her short-term teleporter to jump to the former as soon as it came within range.

Elena was waiting for her, and they embraced, separated long enough for Callie to yank her helmet off, and then grabbed onto one another again. "I thought I lost you," Callie said. "I was so scared."

"I didn't spend as much time being scared, because the nice aliens put us in stasis for a bit while they talked to Drake and Janice, but I was worried, too.

I'm glad you're here. Your crew is really insubordinate. Have you ever noticed that?"

"My XO has been known to take all kinds of liberties. I'm sure you were great." Callie took a deep breath and stepped back. "Okay. We should have a family meeting. My previous plan to attack the secret station and punch Shaper in the head until he told me where you were should be modified to reflect current reality."

"It seems pretty straightforward," Callie said. "Things have gone to hell in this system for the Exalted – the Jovian Imperative is coming, if they aren't here already – so Shaper is probably planning to flee, and to take his frozen Axiom with him. We need to get there first and kill the Cleansing Corps."

"And steal their stuff," Kaustikos said.

"And blow up their stuff. I'd rather not give the Imperative any more Axiom toys, especially ones that belong to the faction dedicated to exterminating life and exploding actual planets and unleashing customized plagues. I don't trust anybody with that kind of technology. The Imperative is already going to get ahold of a scourge-ship or two, and they'll throw every engineer they've got at figuring out how the bridge generators work. I can't stop them from visiting faraway places, but maybe I can stop them from destroying those places utterly when they get there."

"The situation might not be that bad," Ashok said. "I've been trying to figure out how the bridge generators work for ages, and it's still just a magic black box as far as I can tell. I think there's stuff going on inside that violates all the known laws of physics. I'm starting to think there are whole stars or even universes bottled up in those greasy black cubes. We're like cave-people trying to figure out how a Tanzer drive works."

"Put a couple thousand highly trained cave people on the problem and they'll probably crack it eventually," Callie said.

"The stasis field, though – the healers said that has medical uses," Kaustikos said. "Surely we should keep that technology. Think of how lucrative licensing it could be."

"A field that stops time for anything inside it?" Callie said. "That can keep time stopped for thousands of years, maybe longer? That sounds like a tool for domination and control to me. No. Let's make it all go boom."

"Should we just bombard the station as soon as we're within range?" Shall said.

Callie shook her head. "There could be humans there. Who know what Shaper is up to out here. We also need to make sure Shaper is on board, because, if they're not, we have to go after them, wherever they are. I took out two of the three heads of this nightmare system. It will make my teeth itch forever if one of them gets away. We'll approach with the *White Raven* in stealth – the Blaze is more about striking fear than being sneaky, so it can hang back until we need its guns. I'll take an infiltration team, see what we're dealing with, and then I'll give the order to tear the station up once we know. I'll go, and Shall can come in his war drone, and Ashok in case there's engineering stuff, and Lantern in case there's Liar stuff, and Kaustikos."

"In case you need my brilliant tactical insight?"

"No, but we still have you rigged with a bomb, so, if necessary, we can make you explode as a distraction."

"Callie, the station is in sensor range, and… you'd better come look at this thing." Janice sounded more troubled than snarky for once, and Callie hurried up to the cockpit from the galley. She was briefly surprised by seeing Janice and Drake standing at their station on shiny new prosthetics, because she was so used to them operating from within their mobility device, but it was a good kind of surprised. The chair had been good for them, allowing them relative relief from pain and some freedom of movement, but the healers had improved on both those areas. They even said they'd spend more time on Glauketas with the rest of the crew now that gravity didn't trouble them so much, and Callie was happy at the prospect of seeing more of them.

"Show me," Callie said.

The windows turned into screens, filled with a magnified view of the thirteenth station.

"What the hell am I looking at?" Callie said.

CHAPTER 28

"It's biomechanical, we think," Janice said. "It probably started out as one of the Axiom facilities we've seen before, a big nasty branching thing, like the inside of an anthill cast in metal. You can see that basic shape, underneath all the… stuff growing on it."

The thirteenth station was covered entirely in flesh, and, in some places, that flesh was more than a mere covering, and bulged out in immense, tumorous growths. The growths weren't uniform, either, but wildly variegated in color and texture – some sections resembled the slick flesh of a snail, and others the pebbled skin of a starfish, and there were sections of snot yellow and bile green and arterial red. Some sections seemed to pulse. "Is that thing breathing?" Callie said.

"Parts of it are definitely moving," Janice said. "I think it's… well, alive, captain."

"If it's alive, what does it eat?" Callie said, imagining the Exalted feeding captive humans to some hidden maw.

"I think it feeds on radiation," Shall said. "There was

317

a definite physical reaction to some of our scanners, in the form of increased... I don't want to say 'blood flow', but some kind of subcutaneous fluid reaction. If I had to guess, I'd say it metabolizes radiation – galactic cosmic rays, solar wind, maybe other forms produced within the station itself."

"Why would you make something like that?" Janice often sounded disgusted, but she sounded especially disgusted now.

"That is a harder question," Shall said. "The Exalted do seem to enjoy their biological experiments, though."

"Forget why they made it," Callie said. "How are we supposed to board it?"

Janice said, "There seem to be airlocks, here and here." Portions of the screen lit up, and revealed gleaming metal rectangles poking through the flesh, like pieces of shrapnel sticking out of a body. "But if you were planning to take Shall's war drone or Lantern's blister-ship and cut your way through the hull for a sneaky entry... you can try it, I guess, but that skin is thick, and I don't want to think about what would come spurting out if you tried to cut into it. Blood or pus or acid or–"

"I get it," Callie said. "I'll have to do a short-range teleport and open one of the airlocks from inside. I hate coming in the front door. Or any door."

"The Vanir system does seem to demand a lot of

solo infiltration from you," Shall said. "Fortunately, we do still have the element of surprise. The resistance doesn't know about this station, and Shaper doesn't know we have a map of Axiom and truth-teller facilities, so he may not even be watching the entry ways."

"You only know about this station thanks to the largesse of the Benefactor," Kaustikos chimed in. "Lest you forget the reason you're here."

"I have an excellent memory," Callie said. "Do we have any sense of what's going on in there?"

"Axiom stations are resistant to scanning," Janice said. "I'm getting weird readings externally, because of all that flesh – it's warm, alive, and radioactive, or some combination of the three, depending on where I point my instruments. The interior is a mystery, though."

"And everyone knows I like mysteries. I'm going to suit up. Shall, figure out the coordinates for my teleport, would you?" She looked at the biological horror drifting in the void before her for another moment – would this be like entering a space station, or spelunking inside a leviathan? – and then turned away.

Callie emerged from her personal wormhole just inside the nearest airlock. The Axiom stations she'd visited before were vast, and this one was no exception – fortunately, the biological weirdness seemed limited to the exterior. The inside was all dark metal and struts, without meat or goo.

A single scourge-ship was parked in the immense hangar, and, despite its size, it looked like a breadcrumb forgotten on an otherwise empty table. At least now she knew she wasn't alone. Someone was here. Probably Shaper.

Callie needed to make sure that scourge-ship was unoccupied before she opened the airlock, and she approached it under active camouflage. The ship's airlock opened for her, and she boarded and made her way to the cockpit. No pilot on board. She checked the ship's systems and confirmed the presence of half a dozen hunter-drones on board, and after loading Shall's control software, she put them all into diagnostic and repair mode. That was much easier than hunting them down and shooting them on an individual basis.

Callie left the ship and trudged to the hangar's main airlock. The controls were just like those on the first Axiom station they'd discovered, so she knew how to make it open. She didn't like thinking about how many aspects of Axiom technology had become familiar to her.

Opening the airlock would probably set off alarms all over the station, but she didn't mind. This place was enormous. Much better to draw Shaper to her than to spend time looking for him.

She punched in the opening sequence and watched Shall's war-drone fly over with Ashok clinging to his back, followed by Lantern in her blister-ship and Kaustikos floating alone. By the time the hangar doors were halfway open, her boarding team sailed through the gap and landed. Callie shut the hangar door and gathered her troops. "Ashok, go disable that scourge-ship. I don't want anybody slipping away when we aren't looking."

"Permanent disabled or temporary disabled?"

"We've got two ships outside, so I don't foresee us needing this one. Break it like you mean it, but in a non-exploding way. We might need this hangar later."

Ashok snapped off a lazy salute and went humming toward his task.

"Lantern, you and Shall see if you can find any kind of station map, internal life support sensors, things like that. Kaustikos and I will just pick a passage and start searching for Shaper. If you find anything useful, let us know."

Lantern and Shall went in search of a terminal they could access, and Kaustikos floated at Callie's shoulder as she moved toward the nearest access door that led deeper into the facility. They explored empty corridors and rooms full of undisturbed dust in silence for a long time, Kaustikos scouting ahead and returning with news of nothing. Callie periodically checked in with Lantern and Shall, who hadn't found anything as useful as a map, or an explanation of why the station was covered in flesh. "Any useful sensor data?" Callie asked.

"The only life signs we see on board are yours, mine, and Ashok's," Lantern said. "But Shaper could be masking his somehow."

"So in the meantime we search for a particular grain of sand in a mansion. We'll keep trudging."

Kaustikos returned from another abortive scouting attempt and drifted along beside her. "I was surprised you chose me to accompany you. I had the sense you didn't like me."

"I just don't like bullshit, and that's what all your internal components are made of. The Benefactor knew what we were going to find in this system – he even knew the healers who worked on Drake and Janice years ago were here. How? Is he a Liar? A rogue elder from the sect of the truth-tellers?"

"I've only communicated with the Benefactor remotely, captain. He gave me information he deemed necessary to help you with your mission, to destroy the Axiom here, but he hasn't shared the origin of that information with me."

"Kaustikos, you've provided basically zero information. If you hadn't acted as distraction once or twice I'd say your presence here has been totally pointless."

"You wound me, captain. I would have shared more intelligence with you, but you and your crew have proven adept at discovering things on your own, and anyway, your basic distrust of everything I say makes any attempts to help you counterproductive."

Callie grunted. "Can you tell me one thing that's useful, Kaustikos? Just one? Any tidbit that could actually be construed as remotely helpful?"

The probe was silent for a moment. "Just that Shaper is the smartest and most ruthless of those who ruled this system. You should be careful when you face him."

"So that's a no, then. How about the Benefactor? One actual point of data about him?"

"I don't even know if 'he' is the right word. I base that entirely on the fact that his voice seemed masculine when he spoke to me, and there's no reason to believe that's his actual voice. The Benefactor might not even be an individual – they could be a collective of interested parties."

"I don't believe you," Callie said. "I think you know more than you're letting on."

"I have come to realize I cannot influence what you believe, captain."

"I knew Shaper had a secret agenda here, and we figured it out," Callie said. "I'm still wondering what the Benefactor's secret agenda is."

"You're so cynical, Captain Machedo. Do you think you're the galaxy's only altruist?"

"I'm not an altruist. I just have a very expansive sense of self-preservation – one big enough to cover preserving all intelligent life in the galaxy."

"Except the Axiom – they're probably the most intelligent life in the galaxy, and you want to exterminate them utterly, without even having a conversation with them first."

"You don't debate with people who consider first contact an opportunity for genocide. My right to exist isn't open to debate. The Axiom think every other species is vermin to be murdered or animals to be enslaved. When that's your worldview, you forfeit your right to participate in civilization. Believing other people aren't actually people is a dealbreaker. It's a subject that's come up way too often in human history, unfortunately, and as a result, we know how to deal with the sort of people who call wholesale murder 'cleansing.'"

"But these Axiom are harmless – just sleeping. Terminally ill and sleeping, no less."

"Their servants enslaved a whole system and conducted medical experiments on the inhabitants, Kaustikos. Sleeping or not, they're monsters. What the hell are you talking about, anyway? Your boss wants to exterminate the Axiom as much as I do, or so I've been assured."

"I'm just playing devil's advocate," Kaustikos said.

"The devil has a highly qualified legal team on retainer already, so how about you advocate for his victims instead?"

"No one ever wants to debate me," Kaustikos said. "This is a galaxy full of intellectual cowards."

"I brought you along to scout, spaceball. Go do that."

Kaustikos zipped wordlessly along the corridor, leaving Callie alone, which was briefly preferable and then creepy. This hallway was far larger than human scale, more like a tunnel, and was mostly unlit. She turned her suit lights on, but that just revealed hideous organic growths in patches on the walls. The hangar was an exception, then – the biological experiment happening on the outside of the station extended inside after all. There were gooey spots on the floor, too, more and more, slime molds and spongy patches that she skirted widely. "Shall, Lantern, what's the word?"

"– ight – ack – on – ay–" crackled in her suit comms. Ugh. She'd had communication problems on Axiom stations before. She considered going back for their report, but hailed Kaustikos instead. "Find anything?"

His reply came through clearly, at least. "Perhaps. Bear left at the next turning. There's a section of the station that's lit up here."

Callie turned left at the next intersection and the tunnel brightened. Kaustikos floated ahead, in a round room full of transparent glass pillars two meters in diameter. There were hundreds of them, evenly spaced a couple of meters apart, all glowing with soft light from within, rising up from the floor and disappearing into the dizzying heights of the ceiling. Poetically, it was like a crystal forest. Less poetically, it was like a rack full of giant test-tubes. "What is this room for?"

"Who knows?" Kaustikos said. "But look over there." A thin laser pointer beam spiked out of his spheroid body and shone on the floor. Callie grunted. The red light illuminated the wrapper from the same kind of nutrient bars the resistance ate, which were in turn stolen from Exalted supply depots.

"Someone stopped here for lunch. They might still be around. Step carefully."

"I fly." Kaustikos zipped around the tubes and out of sight.

Callie moved through the grove of crystal pillars until she found another doorway. "All clear," Kaustikos signaled, and she passed through cautiously. It would help to have a scout she actually trusted.

The next room was low-ceilinged and illuminated with lights she could barely see they were so far on the red end of the spectrum. There was dust on the floor, lots of it, scuffed and mussed in a trail that curved off clearly to the left. Callie followed the marks and found Kaustikos floating in front of a bright steel plate. The scuff marks on the floor ended at the barrier. Callie considered. "That plate isn't original. Looks like somebody welded it on from the other side, doesn't it?

We'll get Shall in here with a torch–"

"I think I can manage." Kaustikos extruded a manipulator arm, and the end flared with brightness. He began to cut through the plate.

"Kaustikos, stand down. I'm going to get Shall so we have decent firepower when we go in there."

"I'm comfortable with my ability to handle the situation. What do we expect to find, anyway? Sick Axiom frozen in stasis, and a few Exalted desperately trying to escape?" He kept cutting.

Callie had no intention of going into a potentially deadly situation with Kaustikos alone at her side. "You're supposed to obey me, Kaustikos. Or do I need to press the button that makes you go boom?"

The torch turned off, and Kaustikos withdrew the manipulator into his body. "Fine. At least let me go fetch them, since I'm faster than you?"

"Aren't you eager."

"The sooner we deal with Shaper, the sooner we can leave this disgusting system, and I'm eager to return home, that's all."

"Fine. Hustle."

Kaustikos flew away. Callie glanced at her bracelet. Her teleporter was recharged.

She was terrible at being patient, but who needed patience when you could be invisible? She could just pop over to the other side of the barrier in stealth and see what they were dealing with. She could always wait until Shall arrived to actually deal with it.

She found more glass tubes on the other side of the barrier... and inside each tube, a floating body.

Callie had never seen one of the Axiom in the flesh before. Those she'd encountered in the Dream were occupying digital avatars that bore no relation to real anatomy, and she hadn't risked opening the pods where their actual bodies slept – they'd all had intrusion countermeasures anyway – so she'd just destroyed them, sight unseen.

Now she knew what the Axiom looked like. It would have been amusing if they'd been small, pink, big-eyed, and fuzzy, but they were apex predators, and they looked like it.

The Axiom were all nearly three meters tall, with purplish-black skin that looked hard and bark-like. They had long, muscular legs with too many joints, and their feet were multi-jointed, too, tipped with three toes sporting talons, plus a claw on the heel. They didn't have external genitalia, which was a relief. They had tails, thick and doubtless prehensile, with a three-taloned claw on the end. Their torsos were long and lean, and they had two arms on each side (she was reminded uneasily of Drake and Janice's new arms), each with two elbows and a wrist. They had seven fingers on each hand, with surplus knuckles.

Their necks were thick and their heads almost saurian, covered as they were with bony plates and ridges. Their mouths wrapped halfway around their heads and were crowded with teeth made for shredding meat. They had four eyes, all closed in the sleep of stasis – two eyes in the front, like a human, and one on each side, where the ears would have been on a human. They were monstrous.

She was glad they weren't beautiful. It would have been terrible, somehow, if they'd looked like beings of radiance and grace and light.

They were sick, too. She could tell. There were gray patches on their skin, blotting their torsos and legs and faces, ragged and leprous. There were eight Axiom here, silent, still, and frozen in time

Callie would have destroyed them all right then with the weapons in her suit, except the other twenty tubes were full of naked human beings.

CHAPTER 29

"Callie?" Shall said. "Where are you?"

"I teleported to the other side of the barrier."

"Of course you did. Shall we barge in?"

"Barge carefully. There are human captives here."

Callie checked the rest of the room and found no sign of Shaper or any other Exalted, though she did find an operational terminal in a corner. She suspected it contained the controls for the stasis fields.

Had Shaper known they were coming? Or, if not known, had he worried and made contingency plans? She looked at the twenty floating humans. Someone had left a trail in dust and food wrappers, leading right here. An incredibly obvious, impossible-to-miss trail.

Hmm.

The steel plate fell inward with a crash, and Shall's war drone squeezed through the opening, followed by Ashok, Lantern, and Kaustikos. "No sign of Shaper?" Shall said.

Callie shook her head, still thinking.

Ashok wandered among the pillars. "So… this is what's left of the Cleansing Corps? Pretty pitiful remnant of the scourge of the galaxy." He crouched by the terminal – it was set at Liar height – and beckoned to Lantern. "Hey, come tell me if I'm reading this right."

Lantern joined him. "This is a stasis unit. We can release these people, get them to safety, and then… deal with the Axiom."

"Why are these people even here, though?" Callie said.

"Human shields?" Shall said. "The Exalted know we won't blow up facilities with human prisoners on board."

Callie shook her head. "We didn't know there were people here, so it's no kind of deterrent."

"Organ donors on ice?" Ashok said. "Keeping them handy for surgery?"

"I don't…" Callie looked at the leprous patches on the Axiom, and something in her mind clicked. "Ashok, come with me back to the hangar. I think we were supposed to find these humans. I think it's a trap."

"What, are they full of explosives, like me?" Kaustikos said.

"Worse, if I'm right," Callie said. "Keep guard over this area, Shall, and Kaustikos. You should be safe, too, I think, Lantern, but keep your environment suit on anyway." Callie retreated through the hole, followed by Ashok, and they double-timed back to the hangar.

"What's the worry, cap?" Ashok said.

"Those people might be infected with something,"

Callie said. "Shaper led us right to them. I think we're supposed to find those Axiom, kill them, release the humans, and congratulate ourselves on a job well done. Then we'd take the humans back to Vanaheim, and only find out later Shaper left us with a parting gift in the form of an engineered plague meant kill us all." She paused. "Or maybe I'm being paranoid, and everything is exactly what it seems. But when is that ever the case?"

"Whoa. How do we test for an unknown plague? Elena's doing well in her studies, but she's still only about halfway to being an actual medical doctor."

"Shaper could have whipped up a nearly undetectable pathogen, too," Callie said. "I'm not confident in our ability to figure this out ourselves. When in doubt, outsource. Once we're in range of the *White Raven*, we'll call for help."

The white Liars had left contact information with Drake and Janice, and Janice sent out the call. While they waited for a reply, Ashok released all his drones, and Kaustikos and Shall ranged over the station, looking for Shaper. They brought the *White Raven* into the hangar in hopes that its superior sensors might find more from the inside, but it was no good. Searching for life signs was useless, because the grotesque biological portions of the station were alive, generating heat and pulsing with fluids.

Callie and her crew were trying to search a vessel the size of a small city, and, even machine-assisted, it was a slow job. Callie stalked through passageways and ancient empty chambers, looking for some sign of Shaper... and the rest of the Axiom. If she was right, those eight floating in tubes were sacrificial victims, meant to satisfy her and get her to stop looking for the remainder of the Cleansing Corps.

Maybe Shaper was already long gone with the rest of his patients, through a wormhole gate to an unknown destination to regroup and continue his dark work, but that line of thinking didn't do her any good, so she discarded it for now.

"We've got company," Shall called, and Callie teleported back to the hangar bay.

The hospital ship floated just outside. Callie had never seen it, and the others had never gotten a good look at it in its entirety. The ship was beautiful, a smooth, flat-bottomed dome of shiny black, nearly a quarter the size of the Axiom station all by itself. It could have swallowed up the Cleaning Fire and had room to gobble up the *White Raven* and the Blaze for dessert.

The Liar who called himself Metal arrived in a small boarding vessel, carrying a black bag that looked very much like the one their old ship's doctor Stephen had used. "We are here to help," he said, fluttering pseudopods at Callie. "You are the captain who took in our Drake and Janice and gave them meaningful work. We approve you."

"It's nice to meet you." She led the white Liar through the gangrenous corridors to the stasis chamber. Metal gazed at the beings floating in the cylinders for a long time. "These are Axiom. In the flesh. Such have not been seen by many who now live. These ones are very sick."

"And close to death, I hope." Callie stood on the other side of the doorway they'd blasted open. Even with the humans in stasis, and even in her environment suit, she didn't want to get any closer until she knew those people weren't bearing plagues. "I'm told you don't fight, you only heal... but maybe you could see your way clear to euthanize these Axiom?"

"We only do such things at the request of the sick, and even then, with great reluctance. Did you know that no Axiom ever committed suicide? Or so the records say. Even those grievously injured, ones who lost all limbs, even tails, would fight and fight and fight to live. No beings in the galaxy fought so hard to survive. Or perhaps when the Axiom found others with the same will to survive they killed them. That could also be. No, we will not euthanize. They are frozen and no harm now. We will try to help your humans though. Do not attempt to penetrate the quarantine field."

"What field – Oh." The white Liar put down his bag, and when it touched the floor, a dome of sparkling blue light appeared, covering the entire room, with Callie just on the outside. Metal approached the terminal, and then one of the glass pillars stopped glowing and the human boy inside it slumped. The Liar slid open a panel on the tube – Callie hadn't even realized there was a panel there, it was so seamless – and removed the boy with infinite tenderness. Metal gently placed the boy on the deck, and then scanned him with one of his silvery augments, this one mounted at the end of a tentacle. Metal returned to the terminal, then placed the human back in the tube and re-engaged the stasis, making the boy float again.

The white Liar turned off the quarantine field. "Your fears were true and right. These ones are infected, but it is a crude plague, made in haste. It resembles an airborne necrotizing pathogen we have seen before. We can synthesize a cure."

"Necrotizing. So if we'd brought these people down to Vanaheim…"

"The humans would have rotted from the inside to the out. Crude, yes, but very most virulent. You and the other human should return to your ship, for safety. Perhaps your friend the war machine could assist us with moving these patients to the place of rest and healing on our ship?"

Callie and Ashok returned to the stasis room once all

the humans had been taken away and the air cleansed. "Eight Axiom to execute," Ashok said. "Four each?"

"I don't want to give them that much individual attention," she said.

"Firebombs it is." Ashok set to work attaching explosives to the occupied tubes. "Seems kind of cold, cap, killing them when they're sick and unconscious."

"This is the Cleansing Corps. They burned down whole planets before the inhabitants even knew what was happening."

"You make a good point. Timer or remote detonator?"

"Remote. I'll push the button if it makes you feel better."

"I appreciate that, captain."

Once the work was done, and each inhabited tube sported a shaped charge, Callie went to the terminal and deactivated the stasis. According to the white Liars, that field was so powerful that not even an explosion would harm the Axiom if they remained in stasis – there was no passage of time inside that field, and no change, destructive or otherwise, could happen there.

So they weren't killing the Axiom in their sleep after all.

Callie rushed through the pillars as the Axiom began to stir. One howled, a sound with subsonic vibrations that made her bowels clench. Another started to pound at the inside of the tube, trying to get it open. Ashok had already withdrawn, and when Callie hit the doorway, she paused to look back.

She briefly met the open eyes of the Axiom in the nearest tube. The two eyes in front lacked pupils and irises, and shone a single, electric color: blue.

The Axiom opened its mouth wide to reveal rows of serrated teeth. Callie couldn't tell if it was a snarl, a smile, or a yawn.

Callie ran into the next room, ducked around to get her back to the wall, and triggered the remote. The explosions were a series of whump-whump-whumps, and bits of glass and gore spattered through the opening. Callie forced herself to walk back to the entryway and look inside. The tubes beyond were all shattered, and in the foul matter scattered on the floor, she saw no piece bigger than a clenched fist.

"Good enough," she said, and returned to the hangar.

"We've checked every corridor, every hatch, every access duct," Shall said. "We found lots of evidence of past habitation, but nobody's here now. Shaper is gone. We missed him. He left that poisoned bait for us and then took off."

"Why was there still a scourge-ship on board then?" Callie kicked the side of the ship in question and glared at the war drone. "Why is there no evidence of a wormhole opening here recently?"

"They must have had more than one ship. As for wormholes, those traces fade quickly. Or maybe they didn't open a bridge at all, but just left under conventional power before we even got here. We lost him, Callie."

"I hate losing."

"It's mostly a win," Shall said. "We liberated the Vanir system! Sure, the Jovian Imperative will probably handle the cleanup, but, basically, we did it. Even more basically, you did it. Take a minute and bask in your victory."

"We came here to kill the Cleansing Corps, and we failed." She sighed. "Maybe Shaper will hole up on one of the other stations marked on Lantern's map. All right. Let's pack up and go." She looked around. "Where the hell is Kaustikos?"

"Wandered off," Shall said. "I'll track him down."

Back on the ship, Elena tried to comfort her, along the same lines that Shall had – look at all the people they'd saved! Lantern did, too: "Shaper was not able to cure those Axiom, and they are terminally ill, so either they will remain in stasis, or die."

Callie didn't feel any better. She'd been too slow. Also, she'd personally taken out two of the three heads of the Exalted, and the fact that the third had eluded her was an itch in her mind, like an unresolved chord.

Elena came over and put her arm around Callie, snuggling close. She was a comfort, always, but it didn't solve the underlying issue, did it? Callie was lucky to have love. She wanted to have a life where that love could thrive without quite so many existential threats.

They gazed out the observation bay windows as the *White Raven* began to depart the station. The thirteenth station seemed uglier every time Callie looked at it, with those grotesque fleshy growths all over the structure, spanning across its modules and nodes –

"Huh," Elena said. She moved away from Callie, pressed her hands to the glass, and stared. "That's… huh."

"What?" Callie said.

"The station. I was trying to figure out why they bothered to cover it with that stuff. Why make it biomechanical at all?"

"Aliens sometimes do things that are really alien," Callie said.

"Sure, but look… parts of the station are just thinly covered in strange flesh, right? Other parts are all bulbous. Some branches of the station are connected by vast swaths of tissue. Something like a tenth of the station's mass is probably engineered flesh. I know we searched the whole station – but did we really search the whole station?"

Callie looked at Elena for a moment. "Remind me to kiss you later."

"Since when do you need reminders?"

Callie shouted into her comms. "Janice, scan the station again, but this time, focus on the biological parts!"

"It's not like we skipped those before," Janice said. "They're just unidentified organics. Parts of them are warm. It's like a space station covered in tumors and growths."

"Scan the growths for density," Elena chimed in. "Look for hollow places inside."

"Whatever you say, XO. The density of the growths isn't uniform at all, you're right. There are some really big air pockets here or bubbles or whatever you want to call them inside, here." The windows changed into screens and zoomed in on a portion of the station that looked like pebbled starfish skin.

Callie cracked her knuckles. "Shall, get your war drone ready. We're going to do some exploratory surgery."

"Eww," Shall said.

CHAPTER 30

Callie suited up, strapped herself onto Shall's war drone, and they launched toward the station, aiming for a house-sized growth on one edge. Shall's magnetic clamps were useless here, and he had to clamp onto the tumor with claws, digging into the meat of the station.

Up close, the surface was even more horrific – there were cilia growing out of the dark green flesh, and the bumps were irregular and shiny with some sort of oil. "This thing looks like if a pickle had warts," Ashok said in her comm. Callie's suit cam and Shall's sensors were streaming data back to the ship, and she imagined the crew gathered like sports fans watching a big game.

"Cut me a door," Callie said.

Shall extended a manipulator that Ashok had hurriedly fitted with wickedly sharp blades, and it spun, dipping into the meat of the station. Gouts of greenish slime poured out, the fluid boiling and then freezing when it hit vacuum, fouling and binding Shall's blade. That was fine – they'd just needed to get past the thick outer layer, which scans indicated was as solid as a spaceship hull. Shall packed the hole with explosives, then flew them to a safe distance.

The silent detonation flashed light and flung meat. They returned to the now much bigger wound and squeezed inside. The living, organic mass of the interior rubbed against Callie's suit, and, even with that fabric between her, the sensation made her gag. The interior of the tumor was dark, and doubtless damp and foul-smelling, but at least she was spared the latter aspects of the experience. She still felt like they were crawling around in the rotting corpse of a whale, though.

"We've got some kind of tough membrane here, Callie." Shall poked the translucent wall of tissue with a pointed arm. The membrane was pale green and stretched like a rubber sheet, and there was light on the other side.

"Dig in really good, then pierce it."

Shall set his spiked feet in the flesh around them, then tore through the membrane. As Callie had expected, a brutal wind buffeted them as the atmosphere inside exploded out into the vacuum behind them. When the decompression-storm abated, Shall clawed his way inside the first of the hollows.

They were in a round, fibrous chamber, the walls striated like muscle and glowing with green bioluminescence. There were more membrane-covered passages leading off in various directions. The biological equivalent of airlocks? How did they open? "Keep heading toward the big chamber Janice detected," Callie said.

"The membrane we came through… it just healed."

Callie looked behind her and saw the torn flesh had somehow knit itself together. She grunted. "It's a self-healing space station. That would seem wonderful if the whole thing wasn't so disgusting."

"The air pressure in here is equalizing, too. See those glistening slits on the ceiling?"

She looked up, at long, narrow openings like gills above her, the edges fluttering as air passed through them. "I did not need to see that. Nor do I ever need to hear the phrase 'glistening slits' ever again."

Shall tore another membrane open and bulled down the narrow corridor, scraping the sides of the fleshy tube with his bulk, then shredded through a further membrane. The passageway wound around and down and deeper, doubling back on itself, and Callie imagined this as a journey through coils of intestines. The chamber they were looking for was kilometers deep inside this mass, but Shall moved fast. "It's just ahead," Callie. The largest membrane yet, big as a hangar door, bulged before them.

"Let's get in there."

Shall sliced his way through and charged in, and Callie said, "Yes." She loved being right.

This air pocket was as big as a hangar bay, and there

were glass tubes here, too – shorter portable ones, only a few meters long, just big enough to hold their contents. It was hard to count the cylinders because they were so jumbled up, some standing upright, others leaning together, still others stacked up on their sides like lengths of pipe, but she estimated at least two hundred. Each tube held the body of a diseased Axiom, frozen in stasis. The Cleansing Corps, in all its foulness.

"Shaper!" Callie broadcast through her suit's external speakers. "Come out and face me!"

"If it isn't Captain Machedo. The worst diplomat in the galaxy."

The voice came through her comms. She muted that channel and said, "Janice, trace the source of that signal." She switched back. "Shaper of Destiny. How's that destiny working out for you?"

"I have faith in my mission. I am pleased you're here."

"I doubt that. There are too many Axiom piled up here to fit on a scourge-ship. What was the plan, exactly? Hide in this meat-sack and hope I'd go away? Do you have a bigger transport ship coming to meet you?"

"A bigger ship? I have the biggest ship in this system, ready to depart. Admittedly, I was worried about using it, because I feared you would fire on my vessel… but now that you're here, I'm safe. Your allies are unlikely to kill you, the hero of the revolution, just to get to me."

The station lurched, and a few of the Axiom cylinders fell over, clanking together. "What was that?" Callie said.

A great rumble rose up through the floor and the walls, and the whole chamber jerked hard – if Callie hadn't been strapped down, she would have gone tumbling.

"Uh, Callie?" Janice said. "The big ugly tumor you're inside just detached from the station somehow, tore itself free, unfurled some very starfish-looking arms and... Callie, that's not a tumor. It's a ship. It's a ship made out of meat!"

"Life is truly remarkable, isn't it?" Shaper said. "My ship can heal her own damage, feeds on radiation from distant supernovae, produces food from her body sufficient to provision a crew far larger than she needs... she even has a rudimentary sense of self-preservation."

Before Callie could snap out a scathing reply, Shall interrupted her.

"Callie. I'm stuck." Shall tried to move his legs, but they just sank deeper into the organic floor. "The floor turned to slime and I sank, and then it thickened again, and now... I've got goo in my joints. I'm sinking, Callie."

"If this ship is alive, we can hurt it," Callie said. "Fight back."

Shall began firing his weapons at the walls and the

floor. Plenty of his shots struck the Axiom in their stasis tubes, but the projectiles and energy beams didn't do any damage – the stasis fields were so powerful they prevented all harm.

"My ship doesn't feel pain, Captain Machedo. That would be cruel. She senses and repairs damage, but there's no attendant suffering. Firing energy weapons at her is the equivalent of hand-feeding her, anyway. My masters dabbled with creating biological vehicles, but I've surpassed them with my ship. I call her the Scourging of the Skies."

Callie had seen Axiom biological vehicles. She'd even ridden inside one – a train-car-sized insect they'd controlled by manipulating its neural tissue with flashes of light. "So you made a space-faring starfish, huh? How does it propel itself? Some kind of shit-based excrement engine?" She didn't care, but she could tell Shaper liked talking, and talking meant time.

"Oh, various ways. She has membranes that act as solar sails. She can, indeed, expel gas from assorted orifices to aid in maneuvering. There's a more conventional engine, too, grafted into her flesh. The internal atmosphere is created by chemical processes, and there are chambers full of edible plants and flesh, even a pool where I can take my leisure. My ship is a self-sustaining system, a true marvel of biological engineering. I may have failed to cure my masters, at least so far, but I did learn a lot of useful things in my researches."

"I don't think any of this is very interesting, actually," Callie said. "I'm getting bored. I think I'll disable the stasis fields and start ripping the heads off your sick Axiom now."

"Please. The controls for the stasis field are up here with me. You could try to reach my command center, but I don't think you'd make it far. This ship has an immune system, and you and your drone are foreign pathogens to be destroyed. That's why the ship is absorbing your machine. You're next. I only need you alive long enough to act as a hostage to secure my freedom."

"Callie, that meat-ship is opening a wormhole!" Janice shouted. "You have to get out of there!"

"Plan B, Shall," she said. "I'm so sorry."

"I regret that I have but one... wait, five... no, I forgot about the Sunspot. I regret that I have but six lives to give for my galaxy."

While Shall was talking, Callie unstrapped herself from his back and leapt to a heap of Axiom cylinders. They shifted under her feet, but she kept her balance. She pointed herself toward the wall behind her, set her teleporter for max distance, and jumped.

She didn't emerge into space. They'd been too deep inside the ship, too far from the carapace, and she teleported somewhere into its flesh instead. Callie was pinned completely inside a tumor, her arms and legs immobilized by meat, her helmet's view full of pulsing green slime. The flesh was malleable enough that teleporting into it hadn't crushed her, the way appearing inside a concrete wall would have, but she was still stuck like a bug in molasses. She could maybe wiggle enough to trigger her teleporter again... but it needed almost four hours to recharge, and she didn't have anywhere near that long left to live.

What an irritating way to die. At least she had the satisfaction of knowing Shaper would die, too. It was amazing how hard she could hate someone that she'd never even seen in person. And she'd made the galaxy a little safer for Elena – no, don't think about Elena, that hurt too much, think of anything else, it shouldn't be much longer now.

Then the meat around her exploded, and Callie went tumbling wildly into the open. She must have been stuck near the outer layer of the bio-ship, and Shall's explosion had flung the meat that encased her out into space –

But she wasn't in space. There were no stars here, just the dark walls of a tunnel, lit intermittently by bars of light. She was inside the wormhole bridge, floating, watching the starfish ship come apart, great gobbets of meat flying in all directions and smashing into the walls of the tunnel. What would happen to her if the wormhole closed with her inside? It had happened, a few times, due to malfunction or mistake, and the ships in transit were just lost, never seen again. Would the tunnel collapse, and take her with it, or would she just float in empty tunnels until she died of thirst?

A piece of the starfish ship the size of an elephant came flying at her, but it was going in the right direction...

When the fleshy jetsam came near, Callie grabbed onto a trailing length of fibrous meat with both hands and kept holding on even when the speed of its motion jerked her arms so hard she cried out in pain.

The meat was on an explosive trajectory toward the wormhole's opening, and Callie could actually see the *White Raven* through the irregular portal, and the station, with a big ragged wound in its side where the starfish ship had ripped itself free.

The journey through the wormhole only lasted twenty-one seconds. Her sense of time was scrambled, and she didn't know how long ago the portal had opened or the Scourging of the Skies had entered, but she was terrified the tunnel would close with her inside it –

The flying meat saved her. The propulsion in her suit wouldn't have been enough to get her out before the wormhole closed, but hitching a ride on that piece of starship flesh gave her the velocity she needed to get clear. As soon as she returned to normal space, she released the meat, spun around, and watched the starfish ship burn inside the tunnel for an instant before the bridge closed.

"Callie, are you all right?" Elena shouted

"I am here and unharmed, XO," she said. "We had to go with Plan B."

"I liked that war drone," Shall said.

"I still like it." Callie laughed, hiccuped, and sobbed a little, all at once. "That drone saved my life and killed Shaper. Killed the Cleaning Corp, too, assuming that blast took out the stasis module."

"The self-destruct on those drones are designed to bust open reinforced bunkers and flatten hardened command centers," Ashok said. "They're full of boom and shrapnel and the shrapnel is loaded with secondary explosives, so it's a bomb stuffed with a thousand other bombs. You set that kind of weapon off inside what's basically a giant sea creature? You turned that ship into bouillabaisse, cap, along with everything inside it."

"Come pick me up," Callie said. "I need to get this goo hosed off my suit."

"What do we do about the station?" Elena asked. She was in the galley with Callie and the rest of the crew. "The Jovian Imperative is coming, and they'll find this station eventually – then they'll have access to the stasis device, whatever horrible innovations they can extract from the biological tissue, and who knows what other technology."

Callie nodded. "We have to work with the

Imperative. It's inevitable, at this point. We need them. We have the list of Axiom sites we got from the Benefactor, but if we keep on this way, diving headfirst into the unknown, we'll eventually hit our heads on a rock. The failsafe plan was always to let my ex-husband know about the Axiom in the event of our deaths, so he could use the resources of his corporation and the Imperative to continue the fight. I now concede there are advantages to getting them on board before we die."

"Like maybe we could even forego dying entirely?" Ashok said.

"That's one," Callie agreed.

"Allowing the Jovian Imperative access to Axiom technology could be very dangerous," Lantern said. "The truth-tellers perform evil acts, but their ostensible mission was sound – if humans obtain wormhole technology, there's nothing to stop them from going places they shouldn't, where they risk waking the Axiom, or triggering automatic systems that could threaten all life. Nor is that the only concern. With Axiom technology, they could…" She trailed off.

"Become like the Axiom?" Callie said. "Try to dominate the galaxy with their tech? Believe me, the thought of mind-control technology, or the nano-swarm from the Dream, or the kind of plagues the Exalted engineers invented, of any of that getting into the hands of some politician, terrifies me. But… the Axiom technology is out there, floating around, and somebody will pick it up eventually. It's better if we're involved, and can guide the ones who pick it up. At least we understand the magnitude of the Axiom threat.

"Security through obscurity can only take us so far. Keeping the Axiom a secret was the goal of the truth-tellers, and we ruined that when we found the bridge generator in the first place. Pandora's box is open. We've been trying to hold the lid shut, but that couldn't last forever. At least this way, if we see something people shouldn't pick up, maybe we can break it real good first."

"Your arrogance is astounding," Kaustikos said. "Who are you to serve as the ultimate arbiter regarding what technology humans are qualified to possess?"

"I'm Captain Kalea Machedo," Callie said. "Better me than anyone else I can think of."

"She's not all that ultimate, anyway," Shall said. "If she makes bad decisions, we'll shout at her until she stops."

"That's right," Elena said.

Callie smiled. "The question before us right now is, what should we do about the thirteenth station? If no one objects... I say we kill it with fire."

No one objected. The Blaze lived up to its name.

CHAPTER 31

Callie refused to leave the *White Raven* because she'd already been taken prisoner a couple of times on this trip, and she'd had quite enough of that. Her ex-husband Michael and a sour-faced general from the Jovian Imperative met with her and her crew in the galley. Callie kissed Michael on the cheek and shook the general's hand. "I didn't think you'd come through the wormhole personally," Callie said.

Michael chuckled. "When your AI got in touch with me and explained the situation – and provided proof for even the most outlandish of his claims – I called the board of directors, and they unanimously agreed that you were my problem, and I should be the one to deal with you."

Callie snorted. "We got divorced so I wouldn't be your problem anymore." She gestured to a pair of empty chairs.

Michael took a seat, and the general stiffly did the same. "Would you rather talk to me or to uncle Reynaud?" Michael said.

"A fair point. So. What can we do for you two?

Besides re-open the gate and save the Vanir system, I mean, since we did that already."

"The general has a proposal."

She leaned forward, clasping her hands, and cleared her throat. "Captain Machedo. In recognition of your role in liberating the Vanir system, we'd like to offer you and your crew citizenship in the Jovian Imperative, with all attendant rights and privileges."

Callie was shaking her head before the general even finished. "That's nice, but I decline. Anyone else want to join the Imperative?" The rest of her crew indicated that they did not.

"I'm not even allowed to be a citizen, because the Imperative is racist against AI," Shall said.

The general got even stiffer, which was remarkable, and Callie thought, diplomacy. "We do appreciate the gesture, and the rights and privileges are great, but we're not big fans of all the responsibilities. As citizens, we'd be subject to your laws and regulations and authority, and I think it's important, if we're going to work together against the Axiom, that my crew remain as independent operators and partners rather than subordinates. We'd absolutely accept a cash prize, though."

"About that," Michael said. "We're obviously still in the early stages of reorganization here, but the rebel generals are emerging as the obvious local political leaders, and they've put forth a proposal to thank you for their liberation by offering your crew a share of their future prosperity. They want to give you half a percent of the system's profits, in perpetuity."

Callie stared at him. She hadn't expected anything like this. "Half a percent. So... one out of every two hundred lix in profit... would go to... us?"

"That is how the math works out, yes," Michael said. "I'd expect modest payouts for the first year or two, as they build infrastructure, and rather larger dividends after that. This is a system with a wealth of resources." He paused. "I should define my terms. By 'modest' I mean 'the gross domestic product of a small country' rather than 'the gross domestic product of a large country.' With this income stream, you and your crew will have the freedom to pursue whatever projects you desire. No more running errands for corporations like mine."

"I thought I'd be lucky to get a statue," Callie said.

"Being rich won't be much good to you when we're crushed like insects by alien monsters," the general said. "You say you have a map of locations for these Axiom facilities? And of the bases of the so-called truth-tellers who work to cover up the presence of the Axiom?"

Callie nodded. "We'd like to coordinate with the Jovian Imperative to destroy those facilities. We have conditions, though. Any Axiom we find, we kill – no taking them prisoner, no keeping live specimens for study. The Axiom are the enemies of all intelligent life, as we've established with the records provided."

"The xenobiologists won't like it, but personally, I

agree, and I think I can sell that. The Axiom are too dangerous to take prisoner. Anything else?"

"If we find new technology, the Machedo Corporation gets fifty percent ownership. That doesn't just mean we get half the money you make from exploiting that tech – it means we get an equal say in how, or if, that technology is exploited at all."

"Outrageous," the general said.

Callie shrugged. "You're free to wander the galaxy at random and hope you stumble across their facilities. We wish you luck. Making much progress unlocking those bridge generators, by the way?"

Michael gave a thin smile. "Those on the two scourge-ships you left us, one of them partly destroyed, you mean?"

Callie shrugged. "The Cleansing Fire got rid of the ships it could find. I'm not going to apologize for destroying the enemy fleet. It seemed like a reasonable step to take in a war." Callie was only sorry that Shall had missed two of them – the surviving ships had been guarding another Exalted facility. The Imperative got to them first and managed to capture one fully intact.

"The bridge generators work wonderfully," Michael sighed. "Assuming, that is, you want to travel from this system to a seemingly arbitrary point some light years away – an area of space with absolutely no interesting development prospects at all. We've been unable to make the generators open portals to anywhere else, though our engineers are working on the problem."

"So it seems like I've got the only working bridge generator in human hands. I bet I'll be able to reach the targets on my hit list faster than you can, general. I'd like the help, but I can live without it."

The general smiled, an expression as chilly as the surface of an icy planetesimal. "What's to prevent me from seizing your ship, and all of you, as enemy combatants right now?"

Callie raised an eyebrow. "A lot of things, actually. Mainly the nine hundred thousand inhabitants of the Vanir system I just rescued from a century of enslavement. I think they'd object. We're recording this conversation and beaming the data to several remote locations, and, if our talk doesn't go well, we'll transmit the footage system-wide. The Cleansing Fire has an amazing broadcast capability. They use it to demand unconditional surrender loud enough for whole planets to hear, as I understand it."

The general closed her eyes, seemed to count silently to ten, then opened them again. "You are exactly the way Michael described you," she said. "I have to take your proposals back to the ministers, and they're going to stomp and scream and howl, but in the end, they'll take half a loaf over none." She nodded toward Michael. "It's a good thing you have an executive at one of our most powerful stakeholders looking out for you, though, or you'd be in serious danger of assassination, captain. Even so, you might want to make sure your security is well and truly locked down."

"I knew I married you for a reason," Callie said.

"And we finally found out what it was," he said. "Are you going back to Glauketas while you wait for the Imperative to grit its teeth and agree to your terms?"

"We could all use a little down time after all this," Callie said.

"Before you head home, we're going to need our gunships back," the general said. "And we'll have to remove your AI from the systems as well. The Imperative doesn't allow ships to operate with fully autonomous machine intelligences in charge. Which, Shall, is it? I want you to know, that's a policy I personally disagree with. There are more traditional members of the military who think AI can't possibly have the best interests of humanity as a priority, but based on your own record fighting against this Axiom threat, I'd say you make powerful counterexamples. I would have argued to give you citizenship, if you'd wanted."

"Stop, general, or I'll start to like you," Callie said.

The *White Raven* passed through the now-open bridgehead to Jovian Imperative space – they could have used their own generator, but there was a certain ceremonial aspect to using the Vanir system's port authority, and all the fireworks the settlers lit for them were nice.

They left Jupiter behind and began the trek back home to Glauketas. Elena and Callie nestled in bed, and Elena said, "I noticed you didn't mention the Benefactor at that meeting. I noticed Kaustikos stayed in the cargo bay, too. I also noticed you sort of implied that Lantern found the map to the Axiom facilities by hacking into a truth-teller database."

"That is how she found the map. I just left out the part about where she got the access code."

"Why tell the Imperative about the Axiom, but not about the Benefactor?"

"Partly because Kaustikos told me the Benefactor prefers to remain secret, and I can go along with that. He paid us enough. And partly because... I have my own suspicions I need to work out about the Benefactor first."

"Want to share them?"

"They're kind of unformed right now," Callie said. "And if I'm wrong they'll sound really stupid. I hate sounding stupid in front of anyone, but I especially hate sounding stupid in front of people I love, so let me poke at the idea a little more first?"

"Is that the only thing you want to poke at?" Elena asked.

Callie laughed. "I'm usually the crude and suggestive one."

"You must be rubbing off on me."

"I'd sure like to be–"

"Yes, yes," Elena said. "Just come here and kiss me."

"I missed this old lumpy space potato." Ashok spun around in the corridor outside the airlock on Glauketas. "Shall! Did you miss us?"

"I've just merged my consciousness with the version of me on the *White Raven*," the voice of the station said over the PA. "So... not really? Callie, was it really necessary to explode a version of me out there?"

"That was plan B," Callie said. "Of course it was necessary. You never use Plan B if it's optional."

The whole crew was on the station, even Drake and Janice – with their new assistive technologies and modifications from the white Liars, they could finally make use of their quarters here without pain.

Callie turned to face the crew, and Kaustikos. "You all did good in the Vanir system – even you, probe. We saved a lot of lives and changed the face of the galaxy for the better, which isn't bad for a week's work. You're all at liberty. Do what you will."

"I should get back home," Lantern said. "My subordinates have already sent me a dozen priority messages about matters of pressing importance, like not being able to find replacement circuit boards for the pool heaters and running low on their favorite flavor of nutrient slurry." She fluttered her pseudopods in a formal farewell, and Callie did the best to respond with her pitiful human arms. "Let me know when the Imperative is ready to start raiding Axiom stations. Don't destroy the last remnant of the ancient enemy of my people without me."

"I wouldn't dream of it," Callie said.

"We're going to descend into the Hypnos for a while," Drake said. "The healers tweaked our neurology a little, and they think Janice and I can use virtual reality now – and even go into separate virtual environments, albeit with some emotional bleed-through. We just have to avoid one of us doing an erotica sim while the other one does a horror sim, basically."

"Otherwise we're going to start finding all sorts of terrifying things sexy," Janice said. "I could do without all that nonsense. I'm looking forward to a little alone time."

"There's no one I'd rather be with, if I have to be with someone," Drake said. "But it is exciting to not have to be with anyone for a little while."

"Likewise," Janice said.

"How about you, Ashok?" Callie said. "Finally going to visit your family on the moon?"

Ashok chuckled. "They'll just want to know why I'm not married yet. 'I'm married to the stars,' I always say, but that does not satisfy my nani. I think I'll stay here and keep working on that terror-drone fragment we recovered from the Dream. Shall needs a new war drone, after all, and that could be the basis for a really wicked one."

"How about you, Elena?" Callie said. "Want to run away with me to the pleasure domes of the Ennead system?"

"We should really do that sometime," Elena said wistfully. "I'm behind on my studies, though, and I'm so close to certification. I've got a hot date with an educational sim."

"All work and no play–" Callie said

"Makes me an MD as well as a PhD," Elena finished.

"Aren't you curious about my plans?" Kaustikos said.

"I was saving you for last," Callie said. "Going to report back to your boss, I assume?"

"He will be pleased to know how well things went. If you'd just be kind enough to take this bomb out of me…"

"Soon. We need to have a private conversation first."

"Can you remove the explosives before that?"

"That bomb stays in until you're off my station. We'll deactivate it with a drone before you go on your way."

"After all I did, for all of you, you still don't trust me?" Kaustikos spoke in tones of deep grievance. "What does it take?"

"Whatever it takes, you haven't managed it yet," Callie said. "Go entertain yourself for an hour while

I get showered, then we'll sit down and have an exit interview, okay?"

"You liberate a million prisoners, but keep me enslaved," Kaustikos grumbled, and floated away.

"That's it!" Callie clapped her hands. "Everybody get some rest, or at least do work that's more enjoyable than fighting alien monsters. I'll see some of you at dinner probably. It's Ashok's night to cook. No curried eggs, please. The air filtration system on this station isn't good enough for those."

Callie set off toward her quarters, sights set on a shower in her private bathroom. "Any messages while we were away, Shall?"

"One today, from a general in the Jovian Imperative who says discussions are ongoing but the outlook is good. It's nice to know what she was talking about now… We got a note from Stephen and Q on Taliesen, inviting us to visit for a harvest festival. I fear there might be folk music. We also got a message from Uzoma, who's finished up their remedial studies in information technology and is now being headhunted by various companies, including your ex-husband's, because of their off-the-charts scores – they're hoping you can give them some advice about how their talents might best be utilized in the fight against the Axiom."

"Tell Stephen we'll check our calendars but we're a little busy saving the damn galaxy without him,"

Callie said. "I'll call Uzoma back personally. Hmm, if Uzoma takes a job with Almajara, Michael can get them assigned to the division he's setting up to study Axiom technology. I'd feel a lot better having Uzoma on that team... or leading it. How many favors do I have left to call in from Michael, Shall?"

"You get one favor for every time he cheated on you, yes?" Shall said.

"As per the informal but honor-bound part of our divorce settlement, yes."

"You still have an ample supply of favors," Shall said.

"That sounds right. I'm going to get cleaned up. I was stuck inside an alien flesh mass not that long ago, and even though I was wearing a space suit at the time, I still feel grossly contaminated."

"At least you didn't have to actually explode," Shall said.

"It was a pretty near thing." Callie paused. "You were great. You were really brave. Even knowing your consciousness would live on elsewhere, I know it's hard to let an instance of yourself die."

"It's a sensation most people don't get to experience," Shall said. "I don't know how it feels, either, because those instances of me that died took the experience of death with them, and left no memories to integrate. I'm not so different from biological humans that way. I won't know how death feels until I feel it, and I'll never be able to report back."

"On that cheerful note, I'm going to enjoy some privacy and hot water now," Callie said.

Kaustikos floated before her, a silvery orb covered in lenses that somehow still managed to convey condescension and annoyance. Maybe it was the way he bobbed. "I want you to send a message to the Benefactor," Callie said. "I need you to arrange a meeting."

"The Benefactor does not take meetings."

"It can be a virtual meeting, just a couple of avatars in the Hypnos. I'd rather not be in the same room with him anyway."

"I doubt he'll be interested. The Benefactor is content to work at a distance, and through intermediaries. He provides ample value anyway – without his information, the Vanir system would not be free now, and the Cleansing Corps would still pose a threat."

"Maybe I just want to thank him personally, Kaustikos."

"I can convey your sentiments."

"Just tell him we need to meet." Callie forced herself to smile. "And when he says no, tell him I know he's one of the Axiom."

CHAPTER 32

Callie went into the Hypnos parlor and smiled at Drake and Janice, though they were too immersed to smile back. Since the installation of their new assistive technologies, they were able to use a conventional Hypnos pod – the only deviation from the norm was that they had two input cables snaking into the pod instead of one. The healers had done good work. Callie liked the white Liars. They'd talked about taking Elena on for the alien equivalent of an internship at some point, and teaching her some of their techniques. She was in xenobiological bliss at the idea.

Callie went to an empty pod and connected herself to the Hypnos. She didn't like virtual reality – being away from this reality always struck her as a dangerous proposition. What if this reality needed her? Callie had put plans in place to cover things during her absence, at least. For one, Ashok was supposed to keep an eye on Kaustikos, and he had the remote to trigger the explosives attached to the probe. For another –

Well, no use going over it all again. She'd done all she could.

Callie flicked her eyes over the controls and navigated to the private virtual chamber she'd set up for the meeting. In the Hypnos the only limits to the environment were those of imagination, and she had no doubt that Drake and Janice were soaring over crystal castles or exploring prismatic dreamscapes, but she loaded a setting based on one of the old interrogation rooms she'd occasionally used on Meditreme Station. Gray metal walls appeared, scuffed and scratched, with a black mirror across the back wall, also scratched. A metal table bolted to the dirty metal floor, with metal chairs on either side. The one on her side just looked uncomfortable; the one on the prisoner's side actually was. She sat down and waited.

The door opened, and the Benefactor entered. He had to stoop through the doorway because he stood nearly three meters tall. He could have looked like anything he wanted here, but Callie suspected that, like herself, he'd opted for an avatar that reflected his physical reality.

The Benefactor wore a shapeless brown cloak that made him seem rounded and slumped, but he shrugged that off, and let it puddle onto the floor, then stood silent and upright, gazing down at her.

He looked very much like the Axiom she'd seen in the stasis tubes, albeit with skin of a mellow gold-tinged green, like the outer rind of a melon. He was missing one of his front-facing eyes – it was an ugly mass of scar tissue –

and his other eye shone the bright blue of Cherenkov radiation. He looked at the chair, showed his teeth, and then perched on the edge without apparent discomfort. "Callie." His voice was smooth and pleasant. He could sound any way he wanted here, of course, but she was not surprised that he sounded just like Kaustikos.

"Benefactor," she said. "Or do you prefer Kaustikos?"

"Either, though the latter is a close approximation of the title I once held in the empire."

"One who burns?" Callie said.

He gave what might have been a modest bow from his seated position. "When did you realize Kaustikos and I were more like twins than colleagues?"

"Just a guess, until I heard you speak. Once I started to suspect you were Axiom, I wondered if you would really hire an AI based on a human. It seemed more likely you'd want to send a version of your own consciousness along on our mission to the Vanir system."

"Human intuition, hmm? Your people do interest me, I confess. You seem to do a great deal of thinking on a subconscious level, and then insights just... bubble up to the surface. I assume it's because your minds aren't capable of consciously dealing with all the inputs you receive. My people suffer no such limitations. We see and apprehend all things clearly."

"Are you all fucking nudists?" Callie said. "None of you were wearing clothes on the starfish ship either. I'm just glad you don't have nipples."

"Our children are carnivorous and capable of feeding themselves within a day of their birth," the Benefactor said. "We sometimes wear clothes, to indicate rank or function, or for decorations. I am comfortable this way, however. Would it bother you to be naked in front of an insect?"

"I'm an insect, huh? An insect you needed to sting your enemies to death. That was the idea, right? For a while we theorized that you must be an Elder among the truth-tellers, someone who'd decided that protecting the Axiom was a stupid plan. Then I started to think, who hates the Axiom more than I do? Who hates the Axiom more than the people they enslaved do? The answer was obvious." She laced her hands together on the table. "It's 'other Axiom.' You used me to destroy rival factions, didn't you?"

"Among other things."

"You're Axiom," Callie said. "Why use humans to do your dirty work? Why not use a planet-sized deathbot or something to fight your enemies?"

"Various reasons," the Benefactor said. "Shall I enumerate them?"

"Please do." Callie sat back. She wasn't surprised he was a talker. Kaustikos never shut up, and Kaustikos was the Benefactor, or at least a hasty sketched copy of his vast consciousness crammed into a drone.

"For one," the Benefactor said, "why risk myself or my resources when I have disposable things like you to risk instead? If you succeeded, wonderful. If you'd failed, I would have lost literally nothing of value. For another…

I don't have access to the engines of death my people so deftly created. I am, alas, a faction of one. My… call it 'crew' I suppose… was exterminated in the last days of our great war. My allies had a plan to build a time machine and return to the early days of the empire, where we could take over our whole civilization in its infancy. Word got out of our plans, and we'd barely begun construction on our massive, infinitely long cylinder–"

"Insert dick joke here," Callie said.

The Benefactor sighed. "We don't have… those. Ovipositors are fine for our purposes. The machine we wanted to build was a variant on what humans called a Tipler Cylinder, a theoretical object that can create a frame-dragging effect powerful enough to manipulate space-time and permit the reversal of time's arrow. Ask your station computer to give you a child's primer about the science behind it if you're curious.

"For the Axiom, such a device was more than theoretical because we have access to dimensions you can't comprehend. The other Axiom understandably saw our project as an existential threat, and some factions delayed their own hibernation long enough to form a coalition to destroy us. I fled into a wormhole just ahead of the blast wave, and spent millennia hiding in the interstices of known space. Time passes differently in those tunnels, of course, and I needed the time to plan anyway. Imagine my surprise when I saw your ship pass through a wormhole that hadn't been accessed for thousands of years, and never then by anyone besides our slaves and the Axiom themselves. That's when I learned about humans."

"I saw you watching us." She could still recall the fear and confusion she'd felt when a portion of the wormhole tunnel slid aside and revealed that one blazing eye gazing at their passage.

"I meant to be seen. I let another member of your crew glimpse me, too. I had to lay the groundwork for becoming your Benefactor, and being a legend in your mind."

"Is that what you think you are. Tell me, how do the wormholes work? Why do they look like tunnels?"

"I'm not an engineer," the Benefactor said. "How does your Tanzer drive work?"

"It's basically an ion propulsion system, but with the addition of exotic particles–"

The Benefactor shuddered. "Stop, never mind, forget I asked. I simply stole a master key allowing me to access the wormhole system. I gather it was used by the chief of the maintenance crews that kept the lights on inside. I don't know how the system works, and I don't care. I was content to live there and enjoy my freedom."

"So why did you come crawling out of the hole?"

"After you destroyed your first Axiom station I realized you might be valuable, and I tagged along on your journey to the Taliesen system to see how you'd do against a superior threat."

"I caught glimpses of you on the ship. Shimmers."

"My stealth technology exceeds your own, but it's

not perfect... and as I said, human intuition is very interesting. You couldn't see me, but some combination of your senses detected my presence, and transmitted that knowledge to your conscious mind as a sense of unease. Your brains are so inefficient. Your suspicions led me to send Kaustikos this time instead. Why try to hide and stow away when I could accompany you in plain sight? I thought it would be amusing to interact with you directly, too, even through an intermediary. Not that leaving you notes wasn't amusing, too."

"How did you know we'd investigate the things you wrote about?"

"Understanding human psychology is not difficult for me, Callie. Especially yours."

She just let the insults roll off her. Being held in contempt by someone you hated was an honor. "So you followed us to Taliesen, and watched us take out the Dream. Your rivals?"

"I thought you'd die there, honestly. The nano-swarm, the terror-drones... the defenses there include some of our best work. Your plan to infiltrate the virtual reality of the Dream was clever, and the way you defeated the Axiom there by leading an uprising of the suffering slime... that was a bit of a blind-spot for us. Mass cooperation has never been the strong suit of our species, though I believe our competitive spirit is what led us to become rulers of the galaxy."

"Former rulers," Callie said.

"Time will tell, won't it?" The Benefactor showed his teeth again. "The Dream was just entertainment to keep that faction occupied while they booted up something we called a reality engine, a device meant to change fundamental universal constants. The engine would have enabled that faction to survive the heat death of the universe… but it would have also collapsed the wormholes, where I'd been living, so I couldn't have that. I'm not particularly attached to this universe, but I am devoted to surviving in it, and beyond."

"What about the station with the pentachoron key? Why did you send us there?"

"So you could destroy it. I like your willingness to eradicate things you don't understand. It's an excellent quality in an attack dog. The key was necessary to further the plans of another faction. I'm glad you launched it into a star."

Callie nodded. "Fine. So what do you have against the Cleansing Corps? With a name like Kaustikos that seems like it should be your squad."

The Benefactor's face twisted into an unreadable expression. "The Cleansing Corps… are exterminators venerated on your homeworld? The Corps exists to kill infestations. At some point they decided they were important, powerful, guardians of Axiom purity, ha! Leadership by rat-catchers? I think not."

"If you weren't in the Cleansing Corps, what did you do for the Axiom?"

"I was the acid spat by emperors, Callie. I rooted out dissension and treachery, which is always a problem among my people. I served several rulers as personal enforcer, interrogator, and investigator. Unfortunately, during the latter days of the empire, those I served were forced from power. I had many enemies among the newly ascendant factions. Mostly because I'd tortured their former leaders to death. I can't blame them. My position was suddenly precarious. As I said, my allies sought a return to the glory days, to reestablish our unending empire. I still had spies, though, and I got word of the coming attack in time to slip away and save myself." He spread his claws on the table before him. "There. Now you have my life story, or as much of it as you're capable of comprehending."

"So. Where do we go from here? It would be hard for me to work with you now that I know you think I'm an insect. I also can't help but wonder about your goals."

"Peace and quiet are all I want, captain. I used the spies and sources I mentioned to compile an exhaustive map of every Axiom installation, and a bit of research here and there showed me where the truth-tellers are hiding, too – including their leading council. You don't need me anymore, really. Now that you've joined forces with your friends from Jupiter, you can make a concerted attack on my remaining enemies. Then I'll have the satisfaction of being the last Axiom left alive."

"At which point, what, you'll go back to building your time machine?"

"I was an investigator, like you, not an engineer. My satisfaction is wholly negative, not at all positive. I don't get to succeed. I just get to make sure none of the rest of the Axiom do, either. It is some satisfaction all the same."

"That's it? We part ways, and you fade back into the dark?"

"The alternative is you try to hunt me down. That would be amusing. But I can go anywhere, and be anywhere, and hiding from you is so trivial I have stood in your cabin and watched you and your little girlfriend sleep. I suggest you enjoy your success, your acclaim, and your fame. Make the best anthill possible for your fellow insects, and leave me to gloat over the ruins of my enemies."

"I think you're full of shit," Callie said. "I think if anything you just told me was true, it was just cover, to make the lies plausible. I think—"

The Benefactor interrupted. "Ah, but do you know what I think? I think we're done here. I kept you occupied long enough for Kaustikos to complete his mission. I won't see you again, Captain Machedo. I left your people alive, mostly, as thanks for your help... but I would say your goodbyes to them soon. Your universe won't be around much longer."

The Benefactor's avatar flashed out of existence, and Callie ripped herself out of the Hypnos in cold terror at what she might find in the reality beyond.

CHAPTER 33

Callie leapt out of the Hypnos pod, but nothing was immediately wrong – no red emergency lights flashed, no klaxons blared, and there were no urgent messages in her comms. Janice and Drake were still in their pod, and a glance at the monitor showed their vitals signs were fine.

Was the Benefactor just screwing with her? Messing with her head out of pure sadism?

"Shall, is everything okay here?" Shall didn't answer, and the cold at her core spread a little farther. "Shall, answer me. Shall!" She went to a terminal on the wall, in case she was having issues with her comms, but Shall didn't respond to that, either, not even when she input her priority-override-pay-attention-to-me-now code.

She was able to command override the Hypnos pod Janice and Drake were in, leading to confused queries from the latter and swearing from the former. They sat up, pulling away their input leads, and then saw Callie's face. They jumped out of the pod and stood at attention in seconds. "What's the situation?" they spoke with one voice.

"Shall's offline. I think Kaustikos did something to him." I left your people alive, mostly. "Get to the command center and figure out what's happening. I'm going to check on... everyone."

She went to Elena first. She couldn't have done otherwise. When she reached the infirmary she heard pounding and shouting on the other side, and though she couldn't make out the words she recognized Elena's voice. That thawed the ice in her chest, at least a little. The door wouldn't respond – it had been set on quarantine mode, sealing the infirmary off from the station, and it took every command access code she had to make it unlock.

The door slid open, and Elena stood on the other side, sweaty and disheveled and annoyed. She grabbed onto Callie and hugged her, then stepped back with narrowed eyes. "What's going on?"

"Kaustikos," Callie said. "The Benefactor. They're up to some shit. Go join Drake and Janice in the command center, okay?" That was the most secure part of the station if they came under attack. Callie had no idea what to expect. She'd thought she was so smart, and she'd prepared for some eventualities, but clearly not all of them.

Callie went to the cargo bay first, then moved on to the machine shop, where she found Ashok.

She moaned, and everything slowed down. The walk

toward him felt like she was moving through heavy water instead of thin air. "No," she said. "No, no, no." She didn't even call for Elena. She could tell there was no point.

Callie knelt by Ashok. He sprawled on his side, arms and legs at strange angles. He had a burn hole the diameter of a fingertip drilled right between the nests of lenses he had for eyes. Smoke still rose from the hole, and from the corresponding hole on the back of his head.

Ashok had a backup heart. He had two livers. His lungs were self-sealing. He took risks, but he also took precautions, and he could survive a lot.

He could not survive an energy beam passing through his brain.

The extra hearts did not beat, and the improved lungs did not rise and fall. Callie put her face against his chest, and reached with her hand to touch his chin – that part of him was still flesh, and she felt the stubble there, and the coldness of his skin.

Callie allowed herself a single choking sob, and a single stream of fleeting thought – first member of my crew, with me since the salvage days, when his only augmentations were a radiation detector in the back of one hand and a magnetic field detector in the other, my oldest friend, he's gone – and then she blinked tears away and tried to think like an investigator.

Why had Kaustikos killed Ashok? Because he had his finger on the probe's bomb? Or was there another reason? She stood up and looked around the machine shop. A curve of metal rested on the floor – it was the bomb they'd attached to Kaustikos. He'd removed it, somehow. They'd never had a good sense of what resources existed inside his sphere of a body – apparently nano-solvent was part of it. Kaustikos probably could have gotten away any time he wanted. They hadn't realized he was Axiom at first. They hadn't realized what capabilities he might have.

There was a crude eye burned into the surface of the workbench, and when Callie saw it, her heart went dark and hard.

She went to Ashok's safe – they were the only two people who knew the code – and saw it had been sliced open by the same weapon that killed Ashok. That was why Ashok had died. He would have fought to protect the contents of that safe. The dimensional ripper, the device they'd used to enter the pocket dimension that held the strange vault, was gone. Callie groaned, and raced for her room.

The place was wrecked, the bed and dresser and chairs torn to splinters, clothes tossed everywhere, broken glass scattered on the floor like sand at the beach. The safe under her bed was more resistant to energy weapons than Ashok's, but it had been blown completely apart anyway. Normally, that kind of safecracking would be self-defeating, because it would destroy the contents of the safe too…

But not when the only thing in the safe was the pentachoron key. That was indestructible, and now it was gone, in the hands of the Benefactor. Did he plan to open the vault? Was it the last day of the war?

"Not as long as I can still fight," she said aloud.

Shall transferred his consciousness to Glauketas from the *White Raven* and reviewed the security footage. "Kaustikos worked fast. As soon as Callie went into the Hypnos, he accessed a terminal and uploaded some kind of virus that eradicated my consciousness on the station. I've managed to quarantine the virus now, but it's still trying to erase me. With me out of the way, he sealed Elena in the infirmary, locked the Hypnos room, tossed Callie's cabin, and then… then… went to Ashok."

Elena sat in a corner of the command room, quietly weeping.

"Then he opened the safe, got the dimensional ripper, tore a hole in the air, and went through. He's gone."

"But we know where he went." Callie held up her hand, and showed them her wrist, with the teleporter bracelet. "Ashok made some modifications to this. He duplicated the phrase-shifting technology. I can go back to the temple, and to the vault. Ashok built the machine I need to avenge him."

"You can't go alone," Elena said.

"I won't. Shall, boot up the big mining drone in the cargo bay. It's not military, but if it can cut through rock, it can cut through Axiom."

"Yes, captain."

She started toward the cargo bay, and Elena caught her arm. Callie expected Elena to say 'I love you' or 'be careful' or 'come back to me,' but instead, with quiet ferocity, Elena said, "Kill him. Kill both of them. For what they did to Ashok."

"I'd kill them twice each if I could," Callie said.

Once the drone was ready and her other preparations were made, Callie used the bracelet to rip a slash in the air. Shall muscled his drone through the gap first – it made an audible tearing sound at his widest point, which was beyond chilling – and she followed him, the wound in the air closing up behind her.

They were back in the temple. Fluted pillars, white walls etched in ugly Axiom glyphs, a smooth white floor, and a dome that looked out onto an imaginary alien sky. The golden metal vault door still stood, and the Benefactor – really here, in the flesh – stood before the door, holding the key, while Kaustikos floated nearby, doing something to a stack of unfamiliar equipment.

"Callie!" the Benefactor called, voice emerging from a device strapped to one of his wrists – a combination communications device, phase-shifter, and floor-cleaner for all Callie knew. "Kaustikos *said* he thought you'd find a way to follow us here. I really doubted it, but I suppose he has spent more time with you–"

Callie began firing her wrists weapons, and Shall blasted them with an array of mining lasers.

Their beams hit an invisible barrier halfway between them, and the Benefactor made a wheezing, grinding noise that might have been laughter.

"Stasis technology." This time the voice emerged from Kaustikos. "That was the real reason we sent you to the Vanir system. I downloaded the technical specifications for the stasis device while you were running aimlessly around on the thirteenth station. The Cleansing Corps were the only ones who had access to this technology by the end, and it's vital for the completion of our plan."

"The stasis device can create force fields, too, you see," the Benefactor said. "Just a thin slice of air where no time passes, and so no weapon blasts can penetrate. The field can be deployed very selectively. Show them, Kaustikos."

The probe did something to the stack of equipment, and Callie was suddenly encased from the neck down in something soft but unyielding – not unlike the sensation of being squeezed inside the wall of the starfish ship, and just as unwelcome. "What are you doing?"

"We put the air around you in stasis," Kaustikos said. "Slowed the air molecules down until they're as solid as steel." The probe floated over to Shall – who seemed similarly incapacitated – and extruded a manipulator arm, which he plugged into the mining drone's back. "I'm just going to erase Shall's mind. Again. I quite enjoy doing that. I wish I'd had time to eliminate him on your ship. I'd love to get rid of all his backups."

"That's hardly necessary now," the Benefactor said. "They'll all be dead soon enough. There's a line I encountered when I was learning your language, Callie – a process that took most of an afternoon – that I quite like: 'Leave no stone upon a stone.' A reference to the destruction of a city. I can do better than that. I'll leave no molecule upon a molecule. No atom upon an atom."

"What does that key do?" Callie said.

The Benefactor turned to look at the vault door, gazing at it for a long silent moment. Kaustikos finished turning Shall's body into a mindless mining drone and drifted over to join the Benefactor by their machines. The mining drone powered down beside her, slumping – they didn't bother keeping it in stasis now that it posed no threat. Something moved in the corner of Callie's eye, but she couldn't turn her head to get a good look at it.

"The key," the Benefactor said at last. "What does

any key do? It opens a door."

"Fine. What's behind the door, then?" She didn't doubt that the Benefactor would keep her alive at least long enough to gloat.

"The last failsafe of another faction of the Axiom. I didn't need you to kill them – they all died in the fighting a long time ago. I did need you to free the key, though. The field that held the key was specifically designed to stop the members of any other faction from accessing it, and the station emitted a frequency tuned specifically to turn my bones to glass and shatter them in my body. I couldn't come within a thousand kilometers of the place myself, and when I tried to send a facsimile of my mind in a drone like Kaustikos, the station detected the Axiom thought patterns and disintegrated my emissary instantly. Purely automated drones failed to overcome the local defenses and those zealous guards. The countermeasures were ineffective against *you*, though. You really are very good at what you do. I also needed you to acquire a phase-shifter for me, as I had no way to access this place. The wormholes are my playground, but this… little world is something else. Kaustikos stole your shifter–"

"After I killed Ashok."

"Yes, you squashed a bug, how proud you must be. Kaustikos used the shifter to come here, then opened another portal to my location, and I joined him. You never realized the full capabilities of the dimensional ripper. This place, this temple to a dead faction, exists equidistant from all coordinates in ordinary space. You can enter this place from anywhere, and from here, you can *go* anywhere. Doors from anywhere, to anywhere. It makes for a wonderful command center."

"We should get started," Kaustikos said. "We don't need to waste time talking to her."

The Benefactor looked at the drone for a moment, then reached out with both clawed hands, grabbed the sphere, twisted it apart, and flung each half in opposite directions, where the pieces smashed and scattered and sparked. "I can't believe we used to be so alike," the Benefactor said. "Traveling with you changed my artificial counterpart… or perhaps he merely suffered from the limits of processing power and data space in that body. Talking to you isn't a *waste*. You are my last adversary, Callie. The last adversary I'll ever have, almost certainly. Making sure you understand the magnitude of your defeat is a pleasure I would never deny myself. True, it's no more remarkable than a human outsmarting a rat. Any triumph will do in these late days, I suppose."

The Benefactor stepped toward her, holding up the glittering key. "To be used only on the last day of the war. When the final citadel has fallen. When you cannot win, but you want to make sure your enemies lose too. On that day, you insert this key, and the engine of unmaking is activated." He tapped Callie on the forehead, gently, with the shifting end of the key. It was very cold.

Callie kept her gaze on the Benefactor's single blue eye, and didn't let her eyes so much as waver toward the things happening behind him.

"Unmaking, and making. When I turn the key, those doors will slowly grind open. Holes will open all around us, rips in the fabric of space time, connecting this temple to distant parts of the universe. Then, the contents of that vault, energies beyond your understanding, will be unleashed." He showed his teeth, and held his bracelet up to her ear so it could whisper to her. "Those energies will burn the universe down. No molecule left upon a molecule. No atom on an atom. The engine of unmaking will bring about the end of all things."

He stepped back and raised his arms. "And the new beginning! This key destroys the universe, and then *creates a new one*. A universe with the same physical laws and constants, with roughly the same quantity of matter bursting outward from the point of first cause, but in the end, it will be a new universe. New stars, in time. New planets, in time. New people, in time. Only this temple will remain safe and unchanged, this little pocket of hidden reality no bigger than a moon. It will take billions of years for anything interesting to arise out there in the new universe. A long wait for the appearance of life intelligent enough to hail me as a god."

The Benefactor walked over to the stack of equipment and gave it a pat. "Hence my need for stasis. I will turn the key, and then I will activate a stasis field around myself, with a timer set for a few billion years. I will wait here for the new universe to become one worth ruling. I have schematics to make all sorts of useful devices when I wake up, to aid in my dominion. For me, in stasis, the end of this world and the birth of another will take the blink of an eye." The Benefactor bowed. "I couldn't have done this without your help, Callie. I won't even kill you – that's how grateful I am. Of course, you'll starve to death here soon enough. Wait, your kind die of thirst first, don't they? Either way, your last sight will be me, floating peacefully in stasis, awaiting the birth of my empire."

"Can I say something?" Callie said.

"Of course. Some parting words for the universe you're about to lose?"

"Not really. I just wanted to say: Now, Lantern."

CHAPTER 34

"I don't trust Kaustikos," Callie whispered to Lantern. "When we leave the ship, I want you to tell everyone you're going home, then go hide in the cargo bay. You'll be my secret weapon, if it turns out I need one. I got the idea from Kaustikos, actually – when the Exalted boarded the *White Raven* and he said you should hide, since they wouldn't realize you were on board. I don't know if we'll *need* rescuing this time, but I like the idea of having an asset Kaustikos doesn't know about. It won't be long. Just until we send him packing back to the Benefactor."

Lantern agreed willingly enough, slipped away from the group, and took a nap on the cargo bay, inside a crate. The Free didn't need to sleep as much as humans did, but recent events had been exhausting. Her first awareness that anything was wrong came when Callie stopped by the cargo bay to check on her before going to the machine shop… Where she found Ashok dead. Lantern wanted to keen, and mourn, because Ashok was one of the humans she'd grown closest to, and one of the few beings she called a friend. The time for mourning would come, though. For now, she had to focus on avenging him.

Callie and Lantern devised a plan. Lantern hid herself on the underside of the mining drone, out of sight, gripping with her pseudopods as they passed through the hole in the air to the Axiom temple. At first, she thought they'd win easily, but then they were all gripped in stasis. Once Kaustikos erased Shall's mind, though, the drone was released, and once Lantern was able to move again, she scurried away while the Benefactor and Kaustikos weren't looking.

Ashok and Callie had feared this temple might prove dangerous, so they'd returned weeks ago and hidden dozens of Ashok's small drones here – on top of pillars, in the shadows by the gate, and up on the domed ceiling, all disguised by shimmering chameleon tech to blend with their backgrounds. Lantern had the controls to activate those drones, and she hid behind a pillar and slowly moved the scuttling things into better positions while Callie kept the Benefactor talking. He *did* like to talk. Spending millennia hiding in the crawlspaces of the universe would probably make anyone chatty.

When Callie said, "Now, Lantern!" she set off the drones, each carrying its own powerful explosive charge.

She'd moved most of the drones as close as she dared to the Benefactor and his equipment, and the results were explosively effective. The stasis machine was torn apart, whirling fragments tearing into the Benefactor, who howled with his own voice from his own throat.

Now that Callie was free, she sprinted toward the

Axiom. The explosions and the shrapnel had torn off most of the Benefactor's legs and taken both arms on one side, but he wasn't dead – he dragged himself with the remaining arms toward the key, thrown meters away from him by the blast. He growled and snarled with every inch he gained, but Callie beat him to the key, and kicked it away. She pointed a sidearm at the alien's head.

The bracelet on the Benefactor's wrist – now on one of his severed arms, across the room – began to speak. "Callie. My adversary. It seems I underestimated–"

"Nope," Callie said, and fired an expanding ball of plasma through the Benefactor's bright blue eye.

Callie and Lantern stepped back through the tear in space-time to the cargo bay on Glauketas. They couldn't bring the mining drone with them – it was too big and heavy to lift.

Once they were back on the asteroid, Callie tossed her bracelet through the portal. "I'm sorry to lose the short-range teleporter, but I'm happy to lose that… other thing." The hole in the air knit itself up. "I think we're good. The key is in the temple, and there's no way to get to the temple with both phase-shifters locked inside."

"As far as we know," Lantern said.

"A 'yes' would have been more comforting," Callie said.

"Yes," Lantern said. Then honestly compelled her: "Probably yes."

"That's probably the best I can hope for," Callie said. "You know, we've saved people and places before, but this time we saved everyone in the whole entire universe. You know what that means?"

"The good whiskey?" Lantern hazarded.

"The good whiskey," Callie said. "We'll raise a glass to Ashok while we're at it."

Shall called the whole crew to the command center and told them what he'd found.

"Ashok left a will?" Callie said. "That's unusually forward thinking of him."

"It's a video. 'To be played in the event of my totally untimely death,' it's called."

"Let's see it," Callie said. "Dim the lights." She figured if she saw Ashok up on the screen she might cry, and she didn't need anyone else to see that.

Ashok's face appeared, way too close to the screen, his lenses rotating. He stepped back and grinned, which was always unnerving, but also nice. The video had been filmed in the machine shop on Glauketas, which meant he'd recorded this in the not-too-distant-past. "Callie and Shall and Stephen and Drake and Janice and Elena and Lantern and maybe Sebastien if he goes uncrazy and Uzoma and Robin and Ibn and anybody else I forgot, greetings!" So this video was made before they left for Taliesen, when conditions were rather more crowded on Glauketas.

"If you're looking at this I must be dead. Ugh. The worst." Ashok shook his head. "I know the stuff I do isn't always 'safe.'" He made air quotes with one baseline human hand and one nest of manipulators. "I figure there's a good chance I'll die in a wreck, or get eaten by an alien, or maybe I'll plug the wrong piece of experimental tech into myself and turn my gray matter to gray goo. I don't want that to happen, but I'm just an optimist, not an idiot. I know eventually everyone dies. That's why... I got a new upgrade." He thumped his head. "It's sort of a surprise. I've been live-logging myself for basically my whole life, streaming my sensory inputs and memory patterns to a drive. That's good for reliving past glories, and for settling arguments about who said what when. Lately I've been thinking, I have all that data, so maybe I could use it for something? I installed a little black box inside the base of my skull. It sits there quietly mapping my neural patterns, collecting data. It's pretty much the same way Callie's ex-husband mapped his brain patterns to form the seed of our dear buddy Shall, except his tech was external and not as cool."

"Oh, shit," Callie whispered.

"Now, I know turning a mental map and a whole bunch of memory data into a consciousness is not easy or cheap, but I'm leaving whatever assets I have, my shares of the Machedo Corporation, the income from my patents, everything I've got, to start a fund to *save Ashok's brain*! Or consciousness. You know what I mean. I don't need anything fancy – you could put me in a mining drone – I just want a second chance at life. I know an AI based on me isn't exactly the same as me, but then again, is the me who wakes up the same as the me who goes to sleep? That's mind-blowing to think about, right? I took a philosophy class at Luna University, Stephen. Just the one, but it made a big impression."

Ashok cleared his throat. "Anyway. That's it. There are instructions for recovering the mental map and the access code for my life log but uh, definitely check the meta-data and think hard before you watch anything marked 'DOUBLE PERSONAL PRIORITY PRIVATE,' because some things cannot be unseen. I love you all – I can say that now that I'm dead and you're all too sad to make fun of me – and if you want to have a funeral for me that would be great. Everyone can talk about how much they miss me and how great I am. Then you can get to work on bringing me *back*."

The screen went dark.

"Creating an AI is really not cheap," Shall said. "I was an anniversary present from your rich ex-husband, even he could only afford it because his company owns one of the only labs that *makes* artificial intelligences. There are other complications, legal and practical – as far as I know, no one has ever made an AI based on someone who wasn't alive, for obvious reasons. It won't be easy."

"That's true," Callie said. "Fortunately, Michael still owes me lots of favors. I'll cash in every one of them to get this done." She knew a copy of Ashok's consciousness in a computer wasn't the same as getting her friend back. A new Ashok would diverge from the old, changed by not having a physical body, and by the vastness and speed of a mind that lived in machinery instead of bioelectric meat. Michael had formed the basis of Shall, but now, years later, they were entirely different, as distinct as identical twins leading different lives. The same would be true of artificial Ashok.

But like the general said: half a loaf was better than none.

"I've never been to a harvest festival before," Callie said. "It appears to involve getting drunk and setting things on fire, though, so I approve."

Everyone was here for the harvest festival on Owain – they'd even picked up Uzoma, Robin, and Ibn from Ganymede and their colony world, respectively; Stephen and his partner Q met them at that ridiculous spaceport with the mushroom-shaped restaurant and drove them in a land vehicle to their house, a big geodesic dome on sprawling pastoral property surrounded by trees. Their yard was full of dried fruit and vegetables hanging on strings, bales of grass piled up to form mazes and structures, and gracefully carved wooden furniture.

Weirdly enough, given his history in cities and in space, Stephen seemed totally at ease in the country. He looked wonderful, lean and smiling instead of round and doleful. "I credit my new health and outlook to gardening, walking, and eating all these fresh vegetables."

"Getting laid regularly probably doesn't hurt, either," Callie said.

"Propriety forbids comment."

"Whatever. I know it's good for me." She brushed an insect off her arm. "This place is horrible and I'm happy for you."

They had a wake for Ashok – Imperative scientists were still turning his files into a mind – and swapped stories about him, fond and exasperated, while drinking the local booze. Sebastien came to the wake near the end. He approached Callie and said, "I am so sorry. Ashok was one of a kind. I mourn your loss." Then he walked away. That was it. He didn't say anything sarcastic or cruel, and didn't try to make the situation about himself at all. He seemed entirely sincere. Maybe his time on Owain really had changed him for the better.

As the sky grew purple with dusk, the wake segued into a harvest party proper, with various guests from the local settlements gathering around bonfires and sharing good cheer. After making the rounds for a while, Callie sat alone on a straw bale – whatever that was for – and gazed up at the stars. There were lots of them, and she knew there were still monsters lurking in the darkness between them. But now they had a map to those monsters, and the means to destroy them. There was lots of work yet to be done, but Callie and her crew no longer had to do it all alone.

Elena caught up with her old crewmates from the Anjou for a while, but then she came over to Callie and placed a crown made of little yellow flowers on her head. "Perfect." She sat on the bale beside Callie. "How does it feel to be a queen, anyway?"

"Heavy lies the head that wears the crown." Callie wasn't royalty, but she had accidentally become a politician. She'd decided that, if they were making as much money as a small country, they might as well start acting like one. She was a celebrity on the Tangle in every system for her part in liberating Vanir, which helped negotiations with the Inner Planets Governing Council and the Imperative go smoothly. Michael and his company's lawyers had helped too.

As a result, The Trans-Neptunian Authority would rise again. Callie's home, destroyed by the servants of the Axiom, was being rebuilt. Construction on Meditreme Station II was already starting, out near the orbit of Neptune, and Callie had secured exclusive resource exploitation rights from there to the Oort cloud, and the right to offer citizenship, levy taxes, control trade, and make laws for the region.

She hadn't wanted the job, really, but being the head of a nation-state instead of captain of an independent crew gave her a lot more leverage in her partnership with the Jovian Imperative... even if currently the citizens of said nation-state were limited to members of her crew. The Imperative's ministers would have a harder time secretly using Axiom tech behind her back when their partner ran her own country.

"We should get you a real crown," Elena said. "Or at least a tiara."

Callie snorted. "My job is a lot more like being CEO than a queen. Anyway, I'm not really suited for it. We've established that I'm a terrible diplomat. I'm going to talk Shall into taking over the top job pretty soon."

"An artificial intelligence as head of a polity? That's going to shake things up."

"As the head of the newly reconstituted Trans-Neptunian Alliance, I'm drafting a constitutional amendment granting full rights to human-derived artificial intelligences. I'm pretty sure the other senior ministers will ratify, since that's you and Stephen and Drake and Janice and Lantern. The other polities can complain about negotiating with an AI, but they'll suck it up or lose out on trade with us, and once we roll out some benign uses for Axiom tech, like the gravity generators, they'll get over their objections." She took a sip of the sweet, cool wine in her glass. "You know what else that amendment means? It means Ashok, or Ashok the AI, can own and autonomously operate his own ship, flying under TNA colors. I'm giving him the Golden Spider as a rebirthday gift."

"That's… well… I want to say it's nice, but… the Golden Spider is a heap of epoxy and spare parts. It was the one ship so ugly the pirates didn't even bother taking it with them on their last raid before we stole Glauketas out from under them. With the money we're getting from our stake in the Vanaheim system, we could buy him a new ship.

"That would be cruel, Elena. If we gave him a perfect ship, how would Ashok amuse himself? With the Golden Spider, he'll have the endless joy of upgrading, augmenting, and improving himself."

Elena snuggled closer. "Good point. There's a reason you're the captain and I'm just the executive officer."

"There's no one I'd rather have as my XO," Callie said. "There's no one in the world I trust more, and not many I trust as much."

Elena murmured in her ear. "Remember how I told you back on Earth, in the 22nd century, we used to sign our letters 'XOXO' sometimes? Do you remember what that stands for?"

"Why don't you remind me?" Callie said.

So Elena did

AKNOWLEDGMENTS

Thanks to my wonderful son River and my lovely wife Heather for creating a supportive environment that allows me to vanish for hours at a time to write about punching space fascists and kissing the people you love, and for providing such a pleasant reality for me to come home to. Thanks to Ais, Amanda, Emily, Katrina, and Sarah for their kindness and support, and for listening to me go on (and on, and on) about reversals and betrayals and body horror and whether we're allowed to have happy endings, and my rambling doubts about whether I could wrap up this trilogy in a satisfying way. (I think I did. I'm satisfied, anyway.) Special thanks to Ysabeau Wilce and James Thomas for letting me spend several days in seclusion up at Rancho Zopilotes, where I wrote more than half this book, including many of the best parts.

On the professional side, thanks to my longtime agent Ginger Clark for making the business things run so smoothly and for supporting all my weird novelistic whims. Thanks to the team at Angry Robot, especially Marc Gascoigne for believing in this series,

Phil Jourdan for editing the first two volumes so deftly, and Penny Reeve for being a great publicist (and taking care of me last fall when I visited London). They're all gone from the company now, and I miss them a lot, and I wouldn't be here without them. New publicity and editorial coordinator Gemma Creffield has stayed in touch and kept on top of things during this transitional period, Simon Spanton brought his considerable editorial insight and experience to bear on this final volume, and copyeditor Rob Triggs saved me from myself in several places. My thanks to Paul Scott Canavan, who continues to bring the *White Raven* to life in his glorious cover art.

And thanks to you, the readers who joined me on the journeys of the *White Raven*. I'll see you in the stars.